SEASIDE HIGH

Theresa Kelly

Praise God from Whom all blessings flow!

For five of the most wonderful blessings God has ever bestowed: Duncan, Casey, Kira, Cassandra, and Rianne

Cover Illustration by Sandy Rabinowitz.

3558 S. Jefferson Avenue, St. Louis, MO 63118-3968
Manufactured in the United States of America

Library of Congress Cataloging-in-Publication Data

Kelly, Theresa, 1952–
Seaside High / Theresa Kelly.
p. cm. — (Aloha Cove)
Summary: Cass Devane begins her junior year of high school newly situated on Kwaljalein, one of the Marshall Islands in the Pacific, with her new stepsister and stepfather.
ISBN 0–570–05484–2
[1. Stepfamilies Fiction. 2. High schools Fiction. 3. Schools Fiction. 4. Kwajalein Island (Marshall Islands) Fiction. 5. Islands Fiction. 6. Christian life Fiction.] I. Title. II. Series.
PZ7.K2985Se 1999 99–21169
[Fic]–DC21 CIP

---

2 3 4 5 6 7 8 9 10 09 08 07 06 05 04 03 02 01 00

CHAPTER 1

"I can't believe school starts tomorrow." Lying on the floor, Cass Devane glanced up at her stepsister, Tabitha Spencer, who was sprawled on the bed.

"I know," Tabitha said. "It seems like the summer just began, and here we are heading into our junior year."

"And what a summer it's been." Cass grinned. "Did you think when school let out last May that our parents would be married and we'd be sisters before the summer was out?"

Rolling onto her back, Tabitha did a couple of half-hearted sit-ups. "Of course not. I didn't even know you and Mom existed until we went back to Tennessee for Dad's high school reunion."

"Then he ran into Mom, his old high school sweetheart," Cass said, picking up the story, "and they realized the spark was still there. They took up where they'd left off twenty years ago, and the rest is history. Here I am, eight thousand miles from home, living on an island in the middle of the Pacific Ocean, and actually liking it." She shook her head, thinking of the incredible changes she'd experienced in the past two months. "Who'd have thought life could be so unpredictable?"

"And wonderful," Tabitha added. "I love having a mom after all these years." She turned her head to smile down at Cass. "Plus, you're not the worst sister a girl could have," she teased.

Cass stuck her tongue out and drawled, "Gee, thanks. I feel so loved and appreciated."

They both laughed. Tabitha turned onto her side and propped her head on her hand. "So, have you made up your mind what you're wearing tomorrow?"

Cass rolled up to a sitting position, drawing her legs up to lean her chin on her knees. "Nope. I'm still debating between going ultracasual with jeans shorts and a T-shirt or aiming for an entirely new look by wearing the sundress Mom bought me."

"I vote for the sundress," Tabitha said. "You've said you like the idea of starting fresh here on Kwaj. One way you can do that is by changing your tomboy image to something a little more … I don't know—girlish."

Cass snorted. "You sound just like Mom. You're into lace and frills almost as much as she is." Cass glanced pointedly at the lacey pink curtains hanging around Tabitha's windows. They, like the rest of Tabitha's immaculate, very pink and girly room, were in sharp contrast with the plain blue cotton curtains hanging in Cass' messy-but-comfortable room.

"I take it that means you're not going with the sundress."

Cass hesitated. "I like the dress, but it's just not me," she finally decided. "At least not for school. I'll save it to wear to church."

Tabitha groaned. "You're hopeless."

"I know," Cass said cheerfully. "Look at it this way, though. You won't have me competing for the guys' attention tomorrow. They'll run right past me in my T-shirt and shorts in order to drool all over you in your little yellow top and white miniskirt."

Fluffing the blonde curls that cascaded to her shoulders, Tabitha laughed. "Yeah, right. Me in a miniskirt. That'll be the day. I can just picture me trying to sneak out of the house past Dad wearing something that's more than three inches above my knees. He'd make me take it off and burn it before I got two feet out the door."

Gesturing down at her faded green T-shirt, Cass smiled ruefully. "Mom's never had much to worry about with me. My motto is the roomier, the better." She brushed her auburn hair behind her ears and gazed over at Tabitha, her hazel eyes thoughtful. "Are you more excited or nervous about being a junior?"

"Excited, I guess. I haven't really thought about." Tabitha shrugged. "Why?"

"With school starting tomorrow, I'm beginning to realize how nervous I am." Cass rested her hand on her stomach, where the butterflies were having a field day. "It's not just that I won't know anyone. Except for you and a couple of other people, that is," she corrected herself before continuing, "I've always heard your junior year is when you're supposed to start getting serious about things. The teachers push college and ask you where you want to go and what you want to study. I'm not sure I'm ready for that."

"Ready or not, it's going to happen," Tabitha said. "The thought of looking at colleges is exciting to me. Think about it. We'll have our pick of going anywhere on the mainland." Flopping onto her stomach, she peered at Cass through sparkling blue eyes. "If you had your choice of going anyplace you wanted to, where would you go?"

"Somewhere in Tennessee," Cass promptly responded.

"Oh, come on. You can be more creative than that."

"I don't want to be more creative," Cass insisted.

"You know I love Tennessee. In two years, I'm packing up my stuff and heading home, and no one will be able to stop me."

"You just said you like it here," Tabitha protested. "Now you're talking about escaping."

"I do like it here," Cass assured her. "Tennessee is still home, though. It's where my friends are, and Papaw and Mamaw, and my cousins. There's a lot I like about Kwajalein, but Tennessee will always be where I belong."

"I wish I felt that way about a place," Tabitha said wistfully. "I mean, Kwaj is my home, but I won't be coming back here to live after college. Not unless I get a job working for the government—which I doubt. Sometimes I wonder where I'll wind up."

"I'll let you share Tennessee with me," Cass offered, smiling impishly. "Remember when we weren't getting along, and Mom used to say Kwaj wasn't big enough for the two of us? Tennessee's about five hundred miles across. I can live in Jonesborough, and you can live at the other end of the state in Memphis."

Tabitha laughed. "Thanks for the suggestion. As long as Memphis is hot and humid like Kwaj, I'll consider it."

There was a knock at the door, then Mom poked her head into the room. "It's after nine, ladies. Don't you think you ought to start thinking about getting ready for bed? Six-thirty is going to come awfully early."

Cass rolled her eyes at Tabitha. "Honestly, Mom," she said. "We're juniors in high school. I think we can figure out when to go to bed."

"Yeah," Tabitha added.

Mom shrugged. "All right. Just don't come whining to me tomorrow morning about how tired you are." She smiled. "Your Dad and I are going for a walk. We shouldn't be gone more than an hour. In case you're in bed by the time we get back"—she stepped into the room and leaned down to kiss Cass—"I'll say goodnight now." She moved to the bed where Tabitha lifted her face for a kiss. "Don't forget to set your alarm clocks. Since you're juniors," she teased, "you're old enough to get yourselves up."

"She's so great," Tabitha said, still looking at the door after Mom closed it behind her. "I can't believe how lucky I am to have her for a Mom."

"We're not lucky. We're blessed." Cass paused, then smiled ruefully. "Who'd have thought a couple of weeks ago that I'd say something like that? I hated the very idea of you being included as one of *my* mother's daughters. Remember how jealous I was about her relationship with you? I was sure I was being edged out of the picture."

"You were." Tabitha laughed when Cass gave her a startled look. "I tried my hardest to make Mom like me better, but she wouldn't go along with my plan. She refused to play favorites. I was furious at you because I was convinced Dad preferred you."

"Things were really a mess for a while there, weren't they?" Cass glanced heavenward. "Thank God we finally came to our senses. I've discovered I like having someone I can talk with living right in the house. It's so convenient." She yawned. "You know, I didn't feel sleepy before Mom came in to tell us to go to bed. Now I'm having a hard time staying awake."

"Actually, I'm feeling a little pooped myself. Mom wasn't kidding when she said six-thirty will come around sooner than we expect. Tabitha reached over and set the alarm on the clock on her nightstand.

"We haven't discussed what we're going to do about scheduling bathroom time," Cass said with a frown. "You're not allowed to take your usual hour, you know."

Tabitha dismissed the warning with a careless shrug. "I only did that to bug you. Haven't you noticed I've cut down to thirty minutes the past couple of weeks?"

"I thought it was just my imagination." Cass slowly got to her feet and started for the door. "Do you want to use the bathroom first in the morning? As long as I get in there by seven, I can make it to school on time."

Tabitha shook her head. "You can go first. I'd rather ease into the day. Waking up and getting right into the shower makes me tense."

"Good—I'm just the opposite. During the school year, I like to get showered and dressed before I do anything else." She smiled at Tabitha, then headed out the door. "See you in the morning."

Later that night, Cass lay in bed unable to sleep. Her heart raced and her stomach churned every time she imagined walking into the high school the next day. Tabitha had taken her on a tour of the building so she knew she could find her way around. That wasn't the problem. What gave her the jitters was the thought of meeting dozens of new people the next day.

What if they don't like me? Cass thought. *What if the only friends I wind up with are the kids I met this summer? I wish I was back in Jonesborough. If this were the night before starting school at home, I wouldn't be able to sleep because I'd be so excited at the thought of seeing everyone again. Instead, I'm lying here wide awake because I'm dreading having to make new friends. Jesus, please help everything to work out tomorrow.*

She sighed and rolled over one more time. *And please, Lord,* she added, *Don't let me do anything really stupid.*

CHAPTER 2

The moment her alarm went off the following morning, Cass was out of bed and heading to the shower. When she returned to her room, she heard Tabitha's snooze go off again, and then Dad pounding on the door.

"Tabitha Joi, get out of bed," Cass heard him say. He was obviously frustrated. "We're not going through another year of you lying in bed until the last second, then making a mad dash to get to school on time. Come on—Cass is already up and out of the shower."

Cass cringed. She and Tabitha were getting along, but it wouldn't help being compared to each other.

Despite Tabitha's late start, she was ready to leave for school when Cass was. After a quick breakfast, they got on their bikes and joined a line of cyclists heading to the schools. Cass almost laughed at Kwaj's version of traffic. She was still amazed that there were hardly any privately owned vehicles on the island.

A number of the cyclists turned off at the elementary school and junior high, while the rest continued on to the high school. Taking care not to get caught, Cass cast furtive glances at those around her, trying to pick out juniors or seniors. A pair of good-looking guys pedaled past her, and she fervently hoped they would be classmates. She thought to ask Tabitha who they were, but she was too far ahead to get her attention without yelling. The last thing Cass wanted was to was stand out in the crowd.

Once they reached the school, Cass and Tabitha slid their bikes into the rack outside the front doors. Walking to the entrance, they met up with Kira and Micah Alexander, who fell into step with them.

"Did they cut summer short this year?" Kira grumbled. "I could swear we didn't get the full three months we're entitled to."

His teeth gleaming in the morning sun, Micah ruffled his sister's ebony curls. The Alexanders were half-Jamaican, and Cass was jealous of their perpetual tans. "You're just cranky because you had to get up before noon," Micah said to Kira. To Cass and Tabitha, he added, "I've never seen anyone who sleeps in the way she does. She'd stay in bed all day if Mom would let her."

Propping a hand on her hip, Kira stuck her tongue out at him. "Look who's talking," she said. "How many times this summer were you up and going before eleven o'clock?"

"Plenty," Micah shot back. "You just didn't know it because you were still snoozing."

"I don't know why I bother talking to you, Micah." With a withering look for her brother, Kira spun on her heels and stalked toward the front doors. "Are you coming, Tabitha?" she called over her shoulder.

Tabitha broke away from Cass and Micah with an apologetic smile and ran ahead to catch up with her friend. Micah looked down at Cass and shrugged.

"I love my sister, but she gets mad so easily," he said. "Right now, she's probably complaining to Tabitha about how horrible I am."

"You? Horrible?" Cass looked at him in amazement. "Give me a break. You're one of the nicest people I know." She smiled. She knew Tabitha had been in love with Micah for quite some time, even though he only seemed to notice her as Kira's friend. Tabitha had confessed to Cass that she hoped this would be the year he would see her as something more—especially since he'd be going off to college next year.

"Thanks, but you don't have to live with me." Micah gazed fondly after his sister as she and Tabitha disappeared into the school. "Kira and I have had some knockdown, drag-out battles over the years."

Cass shifted her backpack to the other shoulder. "I've learned a little about fighting this summer. Tabitha and I have done our fair share. We're getting along better now, though, so I'm hoping our arguing is pretty much behind us."

"That's what she says too." Reaching the doors, Micah held one open for Cass as she preceded him through it. "What's your homeroom number? I'm down this way." He pointed to the left. "I'll be glad to walk you to your class if you want me to."

"That'd be great." Cass sighed in relief. "The school isn't that big, but I hate the idea of wandering around lost now that I'm a junior. I had enough of that as a freshman."

She fumbled in her backpack for the slip of paper with her homeroom number written on it. Just as she found it, Tabitha and Kira appeared at her side.

"We thought we'd escort you to your class before we head on to ours," Kira announced, pointedly ignoring her brother.

"That's right," Cass said, frowning, "we're in different homerooms." She brightened a bit. "I talked to Rianne, though, and we share the same homeroom." She glanced around the corridor. "I wonder if she's here yet."

"I haven't seen Randy, and they usually come together," Kira said, referring to Rianne's older brother. "Her younger brother, Robby, is a freshman this year. He makes me feel so old," she moaned.

Tabitha elbowed her in the ribs. "That's because you are." She smiled at Cass. "Are you ready to find your class?"

"As ready as I'll ever be." Cass smiled up at Micah. "Thanks for offering to show me the way. I guess I'll see you around."

"With fewer than two hundred students in the school, we're bound to run into each other." He squeezed her shoulder encouragingly. "Don't worry. You'll do fine."

While Micah headed down one hall, Kira and Tabitha led Cass in the opposite direction. There were clusters of students everywhere. To Cass' relief, no one paid any particular attention to her, although someone in almost every group called out to Tabitha and Kira. Cass recognized some people from the youth group Mom had started, but most of the students were unfamiliar to her.

Lord, help me make friends, she prayed quickly as she looked around, *and please don't let me do something embarrassing in the process*.

Tabitha and Kira pointed Cass' homeroom out to her before heading next door to their own class. Taking a deep breath, Cass mustered her courage and stepped across the threshold into the room full of chattering, laughing students.

A quick glance around told her Rianne hadn't arrived yet. That left Cass with the dilemma of where to sit. Spotting an empty desk near the back of the room, she started for it, but was waylaid by a smiling boy in the third row.

"Hi." He unfolded his tall frame from the desk as Cass hesitated at his greeting. Standing, he towered over her. "You're new in town, aren't you?" Before Cass could respond, he gave a rueful laugh. "Talk about your corny pickup lines. Sorry."

Cass relaxed at his self-mocking humor. "That's okay," she assured him with a shy smile. "There are worse ways to start a conversation. Besides, I am new in town. I moved here in July."

"Compared to you, I'm practically a native," he replied. "I've been here thirteen years. My name's Dennis McCrory, by the way."

Cass smiled. "Cass—short for Cassandra—Devane. My mother married Steve Spencer, the radio deejay, over the summer, which makes me Tabitha's stepsister."

"Hey, I've heard about you. Logan Russell said he'd met you and that you seemed like a great girl."

Cass could feel a blush working its way up her cheeks to her scalp. Taken by surprise, all she could do was mumble, "Really? That was ... nice ... of him."

What a totally lame remark, she scolded herself. *Honestly, couldn't you come up with a better word than nice?*

Dennis didn't appear to notice her lack of enthusiasm, however. "Yeah. He said you two have a lot in common. He told me you're really into sports."

"I played basketball on my high school team back home. Logan and I have gone one-on-one a few times."

Dennis nodded. "He told me." Leaning down, he added with a conspiratorial wink, "He also told me you beat him in a couple of games."

Cass laughed. "I think he let me win. He's—"

"Cass!" Rianne Thayer stood in the doorway, waving madly to get her attention. "I finally made it."

Weaving her way through the desks, Rianne came towards them. Dennis shrugged and sat back down.

"Nice talking to you," he said quietly as Rianne approached. "Maybe we can get together after school."

"May—maybe," Cass stammered, astonished.

I've been in school all of—what?—five minutes, and some guy is already acting like he's interested in me?

Rianne reached Cass' side and gave her arm a squeeze. "Isn't it great we're in the same homeroom?" she said. "Let's find some seats so we can look at our schedules and see if we have any of the same classes."

They claimed a pair of empty desks. Before they began comparing their schedules, however, Rianne gave Cass a mischievous grin. Her brown eyes bright with curiosity, she asked softly, "What's with you and Dennis? I didn't know you knew him."

"I don't. I mean, I do now." Flustered, Cass struggled to keep her voice down. She was sure her face was glowing bright red. "He stopped me and introduced himself."

"You're kidding!" Rianne's eyes shot wide open. "Dennis isn't usually very outgoing. In fact, he's pretty shy." She paused. "He just up and introduced himself out of the blue?"

Cass nodded, glancing furtively to see if he was looking at them.

Rianne still couldn't seem to believe it. "How do you do it? First my brother instantly takes to you and now Dennis. I'd appreciate it if you'd share your secret with me. There's a senior I've had my eye on for the past two years, but he doesn't even know I exist."

"I don't know what I'm doing to attract attention. That's the problem." She shrugged. "I was walking to a desk, minding my own business, when he made the first move."

Sitting back, Rianne gave Cass an admiring look.

"Wow, just think what could happen if you set your mind to it. You'd have boys lined up at your door, waiting to date you. We could work a deal where I get the throwaways."

Cass burst into laughter then quickly covered her mouth. "You don't know how funny that is," she declared. "Do you have any idea how many dates I've had in the past two years?"

When Rianne shook her head, Cass held up two fingers. "Two. Count 'em, two." She wiggled her fingers for emphasis. "I'm no math genius, but even I know that averages out to one a year. I've had a really pathetic social life." She raised her hands in confusion. "Then I come here and all of a sudden, guys can't resist me. It's very confusing, especially since nothing about me has changed. Okay, I have a ton more freckles," she conceded. "But I've never known freckles to drive a guy wild."

"Haven't you ever heard the saying, 'don't look a gift horse in the mouth'?" Rianne asked as she smoothed her sleek golden hair behind her ears. "Don't worry about why boys suddenly find you irresistible. Just enjoy it."

"How can I when I don't know if it's going to end as mysteriously as it began?" Out of the corner of her eye, Cass glanced across the room again. She quickly looked away when she realized Dennis was looking at her. "My friends back home aren't going to believe it. I want it to last long enough for me to write and tell them about it."

"My advice stays the same." Rianne picked up the schedule she'd laid down on the desk and opened it. "Don't analyze it—just enjoy it."

The homeroom teacher arrived, and they turned their attention to the announcements. Not trusting herself to remember the information, Cass hastily scrawled notes on everything that was talked about. She knew she'd settle in to the school's routine before long, but at the moment she wasn't going to take a chance on forgetting even the tiniest detail.

When the bell rang, Cass hefted her backpack onto her shoulder, picked up her schedule, and joined the line of students snaking out the door. Once she was in the hall, she turned right, realized after a few feet that she was going the wrong way, and retraced her steps.

Entering her Spanish class, Cass was pleased to find Kira there and went straight to the desk behind hers. Kira turned around to smile at Cass as she slipped into the seat.

"Are you any good in Spanish?" she asked immediately after saying hello.

"I usually got A's back home." Cass set a notebook and pen on the desktop. "Why?"

"Thank You, God," she proclaimed. "Would you consider tutoring me? I barely made it through Spanish 1 last year. English is hard enough as far as I'm concerned. Learning a whole other language is next to impossible."

"I'll do whatever I can to help, but I'm not promising anything," Cass warned. "Just because I do okay doesn't mean I know enough to teach it."

"I'll be eternally in your debt for whatever help you give me." Peering at Cass with soulful eyes, Kira displayed the acting ability she was famous for. "In exchange for your assistance, I hereby promise you my firstborn child."

Giggling, Cass pretended to be alarmed. "You don't have to do that. I'm not sure I'll want my own firstborn. I definitely don't want yours."

Kira laughed. "I see why you drive Tabitha crazy sometimes. You say what you think. She's more the beating-around-the-bush type."

"Well, it takes all kinds." Cass picked up her pen, opened her notebook, and wrote *Spanish 2* on the first page. "Some kinds are just more fun than others."

Kira arched an eyebrow at her. "I'm assuming you mean yourself, as compared to Tabitha." When Cass grinned but didn't say anything, Kira said, "Don't worry. My lips are sealed. As long as you keep me from flunking this class, you can say anything you want about your stepsister, and you won't hear a word of complaint out of me."

"Some loyal friend you are," teased Cass.

"Hey, there's loyalty, and there's keeping yourself out of trouble with your parents."

Cass' laugh was cut off by the bell signaling the start of class. The teacher, who'd been sitting at her desk, stood up and walked around to the front of it. Watching her, Cass took a deep breath.

This is it, she thought. *I'm now officially a junior at Kwajalein High School—known around here as Seaside High*.

Since they were only going a half-day, class periods were shortened to thirty minutes. That gave Cass just enough time to find each room, choose a desk, and take notes about what to expect before heading to her next class.

She quickly discovered that the school was too small for her to get lost, which relaxed her enough to look around for people she knew as she changed classes. She saw Logan Russell, a senior she'd met over the summer, three times. Each time, he immediately caught up with her and walked her to her next class. She felt a little better about herself each time, since it was obvious by the waves and curious stares from other girls that he was well liked.

On her way to her last class, Cass heard someone calling her. Rianne's older brother, Randy, waved to her from halfway down the corridor.

"Wait up," he shouted.

Cass remained where she was while Randy maneuvered his wheelchair around the scurrying students. Having been paralyzed in a diving accident five years earlier when he was twelve, he was quite good at dodging obstacles in his path without slowing down. He reached Cass in what seemed to her to be record time.

"Hey, how's it going?" he greeted her.

"Not bad." Cass fell into step with the motorized wheelchair. "I think I'm going to like most of my classes. I'm not looking forward to physics, but I guess I'll survive. The teacher seems like he's willing to work with you."

"Who do you have?" Balancing his books in his lap with one hand, Randy steered the wheelchair with the other.

"Mr. Stanton." Cass slowed down as she neared her classroom.

Randy nodded. "He's the best. At least that's what I've heard. Last year Mr. Willis taught my class, and I had the feeling he didn't know what he was talking about half the time." He smiled up at Cass. "Which was really bad for me since I never knew what he was talking about."

"I take it you and physics didn't get along."

His laugh was rueful. "That's the understatement of the year. I managed to pass, but just barely. I've never been as happy as I was my last day of physics. I rolled out of that classroom and never looked back."

"Thank you so much for the pep talk," drawled Cass, shaking her head in mock irritation. "I was already worried. Now I'm downright terrified."

"Oh, you'll do fine," he replied breezily. "You seem like the kind of person who takes things in stride." He glanced up at the clock. "Oops, gotta roll. I have less than a minute to make it to class."

Cass hesitated. She didn't want to insult Randy but at the same time ... "Would you like me to—"

Randy silenced her with a stern look. "Don't say it," he ordered, although he didn't sound upset. "If I'm late for class, it won't be because I'm in a wheelchair. It'll be because I spent the time talking to a pretty girl." His grin stretched from ear to ear. "I've waited years to be able to say that. I think I'll be late on purpose just so I can finally use it as my excuse."

Blushing, Cass gave the wheel closest to her a kick. "Get going, pal. I'm not going to be your alibi."

Randy's head swiveled from side to side. "Do you see any other pretty girls around here?" he teased.

"Tons of them," Cass shot back. "So I'm not going to take the fall for you. After all, how many other girls did you stop to talk to before you finally got around to me?"

"None. You were my one and only distraction."

"Oh." Any inclination to joke died on Cass' lips at the earnest look on Randy's face. "In that case, I'll take half the blame." In an effort to bring a little humor back into the conversation, she wagged a warning finger at Randy. "But don't let it happen again."

Laughing, Randy backed up his chair and turned it around. "Sorry, no can do. I intend to talk to you as often as possible."

With that, he raced off down the hall at breakneck speed. Cass saw him whip the chair around the corner just as the bell rang and hoped for his sake that his class wasn't far. Then, realizing she was late herself, she ducked into her classroom and grabbed the first available desk.

CHAPTER 3

"So how did you like your first day at dear old Seaside?" Tabitha asked Cass when they met up on the front steps of the school following the last class.

"I really like being in smaller classes," Cass said, smiling at Kira who came up to stand beside Tabitha. "My high school back home was so big that I felt completely lost in the crowd. One of my teachers never got my name right last year."

"Really?" Kira grinned. "With my grades, not being noticed would probably be a good thing."

As Tabitha and Kira turned to go, Cass asked, "Would you mind waiting a couple of minutes? Rianne's coming home with us for lunch. She just needed to talk with her brothers before she left."

"No problem." Kira flashed Cass an impish smile. "Speaking of brothers, I saw you and Randy walking to class together."

"That's funny," Tabitha chimed in before Cass could respond. "I saw you and Logan walking together."

"Plus, Rianne told me about Dennis McCrory hitting on you." Propping a hand on her hip, Kira made a show of looking Cass up and down. "You're quite the social butterfly. It's probably good you moved away from Tennessee. At this rate, you must have gone through every guy in your school by the end of your sophomore year."

Cass snorted and said, "I wish." She shifted her backpack to her other shoulder and shook back the hair clinging to her face in the noon heat. "Like I told Rianne, I don't know what's going on. I've never had this happen before. Not that I'm complaining," she hastily added at the girls' exaggerated expressions of sympathy. "I'd just like to know what I'm doing so I don't accidentally stop and ruin it."

"You're being yourself," Tabitha said easily, surprising Cass with the compliment. "It's like I found out when we actually started talking intead of fighting. When you're not being a snot, you're a really nice person."

"Thanks ... I think." They all laughed at Cass' puzzled expression.

"What's so funny?" Rianne asked, coming up behind them.

"We'll explain on the way to the house." Tabitha started for the bike racks. "Let's get going. I'm about to faint from hunger."

Dennis caught up with them as they headed off and pedaled alongside Cass until he came to his street. Cass did her best to ignore the meaningful glances her friends were exchanging and to focus on her conversation with Dennis. The situation became even more interesting when Logan joined them about halfway home.

"Dennis." Logan said curtly.

"Hi, Logan. How you doing?" Dennis cheerfully replied. He nodded toward Cass. "Turns out we're in the same homeroom. Small world, huh?"

Logan snorted. "It's Kwaj. Of course it's a small world." Positioning himself on Cass' other side, he asked her, "Do you feel like getting in a little snorkeling this afternoon?"

Feeling trapped between the two boys, Cass frantically searched for a way out of the awkward situation.

"Uh ... I ... uh ... can't. Rianne's coming over, and we ... uh ... we're planning on maybe going to Macy's after lunch."

The excuse sounded lame even to her own ears, but it was the best she could come up with on the spur of the moment. Her one hope was that her friends were too far away to have heard her. Their muffled giggles dashed that hope, however, and Cass felt her cheeks blaze with embarrassment.

I always thought I'd like being the center of attention when it came to guys, she moaned to herself, *but this is more trouble than it's worth*.

As he approached his road, Dennis announced, "I'd like to call you later, Cass, if that's all right."

"That'd be fine," Cass answered in a strangled voice. Risking a peek at Logan out of the corner of her eye, she saw that his expression was thunderous. "Why don't you wait until after three or so to give Rianne and me time to go shopping?" she suggested.

"Will do." Dennis tipped an imaginary hat before breaking off from the group. "Talk to you later."

"Jerk," Logan muttered as the other boy rode away.

Annoyed, Cass shot him a frosty look. "Excuse me? Did you say something?"

Logan had the grace to blush. "It wasn't anything important. I was just thinking out loud."

"Whatever." Cass glared at him for a second so he would know she saw right through his lame response.

Keeping pace with her, Logan flashed an apologetic smile. "Is lunch at your house a girls-only thing or are guys invited too?"

"I don't know." Cass gestured toward the threesome in front. "You'll have to ask them. In cases like this, the majority rules."

As Logan opened his mouth to call to the girls, Kira looked over her shoulder at him and shook her head. "Sorry, pal. No boys allowed. Why don't you head on over to my house and keep Micah company? He said he was going right home."

Logan looked like he was ready to argue, then seemed to accept that he was outnumbered. "Fine," he muttered. "I know when I'm not wanted." Mustering a smile for Cass, he continued going straight when the girls turned left toward Ocean Street. "I'll call you," he told her.

She nodded that she'd heard, then put on a burst of speed to catch up with the others. They giggled when she pulled alongside them.

"Wow," drawled Tabitha. "You're my hero. How many girls can say they have two guys chasing after them?"

"Knock it off," she ordered irritably. "It's not funny. It's actually kind of embarrassing."

"No," Rianne corrected her. "Going around smiling when you don't know you have a piece of food stuck between your front teeth is embarrassing. Watching Logan and Dennis compete for your attention is hilarious. Am I right, ladies?" she asked the others.

Tabitha and Rianne nodded, smiling. Cass just glared at them all. "You're just jealous," she said, trying to get herself off the hook.

"Oh, puh-leeze!" Kira rolled her eyes. "I think the world of Logan, but I can't stand red hair on boys. As far as Dennis goes, he's okay. He's just a little too tame for my taste. I like guys with a bit more pizzazz."

"So what you're saying is you're looking for a dark-haired boy who likes to walk on the wild side," Cass asked.

Kira stuck her tongue out at her. "No, I'm not that picky," she retorted good-naturedly. "A blonde would be fine too."

Cass laughed, Tabitha and Rianne joining in. For all her talk, Kira was actually quite choosy about the boys she spent time with. Micah, who took his job as big brother very seriously, made sure of that.

They reached the Spencer house a couple of minutes later. Parking their bikes on the rear lanai, they made their way into the kitchen and found Mom at the stove stirring a pot of soup.

"You remembered!" Cass said. "You didn't say anything this morning so I wondered if you would."

Setting the ladle on the counter, Mom turned and propped her hands on her hips. "How could you think for a single minute I'd forget?" she demanded accusingly, although her dancing eyes betrayed her amusement. "It breaks my heart that you doubted me."

"Okay, I give up," Tabitha said, looking back and forth between Cass and her stepmother. "What are you two talking about?"

Mom moved to the refrigerator and retrieved cheese and butter. "Ever since Cass started kindergarten," she explained, reaching into the bread box, "I've always served tomato soup and grilled cheese sandwhiches for lunch on her first day of school. It's a tradition. After a while, my boss automatically gave me the day off every year." Smiling, she patted Cass' cheek then Tabitha's. "It's nice not to have to worry about that anymore. I liked knowing I'd be here for my girls when they got home."

Cass felt a quick stab of jealousy at hearing Mom refer to Tabitha as one of her girls. She still wasn't completely used to sharing her mother yet.

"How about you ladies set the table while I grill the

sandwiches?" Mom suggested as she began buttering the bread.

Cass opened a cupboard door to get the plates. "Are you eating too?"

Mom looked up, acting surprised. "You'd actually let me eat with you? I'm honored."

"Well," Cass hedged, grinning, "since you're making us lunch, we'll be nice and allow you to sit with us this time."

Over lunch, the other girls filled Mom in on Cass' conquests at school. Mom eyed her with interest while Cass fidgeted and pretended not to notice.

"I guess you'll have something to write home to Janette about this week," Mom remarked, referring to Cass' best friend in Tennessee.

Cass shrugged and broke off a piece of sandwich to nibble. "It's not that big a deal," she muttered, wishing the others had kept their mouths shut. She'd never hear the end of this.

"Not that big a deal?" Mom said, raising an eyebrow. "You have two boys—three if you count Rianne's brother—pursuing you, and you don't think it's anything to get excited about?"

"It's only because I'm the new girl in town. This will all die down as soon as they get used to having me around," Cass said as she desperately wracked her brain for another subject to distract her mother. "So Mom, like I was telling them earlier—I'm really glad Seaside High is so small." *Okay, so it's not the best thing I've ever come up with*, she thought darkly, but it worked. The conversation drifted to school matters and eventually Mom disappeared onto the porch.

CHAPTER 4

"Hey, Cass! Wait up."

Cass and Tabitha had just started off for school the next day.

Tabitha sent her a questioning look. "Should I go on ahead?"

Seeing Dennis pedaling rapidly in her direction, Cass grinned and nodded. "I'll catch up with you later."

Tabitha shook her head in mock irritation. "The second day of school, and you already have yourself an escort," she said good-naturedly. "Some people get all the breaks."

Cass waited until Dennis halted beside her, the warm breeze ruffling his sun-bleached hair.

"I'm glad I caught you," he said with a smile. "I didn't know what time you left for school."

Cass raised an eyebrow and grinned. "How many times did you circle the block so you could pretend to accidentally bump into me?"

Dennis flashed an embarrassed smile. "I was starting my second go 'round," he admitted. "But that hardly qualifies me as a stalker, you know. I would've had to have circled at least five times for that."

Cass laughed at his guilty expression. "Hey, I'm not upset," she assured him. "I'm actually pretty flattered."

Dennis brightened. "Oh, yeah? Well … good," he finished lamely.

Deciding it was time to let him off the hook, Cass started pedaling. "I guess we'd better head on. It wouldn't look good if I showed up late my second day."

Dennis fell in beside her. "Not to brag or anything, but I'm a favorite with most of the teachers. If you ever get in hot water with any of them, I'll be happy to put in a good word for you."

Cass laughed. "I appreciate the offer, but I don't get in trouble. I'm one of those boring students who never acts up and who always hands her work in on time."

Dennis raised an eyebrow. "Oh, a goody-two-shoes, huh?" He pretended to sigh with regret. "I don't know why I never attract wild girls."

"Who says I'm attracted to you?" She said, hoping she didn't sound as breathless as she felt. "You're the one who tracked me down this morning, remember?" With that, she put on a burst of speed to move ahead of him.

Laughing, Dennis pulled up alongside her. "Saucy, huh? I guess I better watch myself around you."

"If you know what's good for you, you will," Cass said, not quite recognizing the flirting tone that had crept in her voice. "I may not be a wild woman, but I'm no doormat either."

"You've got that right," agreed Dennis. "And I wasn't complaining. I like girls who aren't afraid to speak up for themselves."

Despite the warm sunshine, a shiver tingled up Cass' spine. *Does he realize what he just said?* she wondered. *Is that his way of saying he likes me? We just met yesterday, and he likes me already? Wow! Kwaj really is paradise.*

Reaching the high school, Cass and Dennis parked

their bikes side by side in one of the racks. As they headed toward the entrance, someone tapped Cass on the shoulder.

"Hi. I was hoping I'd see you before homeroom."

Cass turned to smile up at Logan. Although he smiled back, he looked annoyed as his glance flickered toward Dennis. Cass felt herself blush, and she stiffened in response.

I don't have anything to feel guilty about, she assured herself. *I'm not Logan's exlusive property. We've never even had an official date.*

Cass lifted her chin and met Logan's accusing gaze. "Dennis surprised me by coming by to ride to school with me," she explained coolly. "Wasn't that nice of him?" she added, a note of challenge in her voice.

Logan snorted softly. "What a guy." Shifting his backpack to the other shoulder, he lifted a hand in a jaunty wave. "See you."

Cass watched him walk away, her stomach sinking. *Why was I so snotty to him?* she asked herself. Before she could think, Dennis gently touched her elbow and she looked up at him.

"We have six minutes until the bell," he said, looking at his watch. "I don't know about you, but it takes me that long to get to my locker and decide what books I'll need for my morning classes."

"Slowpoke," teased Cass as she fell into step with him. They joined the throng of students streaming toward the entrance. "What you need is a little organization. That way you can be in and out of your locker in two minutes flat."

"Are you volunteering for the job of organizing me?" Although his tone was lighthearted, Dennis' expression was serious as he glanced down at Cass.

Choosing to treat the question as a joke, Cass shrugged and smiled. "You're nuts if you think I'd volunteer for a job like that. If you're willing to pay me, however ..." She left the rest of the sentence unfinished as she sashayed down the hall away from him.

His burst of laughter lifted her on top of the world. *I'm getting pretty good at this flirting stuff*, she congratulated herself. Unfortunately, the sight of Tabitha and Kira leaning against their lockers with identical glum expressions pulled her up short.

"Hey, guys. What's wrong?"

The other two girls exchanged glances, then Tabitha muttered, "You tell her. If I try to talk, I'll just wind up bawling."

Cass' eyebrows shot up in alarm. "What's going on? Is somebody sick? Has there been an accident?"

Kira raised a hand to stop her. "Don't get yourself all worked up. Nothing bad has happened." She shared another look with Tabitha. "Unless, of course, you count Alison Ross."

Cass expelled a relieved breath and turned to her locker. "Who's Alison Ross and why are y'all upset about her?" She consulted the slip of paper she'd scribbled her locker combination on and started twirling the metal dial on the lock.

"She's the new girl in town," Kira said darkly. "She got here four days ago. I'm afraid she's after my brother."

"Uh-oh." Cass stopped spinning the dial on her locker long enough to send Tabitha a sympathetic glance. "Are you sure? You think maybe you're overreacting?" she suggested hopefully.

"Nope." Folding her arms, Kira checked to see who might be eavesdropping and lowered her voice. "She called Micah twice last night, and both times he got off the phone with the goofiest look on his face."

"Is she a senior? She might have called to ask him something about school." Cass searched for a way to put a positive spin on the situation. "After all, she's new to the island."

"Oh, come on," drawled Kira. "Alison Ross didn't call Micah to talk about school. Have you seen her?"

As Cass shook her head, Tabitha emitted a soft groan. "She's gorgeous. She has long black hair down to the middle of her back. Plus, it's so shiny and straight you'd swear it came out of a shampoo commercial." She tugged at one of her own blonde curls. "It's nothing like this frizzy mop I'm stuck with."

Cass' eyes widened in surprise. She'd never heard Tabitha say something critical about her looks. "I thought you liked your hair."

"I did, until I found out Micah prefers brunettes." Tabitha frowned. "All these years, I've waited for him to notice me. Then someone like Alison Ross shows up, and it takes him less than a day to fall for her. Life is so unfair."

"Oh, come on." Cass turned to arch a skeptical brow at her stepsister. "Don't you think you're being rather melodramatic? Micah and this Alison girl just met, and you already have them hooked up."

"You haven't seen her."

"Still—" Cass' protest was interrupted by a shout from down the hall.

"Cass! Don't go anywhere. I want to talk to you."

She spotted Randy weaving his wheelchair through the milling students as he headed in her direction. With a shrug, she retrieved the last of her books from the locker, shut the door, and spun the dial.

"We can continue our discussion after school," she told Tabitha. "Meanwhile, I'll keep my eyes open for Alison. Maybe she's not the threat you think she is."

"Yeah, she's probably even more deadly," Tabitha muttered, then smiled wanly when Randy rolled to a stop a few feet from the group. "Hi, Randy."

"Hi, Tabitha." He nodded at Kira who waved. "Am I interrupting something?"

"Nothing important," Cass said brightly, only half noticing Tabitha's puzzled look. "Besides, we were just about through. So"—she sidled up next to Randy's wheelchair—"what can I do for you?"

Tabitha and Kira disappeared, so Cass accompanied Randy to his homeroom. On the way, after clearing his throat several times, he asked nervously, "Would you like to come over to the house this afternoon? We have a bunch of board games. You know, Monopoly, Clue, those kinds of games. Every once in a while I like to play them again. It reminds me of when I was a kid."

"That would be fun," Cass hedged. Suddenly, she wasn't sure she wanted to commit to a couple of hours with Randy before she knew what her other after-school options might be. She thought quickly. "Uh ... I'll have to check with my mom about coming over." Hoping to ease Randy's obvious disappointment, she flashed him an extra-bright smile. "I'll call you as soon as I get home and let you know. If I can't make it today, let's definitely plan on tomorrow. Okay?"

"It's a deal." Randy halted on the classroom threshold. "See you around. I'll be the one leaving everyone in the dust, or I guess I should say, sand."

Laughing, Cass waited for Randy to enter the room before heading back to her own class. The moment he turned away from her, she stopped smiling and felt her shoulders sag. She tried to banish the twinge of guilt that nagged at her but didn't succeed.

Why didn't I take Randy up on his invitation instead of giving him that song and dance about Mom and Tabitha?

Face it, you wanted to wait and see if you got a better offer, she answered herself.

Oh, I don't think—

Knock it off, the voice ordered. *You might get away with lying to others, but don't even try lying to yourself.*

Cass sighed. *Lord, help*, she pleaded quickly, running through the hall. *I'm starting to make a mess of things!*

CHAPTER 5

Cass made it to her homeroom just as the bell rang and smiled in response to Rianne's wave. From his seat by the window, Dennis also waved and Cass nodded in return. Claiming the desk beside Rianne, she whispered a hurried hello before Mrs. Wilcox began the day's announcements.

Rianne opened a notebook and quickly wrote something down. She slid it across the desk so Cass could see. *Did you talk to Randy?*

Cass nodded.

Did he ask you about coming over? Rianne wrote.

Again Cass nodded, wishing for a way to change the subject.

Are you coming? Rianne drew a happy face, followed by five exclamation points.

Here's my chance to make up for not saying yes to Randy. Cass glanced over at Rianne, intending to nod. What she did, however, was shrug.

"No?" mouthed Rianne.

"Maybe," Cass mouthed back.

"If I could have everyone's attention, please." Mrs. Wilcox said loudly, looked pointedly in Cass and

Rianne's direction. "This next announcement is of particular importance to me since it involves the French Club, which I sponsor."

Sliding down in her chair, Cass tuned her out. The truth was she secretly hoped Dennis would ask her to do something. Across the aisle from her, Rianne sent her several curious glances that Cass pretended not to notice. As soon as Mrs. Wilcox stopped speaking and the bell rang to change classes, Rianne appeared at Cass' side.

"How come you're not sure about coming to the house this afternoon?" There was a note of challenge in Rianne's voice.

Gathering her books together, Cass avoided her friend's eyes. "I explained to Randy I have to ask my mother first. Plus, Tabitha has some problem she wants to discuss with me. I told Randy I'd let him know after I've talked to them."

Rianne's suspicious expression relaxed. "Okay, I understand." Looking sheepish, she went on, "I know I'm overprotective when it comes to Randy. He hasn't had the best experiences with girls, and I don't want him to get hurt again."

Cass leaned down so her hair swung forward to cover her burning cheeks. "You know I wouldn't hurt Randy," she protested in a muffled voice, feeling like a world-class rat.

Rianne gave her a quick hug. "I know. I don't mean to lump you in with all the girls who can't see past Randy's wheelchair. I realize you're different."

Oh, wow, Cass thought uncomfortably. She had to get out of this. "I'd better get to class," she said quickly. "I have Spanish, and I … uh … promised Kira I'd go over some words with her before class started."

Cass slipped into the seat behind Kira a few seconds before the bell rang. Other than a quick glance over her shoulder, Kira didn't acknowledge Cass' presence. Preoccupied with her own thoughts, Cass didn't think it was strange until the teacher told the class to find partners to work on translating a paragraph. Cass tapped Kira on the back.

"How about it? Would you like to be my translating amigo?"

"Are you sure you have time for me?" Kira asked with a sniff.

Cass stared at her blankly. "What's that supposed to mean?"

"Oh, nothing." Kira looked back down at her book. "Forget I said anything. Sure, I'll be your partner."

"Kira, don't lie—" Cass began heatedly then lowered her voice when she realized several nearby students were sending her curious glances. "Look, you're mad at me about something. What's going on?"

"Uh ... excuse me." A boy from two rows over approached her desk. "Do you have a partner already?"

Cass looked at Kira with raised eyebrows, but Kira just stared off into the distance.

Confused, Cass managed to smile up at him. "I think I do, but I'm not sure. If it turns out I don't, I'll be happy to team up with you."

Cass waited until the boy moved away before turning to Kira and hissing, "What is the matter with you? You made me look like an idiot in front of that guy."

"For your information, his name is Alex, and—" Kira tilted her chin in the boy's direction, "he's waiting for an answer."

Cass turned to Alex who was watching her expectantly. Pointing first to Kira then to herself, she said, "It looks like we're partners, after all. Thanks, anyway." As soon as Alex looked away, Cass resumed glaring at Kira. "Okay, start talking. Why are you mad at me?"

Swiveling in her seat, Kira thumped her Spanish book down on Cass' desk and opened it to the page they were supposed to be working on. "We'd better look like we're doing something, or we'll have Mrs. Fleming breathing down our necks." After a brief pause, she whispered, "Okay, here's the deal. I think the way you treated Tabitha before stinks. I mean, you're sisters."

Stepsisters, Cass wanted to correct her, but stopped herself just in time. There was no reason to make Kira even angrier.

"I don't know what you're talking about," Cass said, bewildered. "What did I do?"

"Oh, come on," scoffed Kira. "Think about it. Tabitha was pouring her heart out to you about Micah and Alison, and you seemed like you were interested—for a little while anyway. Then the minute Randy showed up, you took off with him. Tabitha needed you, and you acted like you couldn't care less."

Cass' mouth dropped open in astonishment, and she forgot about pretending to work on the paragraph. After a warning look from Mrs. Fleming, she hastily picked up the pencil she'd dropped and scribbled something on the paper.

"Did Tabitha tell you that's what she thought happened?"

"Well, not exactly," Kira said slowly. She raised defiant eyes to Cass. "But I've known her long enough to know what she's thinking without her having to say anything. And I know she was hurt when you ditched her and went off with Randy," she stubbornly insisted.

"We had finished talking."

"Oh, really?" Kira arched a skeptical eyebrow at her. "Is that why you cut Tabitha off and told her you'd get back to her after school?"

"I didn't—"

"It appears you ladies are doing more talking than working," Mrs. Fleming interrupted. She had come up behind Kira before either of them realized it. "Do I need to separate you two, or can you manage to complete the assignment without any further conversation?"

"We'll do the work," Kira mumbled while Cass lowered her head in embarrassment.

My second day at a new school, and I've already made a bad impression on a teacher, Cass chided herself as she began translating the paragraph. *Way to go*.

Talking only when it was necessary to discuss a tricky word, Cass and Kira completed the assignment on time. While Kira handed it in, Cass stared out the window at a row of palm trees swaying in the breeze. Beyond them, ocean waves licked at the beach in a never-ending rhythm.

She didn't like the idea that she'd upset Tabitha, for a couple of reasons. The first was that she really cared about her stepsister. Secondly, she didn't want Mom jumping on her for mistreating Tabitha, which she'd do if Tabitha complained to her. Along with those two thoughts, Cass realized she'd be irritated if it turned out Kira was right. If Tabitha could get her feelings hurt that easily then, as far as Cass was concerned, she was too sensitive for her own good.

"Where do you go next?" Cass asked Kira after the bell rang. "I'll walk with you so we can talk."

"No can do. I'm meeting Tabitha in the hall. We have U.S. History together." Kira hesitated. "Look, I've been thinking about it, and I might have overreacted before. Tabitha's my best friend, and I'll feel awful if Micah and Alison start going out. It'll be like I'm responsible in some way since he's my brother. I guess I figured if I can't stop Micah from falling for Alison, then at least I should try to stop you from making things worse for Tabitha. Does that make sense?"

Standing up, Cass nodded. "It makes a lot of sense. So—" she gathered up her books and settled them in the crook of her arm, then continued, "are we still friends?"

Kira smiled. "Absolutely. Although how two touchy people like us will ever manage to stay friends without killing each other is beyond me." She gestured toward the hall. "Tabitha's waiting. I'll see you at lunch. If we bump into Micah and Alison before then, I'll be the one sitting in the corner with the hysterical blonde."

Following Kira to the door, Cass was stopped by Alex, who lifted a hand in greeting. "Oh, hi. Did you ever find someone to work with?"

With a foot propped behind him, Alex leaned against the wall and gave Cass a lazy grin. It hadn't registered earlier, but now she couldn't help noticing he had incredibly blue eyes to match his incredibly gorgeous face.

This guy actually waited for me? Cass asked, nervous that he might hear her heart pounding. She desperately wished she had worn anything other than her favorite—but old—pair of jean shorts and a faded green T-shirt.

"I hooked up with Jack Bennett," Alex replied. "Do you know him?"

Cass realized she was staring. "Uh ... no. I just moved here last month, and I haven't met everybody yet."

"Don't you think we should remedy that particular situation—beginning with me?" He smiled. "Alex Johnson at your service."

"I know. Kira told me who you were." For some reason, Cass was having trouble breathing. "I'm ... uh ..." For one horrible second, she was afraid she'd forgotten her name. Swallowing hard, she started again, "I'm ..."

"I know who you are," Alex broke in. "I asked around about you after I saw you yesterday. You're Cass Devane.

Your mother married Steve Spencer. I've worked some at the radio station. Steve's a great guy."

"Yes, he is." Cass frantically tried to think of something else to say. She was sure Alex was on the verge of leaving.

Before she could come up with anything, Alex looked straight at her with his beautiful eyes and asked, "I know you haven't been here long, but are you dating anyone?"

Please don't blush, Cass silently appealed to her cheeks even as she felt them begin to burn. *I don't want Alex to think I'm that pathetically grateful he's paying attention to me, even if I really am.*

"No, I'm not seeing anybody." To her surprise, Cass sounded calm, not at all like the quivering mass of nerves she was inside. Surprising herself even more, she gazed boldy up at Alex. "Why do you want to know?"

"All right," he said, smiling. "A girl who isn't afraid to speak her mind. What a nice change of pace from the girls who think they have to play hard to get."

"I appreciate the compliment, but you didn't answer my question," she teased.

Alex threw back his head and laughed and the light glinted off his blonde hair. "Cass Devane, I think you and I are going to get along great. To answer your question, I wanted to know if you were dating anyone because I'm planning on asking you out myself. How would you like to go to the movies Friday night?"

Her heart began to thud painfully in her chest. *This can't be happening*, Cass tried to convince herself. *Boys like Alex don't ask out girls like me*. She peeked up at him from under her lashes to see if he was laughing at her. He wasn't and a liquid warmth flooded through her.

Licking suddenly dry lips, Cass smiled up at him. "I'd love to go to the movies with you. I'll have to check with my mother first, but I'm sure she'll say it's okay."

"Great." Alex pushed away from the wall. "You know, I'm really good with moms. How about I come by after school and you introduce me to yours? Once she meets me, I guarantee you she won't have any objections to letting you go out with me."

Cass laughed. "You're coming this close—" she held her thumb and forefinger a quarter inch apart, "to sounding like an egomaniac," she warned. "And my mother can spot egomaniacs a mile away."

Alex shrugged. "Not to worry. I'll be so humble and charming your mother won't be able to keep herself from approving of me."

Cass raised an eyebrow. "We'll see."

"Does that mean it's all right for me to come over?" Alex made it sound as if meeting Cass' mother and getting on her good side were the most important things in the world to him.

Eyeing the thinning crowd in the hall, Cass realized she had less than a minute to get to her next class. "It should be, but call first. My mother might have something planned."

"Then call I will." Alex tucked his books under his left arm and with his right hand touched her briefly on the arm. "You'll be hearing from me. See you."

While Alex headed right, Cass scurried three doors down to the left to her English class. She arrived with only seconds to spare and chalked up her breathless condition not to the dash through the hall, but to her encounter with Alex. Across the aisle from her, Rianne smiled as Cass collapsed into her seat.

"Did you get lost?"

Cass shook her head. "Nope. I was … detained."

"From the look on your face, I'm guessing it was by a guy." When Cass nodded, Rianne pretended to sigh with disgust. "Do you plan on leaving any for the rest of us?"

Before Cass could think of a snappy comeback, the bell rang and the teacher motioned for quiet. The rest of the class period left her with no opportunity to talk with Rianne since a prolonged discussion of the previous night's reading assignment was followed by a pop quiz.

The bell signaling the end of the class had barely stopped ringing when Rianne reached over to poke Cass in the arm. "All right, give. Who was it this time?"

"Alex Johnson." Cass managed to keep herself from heaving a blissful sigh. "Do you know him?"

"Uh … yeah." Rianne abruptly busied herself with collecting her books and sliding out of her chair. Standing in the aisle, she fussed with her short corduroy skirt and avoided looking at Cass.

"Uh-oh." Cass wasn't fooled by Rianne's sudden flurry of acitivity. "You don't like him."

"It's not that I don't like Alex." Rianne fidgeted with the strap on her purse, twisting it then straightening it out. "He's a very nice guy. Honest," she insisted at Cass' sniff of disbelief. "It's just … well—" Rianne glanced around. "Alex has a habit of going after the new girls. It's like a game with him. I've never known him to stay with one girl for more than a couple of weeks. He's pretty much the love-'em-and-leave-'em type. I don't want you to get hurt."

"Oh." Her happiness sunk to the pit of her stomach. "I should have known it was too good to be true."

"Hey, don't." Joining Cass as she shuffled toward the door, Rianne butted shoulders with her. "I didn't mean to make it sound that way. Besides, who knows? Maybe Alex isn't up to his usual tricks, and he's genuinely interested in you. Which, if he has any sense, he should be," she added.

Cass gave her a wan smile. "Thanks. You're a good friend."

As the girls merged with the students in the hall, Rianne grabbed Cass' arm and nodded at someone across the hall. "That's Alison Ross," she whispered. "I had a class last period with Tabitha, and she told me Alison's after Micah. Wow, she was right. She's a knockout."

Cass tried not to gape at the girl whose stunning looks drew the stares of everyone else in the hall, especially the boys. To her dismay, Alison was tall and slender with dusky skin and flowing, ebony hair.

"Obviously Alex hasn't seen her yet," Cass muttered, "or he never would have wasted his time going after me."

"Oh, Alex has seen Alison all right," Rianne said confidently. "He makes it his business to check out the new crop of girls at the beginning of the year. The thing is, Alison's a senior. Alex usually goes after the girls his age or younger. I've never known him to date someone older unless the girl chased him."

"I guess he's out of luck then since Alison's going after Micah." Cass made a face. "Life is so strange. Tabitha wants Micah, but she's afraid he wants Alison. I was thrilled thinking Alex wanted me, but I figure, given a choice, he'd rather have Alison." She snapped her fingers. "That's it. The solution is to get rid of Alison. Let's dump her into the shark pit."

"Stop it. You're scaring me." Rianne halted at a door. "Here's my class. I'll see you at lunch."

"I can't wait." Cass spotted Alex coming toward her on the opposite side of the hall and quickly looked away. She leaned in towards Rianne. "After the morning we've had, we're going to have tons to talk about."

CHAPTER 6

Cass paid little attention during trig class, thinking instead about Alex. She felt like the stupidest person on earth—or at least on Kwaj—for falling for his line, but she still couldn't forget the image of him leaning against the wall, his tan, muscular frame highlighted by his khaki shorts and white shirt.

He must be laughing his head off at me, she thought, waves of misery washing over her. *How could I have been so clueless? I suppose I just wanted to believe so badly that he was interested in me. Well, I've learned my lesson. I won't make that mistake again. As soon as I can, I'll tell Randy I'm going over to his house this afternoon.*

After class, Cass stopped by her locker to retrieve the lunch her mother had packed for her before heading to the cafeteria. She'd just crossed into the lunchroom and was scanning the tables for Rianne and the others when Alex blocked her view.

"Looking for me?" he asked with an engaging grin.

"Hardly." Cass made a show of trying to peer around him. When he didn't take the hint, she gazed up at him with an irritated expression. "Have you seen my stepsister, by any chance? We're supposed to eat together."

"Nope. Haven't seen her." Alex gently brushed a strand of hair away from Cass' cheek, causing her skin to tingle. "But I'll be more than happy to stand in for her."

Cass frowned. "You know, I'll bet you say that to all the girls. All the new girls, that is."

Instead of taking offense as Cass had expected he would, Alex laughed. "I see you've heard about my reputation. Who have you been talking to?"

"So you don't deny your favorite pastime is chasing the new girls on the island?"

"Why should I?" Alex shrugged. "It's fun and nobody gets hurt."

"Except the girls who have their hearts broken," Cass said. "But I guess they don't count, huh?"

She tried to brush past Alex, but he moved wherever she did. She finally gave up and glared at him. "This isn't a dance. Will you please get out of my way?"

"What if I told you it's different with you?" Alex asked softly. "That it's not a game and that I think I could really like you?"

Matching his tone, Cass murmured, "I'd say ... yeah, right," she finished scornfully, rolling her eyes for added emphasis.

Once again, Alex laughed off the insult. "See what I mean? You are different. You're funny, you say what you think—"

"And most importantly, I'm smart enough not to get mixed up with the likes of you," Cass interrupted sweetly. "Now, if you'll excuse me, I'm going to find Tabitha and my friends."

This time Alex let Cass by. As she passed him, however, he reminded her, "You said I could call you this afternoon."

"I won't be home."

"Aw, come on. Give me a chance." Alex paused. "Please?"

He sounded so serious that Cass stopped and turned. "Why me? Why don't you pick on somebody else?"

"Because you, Cass Devane," Alex leaned in so close that she could feel his warm breath on her cheek, "are special. You're not like anyone I've ever met. I want to get to know you better."

"And you, Alex Johnson," Cass purred, "are full of it." Reveling in his stunned expression, she swept past him. "But I've decided you can go ahead and call me if you still feel like it," she added over her shoulder. "I'm enjoying myself so much, I believe I'd like to get to know you better too."

Her head held high, Cass walked away without giving Alex a chance to reply. She wondered if he'd call, then mentally shrugged. Either way, she figured she came out a winner. If he didn't call, it meant it was just a game after all and she was better off without him. If he did call, it meant he really was interested, and her heart raced at the possibility.

"What were you and Alex talking about?" Tabitha demanded the moment Cass sat down at the table she and the others had claimed. "Rianne told us he's after you."

"I do believe I just managed to put old Alex Johnson in his place," she announced proudly.

Kira applauded. "Way to go. It's about time. If you ask me, that boy's been allowed to run wild for way too long." Taking a bite of her sandwich, she leaned across the table and fixed Cass with an eager stare. "Start from the beginning, and tell us exactly what happened. Don't leave anything out."

By the time Cass finished, the lunch period was half over, and she'd only eaten a couple of potato chips. "Okay, it's somebody else's turn to talk. I'm starved."

While the others discussed their various Alison Ross sightings, Cass listened with one ear and allowed her gaze to roam the cafeteria. Other than Alex, she only spotted Dennis, and concluded Randy, Micah, Logan, and, unfortunately, Alison were scheduled for the second lunch period.

Cass eyed Tabitha with sympathy. *I'm sure it doesn't help much for her to know Micah and Alison could wind up eating lunch together every day.*

"Hello? Earth to Cass." Kira snapped her fingers under Cass' nose.

Cass blinked in surprise. "I was just checking to see who else has lunch this period."

"Logan does." Tabitha wiggled her eyebrows, making the others laugh. "I know you have a herd of guys stampeding to date you, but I hope you haven't forgotten about Logan."

Cass felt her temper flare briefly. "What's there to forget?" she asked somewhat testily. "It's not like Logan and I were ever an item."

"An item," echoed Rianne. She grinned at Kira and Tabitha. "I love it. It's such an old-fashioned term."

"Not that anyone could ever accuse Cass of being old-fashioned." Tabitha traced a design in the frosting of the cupcake Mom had included in her lunch. "Old-fashioned girls don't date three or four different guys at the same time."

Cass struggled to hold her irritation in check. "Excuse me, has anybody here seen me go out with anyone recently? Or ever, for that matter?" When her friends shook their heads, she smiled. "I rest my case."

"It's not the number of guys you've actually dated," Tabitha insisted. "It's the principle of the thing."

"What are you saying?" Cass challenged. "I'm not even supposed to talk to anyone but Logan?"

Tabitha shrugged. "Well, no. It's just—I don't know—it looks bad for you to be flirting the way you have been the past couple of days. I'm worried you're going to get a reputation."

"First of all, you make it sound like you've seen me talking to dozens of guys. There have been two—count 'em, two—Dennis and Alex," Cass pointed out. "Secondly, they approached me. I didn't go chasing after them. What should I do when a boy starts a conversation with me? Ignore him? Besides, what kind of idiotic place is this if just talking to a boy earns a girl a bad reputation?"

"Okay, that's enough," Rianne broke in. "This conversation is going nowhere. Personally, I couldn't care less about Logan, Dennis, or Alex. All I care about is whether or not Cass is nice to my brother. As long as she's nice to Randy, she can date a hundred guys and it wouldn't bother me one iota."

The others laughed and the tension lifted. Cass and Tabitha exchanged apologetic smiles. Before they knew it, lunch was over and it was time to go their separate ways to their afternoon classes.

Logan caught up with Cass as she was exiting the cafeteria. "Hi."

Flipping her hair over her shoulder, Cass nodded at him. "Hey."

"Did you have a good lunch?" Logan stepped aside and let Cass precede him through the doorway.

Cass smiled. "It was great. Now that Mom doesn't work, she's really into cooking and stuff. She gave Tabitha and me egg salad sandwiches on homemade bread and cupcakes she baked herself. It's nothing like the peanut butter-and-jelly lunches I used to eat, that's for sure."

"Tell your mom I won't complain if she feels like throwing in an extra sandwich or two for me every now and then." Logan paused at the point where the hall forked. "Where are you headed?"

"Uh—" Cass stopped and checked her schedule. "Physics. Room 204."

"That's upstairs. My next class is on this floor." He hesitated, picking at the corner of one of his textbooks. "Are you doing anything after school?"

What is this? Cass wondered, half-exasperated, half-amazed. *For years I've been the invisible woman as far as guys are concerned. Now three of them want me to do something with them the same afternoon.* She smiled to herself. *Not that I really want to complain.*

She remembered Logan was waiting for an answer. "Actually, I do have plans. Maybe we could do something tomorrow," she suggested. "We could get everybody and go to the pool or the lagoon."

If Logan was disappointed that she didn't suggest an activity involving just the two of them, he didn't show it. "Sounds good. I'll call you later. Even better, I might drop by after supper."

Cass, distracted by Dennis calling her name and waving to her, almost forgot to respond. "Oh … uh … yeah, either way will be fine." She started to edge away. "I've got to go. See you." She left with a quick wave, not looking back.

CHAPTER 7

Cass and Tabitha rode home together after school while Kira and Rianne went to their houses. Once again, Dennis accompanied Cass and Tabitha part of the way before veering off at his street. The moment he was out of earshot, Tabitha turned to Cass.

"You sure gave him the runaround when he asked about coming to the house," she remarked. "What's up? Have you decided you don't like him after all?"

"No. Dennis is great." Cass briefly lifted her face to the sun, savoring its warmth after the school's frigid air-conditioning. "The problem is I'm still trying to figure out what to do about Randy and Alex. Things are complicated enough without adding Dennis to the mix."

"What do you mean?" Tabitha asked.

Cass quickly explained the situation to her. Tabitha remained silent as they parked their bikes behind the house. When Cass started toward the porch, Tabitha caught her by the arm.

"You realize what you should do, don't you? I mean, it's obvious."

Shrugging, Cass mumbled, "I don't think it's all that clear-cut."

Tabitha gave Cass' arm an impatient shake before releasing it. "Yes, it is. Randy asked you first. It's only right that you should tell him yes when he calls."

Cass just looked at her. "But I'd rather spend time with Alex."

Tabitha's eyes narrowed. "Why?" Her voice was tense with emotion. "Because Randy's in a wheelchair?"

Cass met Tabitha's challenging gaze without flinching. "No, and I can't believe you'd say something like that to me. You know how much I like Randy. He could be armless, legless, and—and—bald, for all I care. It's just—"

"Go on," Tabitha urged when Cass left the rest of the sentence unfinished. "It's just what?"

Cass took a deep breath before continuing, "Randy and I will never be anything more than friends. It's different with Alex. It could develop into a boyfriend/girlfriend thing with him. He asked me to go the movies Friday," she confided.

Tabitha dismissed Alex's invitation with a breezy wave. "Big deal. He's taken half the girls on the island to the movies. I want to know why you could never be anything but friends with Randy. It *is* the wheelchair, isn't it?"

"No!" Cass fairly shouted, despite the uncomfortable jab from her conscience. "It's—he—we—" Frustrated, she threw her hands up in the air. "Forget it. I'm not going to bother trying to explain how I feel since you probably wouldn't understand anyway. Go ahead and think whatever you want to think. The important thing is *I* know the truth."

As best she could on the scraggly grass and wearing a pair of flipflops, Cass stomped into the house.

She hadn't been inside two minutes when the phone rang. Mom answered it, then handed her the receiver.

"It's for you." She winked. "It's a boy."

As though whoever it was could see her, Cass smoothed her hair before taking the phone. "Hello?" She silently chided herself for sounding out of breath.

"Hi, Cass. It's Alex."

Yes! Cass thought with exultation.

Aloud, she said calmly, "Hey, Alex."

"Was that your mother who answered the phone?" he asked.

"Uh-huh. Why?"

"Because I missed my chance to start charming her," Alex said with a laugh. "Are you surprised I called?"

Enjoying herself, Cass wrapped the phone cord around her finger then let it unravel. "Not really. Everybody keeps telling me you're smarter than you look."

He laughed again. "So, is it okay for me to come over?"

"Hold on. Let me ask." Cass covered the mouth of the receiver with her hand. "Mom, it's a boy from a couple of my classes. He wants to come over for a while. Is that okay?"

Mom didn't hesitate. "Absolutely. Tell him not to eat anything. I'll be happy to fix you two a pizza."

Cass returned to the phone. "My mother said you can come. She also said not to eat anything because she's making us a pizza."

"Great," enthused Alex. "Pizza's one of my favorites. I'll be there in about ten minutes."

"See you." Cass hung up the phone and turned to discover Mom watching her with curiosity, her elbows on the counter her chin on her hands. "Who's the boy? I want to know all about him."

Cass darted a glance at Tabitha who lounged against the refrigerator, frowning. "His name is Alex Johnson, and he's a junior. That's really all I know. Steve knows him," she added. "Alex has done some work around the radio station."

"Aha!" Mom straightened and headed to the phone. "I think I'll call my husband and do a little snooping."

"Mom," Cass protested, "I don't want it getting back to Alex that you've been checking up on him."

Mom shrugged as she dialed the phone. "How would he find out? The only way would be Steve, and he won't say anything. You have nothing to worry about." She turned away from Cass and said into the phone, "Steve? Is this a good time? I have a couple of questions I want to ask you."

Cass left the kitchen, deciding to change her clothes instead of eavesdropping on the conversation. When she reached her room, she discovered Tabitha had followed her.

"I take it our little chat outside didn't do any good," Tabitha said, leaning against the door.

Cass shot her an irritated glance over her shoulder. "I told Randy I didn't know if I had plans. Alex called before I had a chance to talk to Randy, so now I have plans. I won't be lying when I tell Randy I'm busy."

"That is so cold." Tabitha shoved her hands into her shorts pockets. "What do you think Rianne would say if she knew how you're treating her brother?"

Cass whirled around from the closet. "Is that a threat?" she growled. "Are you saying you'll tell Rianne if I don't do what you want me to do?"

Raising her hands, Tabitha backed up a step. "No way. I wouldn't sink that low. I just thought you might want to consider how Rianne would feel if she found out you ditched Randy for Alex. It could get back to her, you know."

"If it does, she'll understand." Even Cass heard the

lack of conviction in her voice. Turning her back on Tabitha, she pushed through her clothes until she found something that seemed appropriate for Alex. "Rianne knows I like Randy as a friend, nothing more."

"She also knows you don't treat friends like trash." Tabitha stepped into the hall. "Think about it." As she turned to head back to the kitchen, she almost ran into Mom. "Oops, sorry."

Mom smiled. "No harm done." Directing her attention to Cass, she held out the cordless phone. "I switched phones because Steve wants to talk to you. I'll be in the kitchen getting the pizza ready when you're done."

Cass accepted the phone with a hollow feeling in the pit of her stomach. She still wasn't used to having a father and especially not when it came to dealing with his reaction to her dating. Swallowing hard, she lifted the phone to her ear.

"Hello?"

"Hi, sweetie. How are you?"

"Pretty good." Cass pulled her T-shirt off and shrugged into the shorter purple shirt, buttoning it with her her free hand. "How about you?"

"I'm ready to call it a day. All I've done is field phone calls from people wanting to know when the mail's going to get here. Other than that, I can't complain. Listen," Dad went on, "your Mom tells me Alex Johnson is coming by to visit in a little bit."

"Uh-huh," Cass said cautiously.

"I just wanted you to know I approve."

Cass heaved a sigh of relief, and the knots in her stomach loosened. "Good. I'm glad to know that."

"I've always found Alex to be polite and respectful and very good company. I hope the two of you have a good time this afternoon."

"Thanks. I'm sure we will." Cass finished buttoning her shirt and started to tuck it in. "Do you want to talk to Mom again?"

"I'd like to, but I can't." He laughed. "Duty calls. Two other lines are lit up on the phone here. Just tell your Mom I'm crazy about her, and I'm counting the seconds until I see her again."

"Oh, yuck! Like I'd actually deliver a message like that," Cass scoffed good-naturedly. "Love has definitely scrambled your brain. I used to think you were a pretty smart person."

"I didn't think you'd do it, but I figured it was worth a try," Dad replied cheerfully. "Anyway, I'll see you when I get home. Bye now."

"Bye."

Cass pushed the off button and tossed the phone on her bed. Walking to her bedroom door, she closed it so she could check herself out in the full-length mirror hanging on the back. Although she looked fine, she wasn't entirely happy with what she saw staring back at her.

"Maybe Tabitha's right," she whispered to her reflection. "Maybe I should have gone over to Randy's and put Alex off until tomorrow. But, dang it all," she argued with herself, "we're talking about Alex Johnson. He's just about the best-looking guy I've ever laid eyes on. Janette and the rest of my friends back home would die if they ever saw him. No," she decided, "I did the right thing by choosing to see Alex. I'm sure of it."

As Cass left her room to join her mother and Tabitha in the kitchen, she realized there was one little problem with the pep talk she'd just given herself. If she was so sure about her decision, why did she feel like she was somehow betraying Randy and, even worse, Rianne?

The phone rang again as Cass reached the living

room. Yelling, "I'll get it," she ran back to her room and snatched the cordless off the bed. It was Randy.

Here's my chance to make things right, she told herself. *I'll tell Randy I'll be over in a little while, then I'll make sure Alex doesn't stay longer than an hour or so.*

Pleased with herself for having come up with a workable solution, Cass greeted Randy warmly.

"Cass, I'm afraid I'm going to have to take a rain check on getting together today," Randy said a few seconds later. "My mother's in the middle of a cleaning frenzy, and she doesn't want company. She said tomorrow would be fine, though."

Cass tried to sound disappointed, but she couldn't help smiling. "I understand. Tomorrow will be fine." Deciding a little white lie couldn't hurt, she added, "I'm sorry it didn't work out for today. I was looking forward to it."

"Yeah, me too." In contrast to Cass, Randy sounded genuinely let down. "I guess I'll talk to you later then."

"I'd like that," Cass responded and meant it.

After hanging up, she couldn't wait to tell her worrywart stepsister how things had turned out. More importantly, she could spend time with Alex and not worry about who might find out.

Yup, Cass mused, dancing as she exited her room, *life is definitely looking up. It's proof that things work out if you just play your cards right.*

CHAPTER 8

"Cass, are you busy?" Tabitha asked hesitantly, hovering in the doorway of Cass' room.

Cass looked up from the magazine she was reading. "Nope. Come on in. What's up?"

Tabitha shuffled into the room and sank down onto the bed. She wondered if she looked as awful as she felt. "Kira just called," she said, forcing the words past the pain in her throat. "It's official. Micah invited Alison Ross over to his house after school today. She should be there in a couple of minutes. Kira promised to keep an eye on them and report everything they say and do."

"Oh, Tabitha," Cass said, tossing the magazine aside, "I'm so sorry. Are you sure Micah asked her, though? That Alison didn't invite herself, and he was stuck with having to be polite?"

"No. Kira was very definite that Micah asked her."

"Well, things aren't always what they seem," Cass said, far too brightly as far as Tabitha was concerned. "Maybe Micah ... uh ... maybe he ... you know—"

"Forget it. In this case, it's exactly what it seems to be." Tabitha laid back on the bed, clutching her stomach. "Micah's known Alison four days and he's on the verge of asking her out. He's known me eight years, and I mean absolutely nothing to him."

"That's not true and you know it," argued Cass. "Micah thinks the world of you."

"Yeah, as his kid sister's best friend," Tabitha sighed. "But as a girl he'd be interested in dating?" She shook her head. "No way."

"I can't believe you're just giving up like this." Cass sounded indignant. "If you like Micah as much as you say you do, why aren't you fighting for him?"

"Yeah, right." Tabitha snorted. "You try fighting somebody like Alison Ross. It would be like going into battle without any weapons. How can I compete with someone like her? She's everything I'm not. All these years I never knew Micah preferred tall, dark-haired girls. I guess a blonde shrimp like me doesn't stand a chance."

"I don't like it when you put yourself down," Cass said, surprising Tabitha. "You're not a shrimp. You're petite. Besides, as far as Micah not liking—"

The doorbell rang and Cass abruptly broke off. Neither of them spoke as they listened to Mom answer the door, followed by the rumble of a male voice. Tabitha glanced at Cass, thinking at first it might be Micah—then, stomach sinking, realizing it couldn't be.

"Cass!" Mom came down the hall and poked her head into the room. "A boy named Dennis is here to see you."

A pleased smile lit up Cass' face. "Really? He didn't say anything about coming by. Tell him I'll be right there," she said.

Mom shook her head, grinning at Tabitha. "Do you have any idea what's going on with my daughter and all these boys? All I used to hear when we lived in Tennessee was complaint after complaint about how no guy ever gave her a second look."

"Thank you so much for sharing that, Mother," Cass drawled. "Now, if you two don't mind I'd like some privacy so I can change. Dennis is waiting, you know."

"I recognize a hint when I hear one. How about you?" Mom motioned for Tabitha to join her. "I guess we'd better leave before she throws us out."

Once in the hall, Tabitha turned to go to her own room. Mom seemed surprised. "Aren't you going to say hello to Dennis?"

Tabitha shook her head. "I don't feel like being social right now. I think I'm going to my room to lie down for a while."

A worried frown creased Mom's forehead, and she reached out her hand to check Tabitha's temperature. "Are you feeling okay? Does anything hurt?"

Tabitha eluded Mom's touch by inching toward her room. "I'm fine. I'm just tired." She smiled wanly. "You know how it is, trying to get back into a routine the first week of school."

Tabitha closed the door, trying to give Mom a bright smile to convince her she was okay. She should have known it wouldn't work. A few minutes after Tabitha heard Cass and Dennis leave, Mom tapped on her door. "It's your favorite cookie lady," she called cheerfully. "May I come in?"

"Sure," Tabitha said hesitantly. She was sitting at her desk, her physics book open in front of her.

Mom let herself in. "I thought you were going to lie down."

"I tried, but I couldn't relax," Tabitha said. "I realized I have too much to do. The teachers are already piling on the work."

Mom walked up behind her and rested a hand on her shoulder. "So you've been slaving away in here?" She set the cookies and milk off to one side of the desk.

"Not really." Tabitha waved a hand over the book. "It's physics, so I'm basically clueless. I've been staring at the same page for five minutes now, and nothing makes sense."

Mom gave a rueful laugh. "I wish I could help you, sweetie, but physics and I never got along either."

"Great. Dad already warned me he won't be much help." Tabitha nibbled at her cookie. "I was planning on getting Micah to tutor me," she said casually, "but I guess he's out of the picture for the time being."

"Oh, really?" Mom matched Tabitha's nonchalant manner. "Why is that?"

"Let's just say he's too busy to spend time with the likes of me," Tabitha said, trying to keep the bitterness out of her voice.

Mom sat down on the corner of the bed. "Oh? Did the two of you have a falling-out?"

"Hardly," Tabitha scoffed. "He'd have to actually notice me before we could have a fight."

Mom frowned. "I thought you and Micah were great friends. He certainly spent a great deal of time with you this summer. Maybe you'd better start at the beginning and fill me in on what's happening. I seem to be missing something."

Tabitha sighed, not sure how to explain. "Okay, here's the deal. Micah has taken up with a new girl in his class."

Mom frowned. "Exactly what do you mean when you say he's taken up with her?"

"According to Kira, they've had several phone conversations over the past few days. Then today Micah invited her to the house."

"I see," Mom said softly. "Have you met her?"

"No, but I've seen her." Tabitha picked up her pen and twirled it in her fingers. "Her name's Alison Ross and she's drop-dead gorgeous. Kira says she's from Abilene, Texas, so she has that way of talking." At Mom's raised eyebrows, Tabitha hastily explained, "Not that a southern drawl is a bad thing. It's just that boys really seem to fall for it, and it's one more thing Alison has that I don't."

"I take it you feel inferior next to her," Mom said quietly.

"Not to be rude or anything, but gee, Mom, duh." Her short bark of laughter was harsh. "You'd have to see Alison to understand. She looks like a model. Everything about her is perfect. Even her skin is perfect. I'll bet she's never had a bad hair day in her life."

"Now, sweetie," Mom said gently. "I'm sure the last thing you want to hear right now is a sermon, but don't you remember when the youth group discussed self-esteem? We talked about the foolishness of comparing ourselves to others and the need to remember we get our worth from being children of God."

"That's easy to believe when you're feeling pretty good about yourself." Tabitha made a face and broke another cookie in half. "It gets a lot harder when you run up against someone like Alison. We may both be children of God, but the problem is He made her ten times prettier."

"I've never heard you talk so much about appearances. I thought it didn't matter to you what other people look like." She hesitated. "Perhaps it doesn't matter as long as you're the more attractive one."

Tabitha jerked her head around to glare at Mom. "What's that supposed to mean?" she demanded icily.

Mom motioned for her to calm down. "Don't get huffy until you hear me out. My guess is you're used to being the pretty one in most groups. You're a very attractive young lady, and I think you take it for granted that you're better looking than a lot of girls your age."

"Are you saying I'm stuck-up?" Tabitha had a hard time getting the words around the lump of indignation lodged in her throat.

"Not at all," Mom assured her. "I don't believe it's something you usually spend much time thinking about. Now that Alison's appeared on the scene, however, you feel like you're coming up short when you measure yourself against her. That's a new experience for you, and not a very pleasant one, I would imagine," she added sympathetically.

"It's not." Tabitha paused, puzzled. "I'm not sure why you're telling me this."

"Would you want some girl to feel bad about herself because she's not as pretty as you are?"

Tabitha didn't hesitate to respond. "Of course not."

"Then don't beat yourself up over Alison."

"But—"

"But nothing," Mom interrupted. "I know what it's like to drive yourself crazy worrying about how pretty you are compared to someone else. Way back when your Dad and I were in high school, I lived in constant fear he'd drop me for a prettier girl. I didn't understand then that he liked me for the person I was inside, not for what I looked like on the outside." Laughing, she made a show of playfully fluffing her hair. "Of course the outside wasn't bad, if I do say so myself."

Tabitha gave her a sad half-smile. "At least you and Dad were dating, though," she said. "Micah and I haven't even gotten that far. I guess he doesn't like my inside any more than he likes my outside."

"Oh, sweetie, he likes you very much." At Tabitha's skeptical snort, Mom insisted, "I can tell by the way Micah looks at you that he cares a great deal."

Tabitha still wasn't convinced. "Then why hasn't he

ever asked me out?" she asked.

Mom hesitated. "Perhaps he doesn't know you're interested," she said finally.

Tabitha just stared at her. "How could he not know? I've been giving off obvious 'I'm available' signals for years now."

"Just because they were obvious to you doesn't necessarily mean Micah recognized them," Mom said. "Think about it from his point of view. He likes you, but you're his sister's best friend. He must have thought about what would happen if he put the move on you, and it turned out you weren't interested. Imagine how awkward and embarrassing it would be for him to have you still coming around to spend time with Kira."

"But I wouldn't turn him down," protested Tabitha. "I'd go out with him in a heartbeat if he'd only ask."

"Micah doesn't know that," Mom said calmly. "My guess is he decided to play it safe and not run the risk of upsetting your friendship with either him or Kira."

"And now it's too late to try to convince him that dating me wouldn't mess anything up." She raised unhappy eyes to Mom. "Do you have any advice for me?"

"Well, let's see." Mom reached for a cookie. "I suppose my only advice is to not give up. Just because Alison has entered the picture doesn't mean you have to roll over and play dead. Figure out a way to let Micah know you're as interested in him as Alison is, actually, even more so."

Despite her misery, Tabitha managed a laugh. "It's easy to tell that you and Cass are related. She gave me pretty much the same advice. She told me not to give up without a fight."

Mom smiled smugly. "Well, there's no way both of us could be wrong." Turning serious, she asked, "All kidding aside, are you okay? Do we need to talk any more?"

Tabitha sighed. "I'm fine, but I'm also kind of sick of the subject right now. Plus, I have a ton of homework."

"In that case, I'll go start dinner. Your Dad put in a request for meatloaf and potatoes tonight." Mom leaned down and gave Tabitha a brief, hard hug. "Keep your chin up, sweetie. If you decide you do need to talk some more, I'm just a holler away."

Tabitha returned the hug. "I know. Thanks."

After Mom left, Tabitha stared out the window. *It's nice to have a mother to talk this kind of thing over with*, she mused, *but it doesn't change anything. Chances are I'm not going to do anything about letting Micah know how I feel. That would be like throwing myself at him, and I'm too chicken for that.*

Suddenly restless, Tabitha jumped up and walked to the window. "Why did Alison have to show up now?" she wailed in an anguished whisper. "This is Micah's last year on Kwaj and my last chance to get him to notice me. Why couldn't her parents wait one more year before moving here?"

Tabitha leaned her head against the cool glass. "God," she murmured, "I'm still new at this prayer thing." She laughed softly to herself. "Like You don't already know that. Anyway, I'm not really sure what I should be praying for. I mean, I know I'm supposed to pray for Your will to be done, but where does that leave me and what I'd like to have happen? It's probably too much to ask that You magically whisk Alison back to Texas. But what about making Micah realize she's not his type after all? Is that allowed?" She briefly closed her eyes against the brilliant sunshine, then opened them to gaze up at the cloudless sky. "I'm trusting You to work this out somehow, God."

CHAPTER 9

Feeling somewhat better, Tabitha returned to her homework. After finishing off the remaining cookie and drinking the milk, she settled down and tried again to unravel the mystery of physics. Ten minutes later, she tossed her pencil onto the desk in frustration.

"I give up," she growled.

As she shoved her chair back from the desk and prepared to stand up, the doorbell rang. Tabitha made a face. *Probably another guy for Cass*, she thought sourly. *Who is it this time? Alex? I wonder how he'll feel when he finds out Dennis got here first.*

Taking her time, Tabitha closed her books and stacked one on top of the other. After pushing her chair back into place, she walked to the door and opened it. Logan stood on the other side with his fist raised, ready to knock.

Tabitha jumped back. "Oh my gosh! You scared me."

Logan's smile was apologetic. "Your Mom told me it was all right to check and see if you were busy."

"It's fine," Tabitha assured him. "I wasn't expecting you, that's all."

Logan gestured toward the desk. "Your Mom said you

were working on physics. Are you finished?"

Tabitha rolled her eyes. "Yeah, right. I can't even get past the first problem. I've just about resigned myself to flunking the class and never making it out of high school."

Logan laughed. "Don't throw in the towel yet. You've only been at it three days. Besides, have I ever mentioned I got an A when I took physics last year?"

"You're kidding!" Tabitha suddenly brightened. "How would you like to be my knight in shining armor and rescue me from the evils of physics?"

"I'd be honored." Logan laughed. "When would you like me to suit up so we can start?"

"Definitely not right this minute." Tabitha shuddered. "I'll go crazy if I have to spend any more time looking at that book. Let's sit on the porch and talk awhile so I can rest my weary brain cells."

"I have a better idea," Logan said. "How about we go for a walk?"

About to agree, Tabitha suddenly frowned. "You're not thinking about going to Eamon, are you? I think Cass and Dennis went there."

"Yeah, your mom told me. But believe me, I have no intention of going anywhere near the place. The last thing I want to do is spy on Cass."

Tabitha smiled in relief. "Good. In that case, I think a walk is a great idea. Let me get my sandals and we're out of here."

Once outside, Tabitha and Logan headed up the beach toward the airport. They walked in silence for a few minutes, Tabitha's thoughts lost in the muted roar of the distant surf and the peeping of the sandpipers.

"Cass says she misses birds," she finally said. "She says Tennessee has all kinds of birds—cardinals, bluejays, mourning doves—and they all have their own songs.

She thinks the pipers are a poor excuse for real birds because all they do is squeak."

Logan nodded, his eyes on the beach. "I agree with her. In a way, I'm still not used to how quiet it is here. Back home, we had birds and these incredibly loud insects. But you know what I miss the most?" His voice took on a faraway quality. "Fireflies. I used to like watching the fireflies on summer nights."

"You don't talk about Pennsylvania much. At least not the way Cass talks about Tennessee." Tabitha shook her head. "Sometimes she goes on and on so much about the place that I want to strap a muzzle on her."

Logan stopped and bent down to examine a shell in the sand, then tossed it aside and straightened up. "It used to bug me that Cass talked so much about Tennessee. It reminded me of Pennsylvania, and I didn't want to think about home. I've told you how tough things were after my father lost his job and before we moved here. After awhile, though, it got so I liked listening to Cass talk about Jonesborough because it helped me remember the things I liked about living in Pennsylvania."

"You really like her, don't you?" Tabitha asked softly.

Logan's expression was bleak as he stared out at the horizon. "Yeah, I really do." He kicked at a broken piece of shell. "But I guess I waited too long to tell her."

Tabitha gave a short, humorless laugh. "You and me both, pal."

Logan glanced down at her, looking uncertain. "What are you talking about?"

"I've been kicking myself all afternoon for not letting Micah know he's not just Kira's big brother to me." Shrugging, Tabitha slid her hands into her pockets. "It's no fun torturing yourself with what if's, is it?"

"Tell me about it," Logan agreed. He hesitated a few

seconds before asking cautiously, "What do you think is going on with Micah?"

Tabitha shot him an irritated glance. "You don't have to play dumb with me," she said darkly. "I know Micah invited Alison Ross over this afternoon. Kira told me."

"Oh." Clearly uncomfortable, Logan looked everywhere but at Tabitha.

"Don't worry," she drawled. "I'm not going to pump you for information or pressure you into revealing any deep, dark secrets Micah might have shared with you about how he feels about Alison. I mean, it's obvious, isn't it? Plus, I won't ask you for advice on how to get him back. Mainly because thanks to my own stupidity, I never had him in the first place."

"I wouldn't mind giving you advice." He smiled at her. "I was planning to ask you what you thought I should do about Cass. Maybe we could trade suggestions."

Despite her blue mood, Tabitha laughed. "You can be downright irresistible when you put your mind to. You've got yourself a deal. Who goes first?"

"You do," Logan said quickly. He pointed to the right at the road that led to the island's shopping area. "But not before we stop in at the Ten-Ten for something to drink. I'm about to die of thirst."

"Same here." Tabitha gazed up at Logan with her most winsome expression. "Buy me a soda and I'll give you a foolproof plan for worming your way into Cass' affections," she promised.

Logan yanked one of her curls. "One soda coming right up, little lady."

After choosing their drinks and deciding to split a bag of pretzels, they walked from the convenience store to the nearby department store, jokingly named Macy's. Locating an empty bench at the far end of the store's porch, they sat down and opened the soda and pretzels. Logan gulped down a long swallow of his drink.

"Ah! There's nothing like an icy cold cola on a hot day."

"Every day is hot around here," Tabitha pointed out. She took a sip of her drink. "Sometimes I think it would be fun to live someplace cold for a while and drink hot cocoa. I don't think I've ever had hot cocoa."

Logan stared at her. "You're joking, right?"

Tabitha shook her head. "I know for sure I've never had it here. Maybe my dad used to make it when we lived back on the mainland and I was too young to remember."

Logan just shook his head. "I don't know which way is better to drink it, with marshmallows or whipped cream on top."

"Stop," Tabitha laughingly ordered. "You're making me drool. I guess I'm going to have to add hot cocoa to my list of things I want to experience someday."

"You really have a list like that?" Logan dug a handful of pretzels out of the bag and popped several into his mouth.

"Only in my head. Even though I love Kwaj, I realize there are things I've missed out on by living here. I suppose keeping track of them must sound silly to you."

"No, it doesn't," Logan assured her. "But—" he teasingly wagged a finger at her and continued, "you're not going to get out of giving me advice about Cass by talking about them. A deal's a deal. I bought you a drink. Now it's time you started talking."

Distracted by hearing her name called, Tabitha waved to a couple of girls entering Macy's, then turned her attention back to Logan. "First of all, I think you need to let Cass know you like her as a girl, not just as a friend."

"Right," scoffed Logan. "And have her laugh in my face? Or even worse, take pity on me? No way. Next suggestion."

"I'm serious," Tabitha insisted. "I'll bet you she has no idea you think of her as anything but a friend."

"In case you've forgotten, she has Dennis and Alex after her," Logan reminded Tabitha. "Dennis I could probably deal with. But Alex?" He vigorously shook his head. "No way, man. When he decides he wants a girl, he doesn't quit until he gets her. Plus, let's face it. He's got it all over me in the looks department."

Recalling her conversation with Mom, Tabitha squirmed. "You shouldn't compare yourself with other people, you know."

Logan shot her a scornful look. "Yeah … whatever."

"Look, you're a great guy. Any girl would consider herself lucky to be going out with you."

Logan just raised his eyebrow, doubt evident on his face.

"I mean it. I've known Alex a long time, and he's nothing but a pretty face." Tabitha shrugged, ignoring Logan's derisive laugh. "Cass is smart. She'll figure that out before too long. As far as Dennis goes, he's a nice enough guy, but he doesn't have a lot of personality. Cass likes people who make her laugh."

"So I should wait for her to wise up about what Alex and Dennis are really like and come running back to me?" Logan sounded confused. "What about telling her how I feel?"

Tabitha heaved an exasperated sigh. "I thought you didn't want to do that."

"I don't."

"Then it looks like waiting is your only other option," Tabitha pointed out with exaggerated patience.

Logan lapsed into a frustrated silence. "What if I wait too long and someone else comes along?" he finally demanded.

"I guess that's a chance you'll have to take." Tabitha selected a pretzel and crunched into it.

"What do you think about asking her out?" Logan asked hesitantly.

Tabitha pretended to consider the idea. "That's an interesting possibility, but I don't think she'd go out with me."

A couple of seconds passed before Logan realized she was kidding. He gave her a playful shove. "Very funny. Now answer the question. Do you think she'd go out with *me*?"

Munching on her pretzel, Tabitha took her time studying Logan from head to toe. "Sure, why not? You're not too repulsive." She grinned. "But then again, you're no Alex, either."

"You sure know how to build up a guy's ego," Logan good-naturedly griped. "All joking aside, though," he went on, "do you think I should ask her for a date?"

Tabitha nodded. "Absolutely."

"Okay." He rubbed his palms on his shorts. "I'll do it. I'll ask her to the movies tomorrow night."

"Uh ..." she hesitated, hating to break the news to him. "She's already going with Alex."

"Great." His mouth set in a grim line, Logan flung down a pretzel and crushed it beneath his sandal. "I finally get up the nerve, and it turns out she already has a date."

"What about Saturday?" suggested Tabitha.

Logan snorted derisively. "Like she'll want to go out with me after being with Alex the night before. Get real." He dropped another pretzel and stomped on it.

Tabitha grabbed the bag of pretzels off the bench

between them and placed it on her other side, out of Logan's reach. "So now you're back to feeling sorry for yourself because you don't look like Alex."

"Hey!" There was a nasty quality to Logan's smirk. "If you're allowed to feel sorry for yourself on account of Alison, I figure I'm entitled to throw myself a pity party or two."

Tabitha stared at him in astonishment. "What a low-down ... rotten ... completely mean thing to say," she sputtered.

"I know." Logan was instantly contrite. "I'm sorry. I shouldn't have said it." Sliding across the bench, he took Tabitha's hands in his. "You have every right to be mad at me, but don't be. Please. What can I do to make it up to you?"

Tabitha wanted to stay angry at him, but she couldn't. Summoning a wan smile, she mumbled, "It's okay. I mean, we all say things we regret."

"I do regret it," Logan assured her. "But I still want to make it up to you. What do you want me to—"

"Hi, you guys," interrupted a familiar voice.

Tabitha looked away from Logan to see Micah, followed by Alison, approaching them. When she noticed his gaze flicker to her and Logan's clasped hands, she abruptly snatched hers back and folded her hands in her lap.

Logan glanced over his shoulder to see who had joined them.

"Hello, Micah." Tabitha returned his greeting with all the calm she could muster. Although it nearly killed her to do so, she nodded politely to Alison.

"Hey, Micah, Alison." Logan stood up as they approached. "What are you doing here?"

"My mother sent me to see if we had any mail come in." Micah jerked a thumb over his shoulder at the rows of post office boxes that lined the wall at the other end of the porch. "Alison volunteered to come along, and here we are. What are you guys up to?"

Before Logan could reply, Tabitha stood up, holding her can of soda in one hand and the bag of pretzels in the other. "We decided we needed a snack."

Micah scanned the porch. "Is Cass around here somewhere?"

"Nope. She's at Eamon with a friend." Tabitha smiled so brightly that it made her cheeks hurt. "Logan and I are here by ourselves."

"Oh." Micah was obviously surprised. He suddenly seemed to remember Alison and drew her forward. "I don't know if you two have met."

"We haven't." Tabitha gritted her teeth and forced herself to say, "I'm Tabitha Spencer. Kira's my best friend. I'm a junior too."

"I know. Micah's mentioned you." Alison smiled, but only looked at Micah.

Mentioned me? Tabitha seethed. *We've known each other eight years, and all he's done is mention me? Thanks a lot, pal.* She shot him a withering look.

"I'm Alison Ross, by the way," she continued, finally looking away from Micah. "I moved here from Texas last week."

No joke, Tabitha silently sneered. *Like that accent of yours doesn't give you away.* Aloud, she said sweetly, "Well, good for you. How do you like Kwaj so far?"

Alison smoothed red-tipped fingers through her ebony hair. "I like it just fine." She smiled again at Micah. "The people I've met are very nice."

After returning her smile, Micah glanced uneasily at Tabitha. She sniffed and looked away. He cleared his throat. "I guess I should go check the mail. My mom's waiting. I'll see you guys later," he added, looking at Tabitha.

She ignored him. "It was nice meeting you, Alison."

The girl wiggled her fingers at Tabitha. "The pleasure was all mine." She flashed Logan a bright smile. "I'll see you in class tomorrow, Mr. Russell. I hope you've done your history assignment."

"Not yet," he said. "But I will."

Tabitha frowned at the goofy expression that spread across Logan's face. It was all she could do to keep from elbowing him in the ribs.

"We ought to be going, too," she announced, more sharply than she intended.

"What?" Blinking, Logan suddenly seemed to remember Tabitha was there. "Oh … uh … right. Okay."

Micah hesitated, even though Alison had already turned away. "Where are you off to?"

When it became clear Tabitha wasn't going to respond, Logan answered, "I guess we'll finish our walk then head back to Tabitha's house so I can help her with her physics homework."

"There aren't too many places to walk around here, are there?" Alison asked suddenly.

Tabitha bristled at what sounded to her like a criticism of her beloved island. "Not for somebody from Texas with all that wide, open space," she drawled. "But those of us who have lived here awhile don't mind." She fixed Micah with a challenging stare. "Isn't that right, Micah?"

He shuffled his feet and glanced back and forth from Tabitha to Alison. "Well, yeah. We're used to it. But," he added uncomfortably, "I can see how it might seem cramped to someone who just got here."

"Hey, I'm not complaining," Alison hastily assured them. "I think Kwajalein is wonderful." She lifted the hair off her neck in such a way that it made Tabitha want to yank it out by the roots. "I love the weather."

"It's not too hot for you?" Logan asked, with a touch too much concern as far as Tabitha was concerned.

Alison laughed. "There's no such thing as too hot, silly. I do believe I'd be perfectly happy living in the middle of the desert."

Be my guest, Tabitha thought darkly. *I'm sure the Sahara has lots of room.*

"Tabitha's a hot-weather fan too," Micah told Alison.

She smiled at Tabitha. "I wonder what else we have in common."

Hmm, let's see. Micah maybe? Tabitha's eyes narrowed as she regarded Alison. *Why do I have the sneaking suspicion you already know that?*

Logan touched her elbow to get her attention. "We need to get going. Don't forget you're eating early tonight."

"I haven't forgotten." Tabitha clamped down on the anger building inside her. "Okay, we're really off this time." Mimicking Alison's wave, she wiggled her fingers. "Have fun getting the mail."

"We will." Alison leaned against Micah and stared defiantly at Tabitha. "And you two have fun ... walking."

"We'll probably do more jogging than walking," Logan said, completely missing what Tabitha heard as a nasty innuendo, "since we need to get back so we can work on Tabitha's physics assignment." He punched Micah on the shoulder. "Talk to you later, buddy."

"Yeah. See you." Once again, Micah's gaze was directed at Tabitha.

Dumping their soda cans and the empty pretzel bag in the nearest trash bin, Tabitha and Logan left the porch and headed back toward Ocean Street. Tabitha fought the urge to glance back and see what Micah and Alison were doing.

"Do you want to stick to the road or go by way of the

beach?" Logan asked as they neared the spot where they either needed to turn left or go straight.

"Let's walk on the beach," decided Tabitha. "I don't want to risk running into somebody and having to be sociable."

"Alison put you in a bad mood?"

"It was the combination of her and Micah." Tabitha growled low in her throat. "I thought he had more sense than to fall for somebody like her."

Logan shrugged. "What do you mean? She seems okay to me."

"Of course she does." Tabitha tossed her head and sniffed with disdain. "You're a guy. All you see when you look at her are the long, black hair, the big, brown eyes, and the beautiful face and figure."

Logan hesitated. "So what's wrong with that?"

"They hide what she's really like." Tabitha didn't bother trying to mask her impatience. "Didn't you notice the way she hung all over Micah, then checked to make sure I was watching? And that crack about us having fun walking. She wants Micah to think something's going on between us because she wants me out of the picture."

"Aw, come on," Logan protested. "You're reading way too much into an innocent little comment."

Tabitha glared at him. "Girls know when other girls are sending them messages, and that one was loud and clear. Alison was warning me she's going to fight for Micah."

"Then why don't you fight back?"

Tabitha threw her hands up in the air. "You're the third person this afternoon to say something like that. What is this, some kind of conspiracy?"

"I haven't talked to anyone else so, if it is, I'm not in on it." Logan draped a friendly arm across Tabitha's shoulders. "You advised me about Cass. Now it's my turn to give you some helpful hints about Micah. Even if he is interested in Alison—and I'm not saying he is—don't forget the two of you go back a long way. You can build on that. But nothing's going to happen if you throw in the towel and walk away. That would be handing him to Alison on a silver platter."

"Yeah, but don't you think Micah would have done something by now if he considered me girlfriend material?" argued Tabitha. "Written me a note, asked me out, something?"

Logan said nothing.

Tabitha jumped on his silence. "You know something, don't you? Micah's talked to you about me."

He hesitated, then nodded reluctantly.

Tabitha jumped out in front of him and grabbed his arms. "What has he said? Is he interested, or am I just Kira's friend to him?"

Logan shrugged her off. "Tabitha, I ... that is, Micah—" He shook his head. "I'm sorry. I can't say anything."

"Aha! That means there's something to say." She grabbed his arm again. "Come on," she urged. "You can tell me. I won't tell Micah you said anything. I have to know what he's said about me."

Logan looked away from her pleading expression and stared out at the ocean. He sighed, indicating his frustration. "I thought you said you wouldn't pressure me into revealing any of Micah's deep, dark secrets."

"I was referring to conversations you might have had about Alison, not me." She shook his arm. "Out with it. Tell me everything he's said."

Suddenly she realized how hard she was shaking Logan's arm and abruptly moved away. "Sorry," she said softly. "I obviously need to get a grip when it comes to

Micah. I shouldn't have tried to force you to tell me stuff the two of you have talked about."

Logan crossed the distance between them and put his arms around her. After a moment, she rested her head against his shoulder.

"It's all right," Logan assured her. "I've found myself heading over the edge a time or two thinking about Cass. Everybody's entitled to act a little nuts every now and then."

Sliding her arms around Logan's waist, Tabitha gave him a squeeze then stepped back. "You really are a good guy. Cass had better come to her senses soon before some other girl snatches you up."

Logan smiled, looking slightly embarrassed. "You're not so bad yourself."

Tabitha laughed. "Now that's about the nicest thing anybody's said to me in a long time." She curtsied. "Thank you, kind sir."

Logan looked down at her and grinned. "I am your knight in shining armor," he reminded her.

"Yes, you are," Tabitha said softly, then abruptly switched moods. "Let's go. It's time for you to perform your knightly duties. I've decided I'm going to pass physics if it's the last thing I do."

Logan laughed. "Well, lead on then, fair maiden. I'm right behind you."

CHAPTER 10

"I hear you both had busy afternoons," Dad said at dinner that night, smiling at Cass and Tabitha. "Did you have a good time at the lagoon?" he asked Cass.

Cass nodded. "We got so hot after a while that we wound up going in the water up to about our knees. I still can't get over how clear the water is. It's one of the best things about living here."

"Along with Dennis?" Dad asked.

"He's okay." Cass pushed some peas around her plate and avoided looking at the others. "It's just he doesn't—"

"Have much personality?" Tabitha finished for her.

Cass was surprised. "Yeah. How did you know?"

Tabitha shrugged. "I've had a few conversations with him over the years."

"He's so serious." Using her fork, Cass squashed several peas into green mush. They were not her favorite vegetable. "You know how I like to kid around. I kept having to explain when I was joking." Abandoning her peas, Cass speared a roasted potato. "Still, he's nice. I talked to him about the youth group."

Mom looked up from her plate. "Oh, good. Do you think he'll come?"

"I doubt it." Cass bit into the potato, chewed quickly, and swallowed. "He said he's really not too keen on religion and stuff."

Dad frowned. "Your Mom and I don't want you girls dating anyone who isn't a Christian."

"I know that." Cass' tone was a bit on the testy side. "That's why I mentioned it, because it's one of the reasons I want us to just be friends, nothing more."

"That's very wise of you," Mom said, after a brief moment of stunned silence.

"I agree. I'm impressed with your common sense." Dad shifted his attention to Tabitha. "Now tell me about your outing with Logan."

Cass stared at her stepsister. "Logan came over? Why didn't you tell me?"

"Because this is the first time we've seen each other since you got back from Eamon," Tabitha said.

Cass frowned. "Did Logan come here looking for me or did the two of you have plans?"

"He was hoping to spend some time with you," Mom said before Tabitha could answer.

"Did you tell him where I was?"

Mom shrugged. "Of course I did. Do you have a problem with that?"

Cass thought a moment, then slowly shook her head. "I guess not. Did he seem upset when you told him?"

Mom shrugged. "I don't think so. Tabitha, did he say anything to you?"

Tabitha crammed a forkful of meat loaf into her mouth then shrugged and muttered around her food, "Sorry. Can't talk with my mouth full."

Cass was instantly suspicious. "He said something, didn't he?"

Tabitha widened her eyes in an attempt to look as innocent as possible. Before she finished chewing the first bite of food, she shoveled another forkful into her mouth.

Cass huffed in exasperation. "Why won't you talk to me? What are you hiding?"

Mom reached out to pat her arm. "Now, sweetie, don't badger her. I'm sure Tabitha will tell you what she can when she's ready."

"What do you mean by 'what she can'? We're sisters. She shouldn't keep anything Logan said from me. If y'all wanted me to, I'd tell you word for word every single thing Dennis and I talked about this afternoon."

"Cass, you know it wouldn't be right for Tabitha to break Logan's trust," Mom responded calmly. "If he asked her not to repeat their conversation, then she should honor his request."

"But—" At a warning look from Mom, Cass' argument died on her lips. Slumping in her chair, she sullenly studied Tabitha. "So where did you and Logan go? If you're allowed to talk about it, that is," she added, darting a wary glance at Mom.

Tabitha took a drink of milk. "We walked up the beach, then cut across to the Ten-Ten, and got soda and pretzels. We sat on Macy's porch while we ate."

"Oh." Cass desperately tried to think of a way to get Tabitha talking. "Did you see anybody while you were there?"

The disgusted expression that flitted across Tabitha's face told Cass that she had. "Unfortunately, yes. Micah and Alison showed up."

"No!" Cass temporarily forgot about her own situation. "What did you do?"

"There wasn't much I could do. I had to talk to her."

Cass leaned forward eagerly. "Is she as pretty up close as she is from a distance? Or does she have some horrible flaw?"

Before Tabitha could respond, Mom jumped in. "Honestly! You're both obsessed with this girl's appearance. If I didn't know better, I'd say both of you were jealous."

"I am not jealous of Alison Ross," Cass said. "I'm just curious about her, that's all. She's too good to be true. There has to be something wrong with the girl."

"I'm jealous as all get out of her," Tabitha admitted without embarrassment. "It's intimidating to be around someone who looks like her."

Mom gave them both a stern look. "Girls, obviously you don't have to like everyone you meet, but at least judge people by who they are, not what they look like."

"Well I don't know if this is who she is," Tabitha said, "but she was almost mean to me today."

"She was?" Cass asked quickly, ignoring the warning look from both parents. "What did she do?"

"Girls!"

Both turned to stare at Steve. Obviously the parents did not want to be part of the discussion. Tabitha gave her a "I'll tell you later look," so Cass silently turned back to her food.

"Are you still down because of Micah and Alison?" Cass asked later as she and Tabitha were doing the dishes. Tabitha had been quiet for quite some time.

Tabitha shot her a look, but didn't bother to answer.

Cass frowned. "I only asked because it seems to me that if you are, it's a waste of time."

Tabitha sighed impatiently. "Didn't you tell me I should fight for Micah?"

"Yes, but getting your feelings hurt because you saw him and Alison together isn't fighting for him." Cass leaned against the counter. "Either do something about the situation or quit pretending you're going to, and let Alison have him. You can't have it both ways."

"This from someone who's trying to have it three or four different ways," Tabitha retorted.

Cass stiffened. "What are you talking about?"

Tabitha dumped a handful of clean silverware into the drainer. "You want to see where things might go with Alex and Dennis and maybe Randy. Plus, you want to keep stringing Logan along. You should have seen the look on your face when Dad said Logan and I had gone out."

"What look? I didn't have any look," Cass hotly denied. "I was surprised, that's all. That was the first I'd heard that Logan came by."

"It was more than that and you know it." Tabitha turned the water on and began rinsing the things she'd already washed. "It really bothered you that Logan and I did something together. You may not want him for yourself, but you don't want anyone else to have him either."

Cass stared at Tabitha for several long seconds, debating with herself about asking the question that was on the tip of her tongue. "Are you telling me you're interested in Logan?" she finally asked.

Tabitha shrugged. "What if I am?"

Cass opened and closed her mouth a few times, unable to think of a response. When the phone rang, she ran to answer it, grateful that she'd been rescued.

"Hello?"

"Hi, Cass. It's Randy. Are you busy?"

"Hey, Randy. You caught me at a good time. I'm not doing a single thing." Cass made a face at Tabitha who was watching her from the sink. "At least not anything important." She turned away. "What do you want?"

Tabitha's response was to turn on the radio. *Fine*, Cass thought, *who needs her anyway?*

CHAPTER 11

A quick look through her closet the next day had changed Cass' mind about needing Tabitha. Cass owned nothing that would work for her date with Alex, so she had gone to beg Tabitha for something appropriate.

"Are you excited about tonight?" Tabitha asked.

Cass broke into a huge grin. "I know I've said it before, but I can't believe I'm actually going out with someone like Alex. I wish you could secretly take a picture of us so I could send it to Janette back in Tennessee. It would probably come back with drool all over it, but it would be worth it."

Tabitha looked slightly troubled. "What do you like about Alex, other than the fact that he's gorgeous?"

"I need another reason?" Cass asked, grinning. She hugged the blue sundress Tabitha had let her borrow.

Tabitha didn't seem to share her amusement. "I'm serious. Going out with somebody because of his looks isn't a very good idea."

Cass frowned. "Now you sound like Mom," she said. "What do you have against Alex? I know you think he's only going out with me because he dates all the new girls, but there has to be some other reason why you don't like him."

"He's a phony," Tabitha responded immediately.

Cass' laugh exploded from her in surprise. "Are we talking about the same Alex Johnson? I've spent a lot of time with him this week, and he's as real as they come. Even Mom liked him when he came by yesterday to meet her."

"Alex can be extremely charming when he puts his mind to it. I'm not saying he's not likable." Tabitha hesitated, then went on, "But it's like he's acting all the time. He figures out what will work best with each person, and that's how he acts when he's around them."

Cass narrowed her eyes in suspicion. "Are you sure you're not jealous? It sounds to me as if you'd like Alex for yourself."

Tabitha laughed. "Hardly. Don't forget I've watched Alex operate over the years. He's good, but it's all a game to him. Tell me," she tilted her head and regarded Cass with a steady gaze, "has he talked to you about church and stuff?"

"You know he has." Cass was annoyed at the possibility that Tabitha was trying to trip her up with a trick question. "You were there last night when I mentioned to Mom that he's thinking about coming to the youth group."

"Which is precisely my point," insisted Tabitha. "I've never known Alex to be interested in religion. In fact, during a debate in English class last year, he argued that atheism can be a good thing."

"I know. He told me." Crossing her arms, Cass leaned against the footboard of Tabitha's bed. "He also told me he's changed his mind since then, and he wants to learn more about God. That's why he wants to come to a youth meeting."

Tabitha snorted. "Yeah, right. He hasn't changed. Think about it." Holding up her hand, she ticked off on her fingers each point as she made it. "Alex is pursuing you. Your parents head up a church youth group that you helped start. One surefire way for him to get your attention is to attend a meeting. He shows up at a meeting. Voila!" She lifted her hand high and waved it. "You're so pleased you fall into his arms, and the two of you live happily ever after. Until he finds some other girl to chase, that is," she added, "and the game starts all over again."

Cass, who had brightened at the thought of her and Alex living happily ever after, glared at her stepsister. "You and I both know Alex doesn't have to work that hard to get me to notice him. I figure he knows it too. It's obvious I'm dying to go out with him. So why would he go to all the trouble of pretending he's interested in the youth group when he knows it isn't necessary?"

"Everything is a game to Alex," Tabitha replied. "He doesn't want you to just go out with him. He wants you to really fall for him. It's an ego thing."

"If that's true, it's really sick." Closing her eyes, Cass thought about what Tabitha had said. She recalled her several conversations with Alex and how he seemed to genuinely enjoy her company. She refused to believe he'd been faking it.

"You're wrong," Cass said, making sure she sounded more confident than she felt inside. "Maybe he's acted like that in the past with other girls, but it's different with me. I don't know how I know it is, but I do. Alex honestly likes me, and I feel like the luckiest girl in the world." She giggled. "Or at least on Kwaj."

Tabitha sighed. "I give up. Don't come crying to me when Alex dumps you." She fixed Cass with a steely stare. "And he will. So don't tell me I didn't warn you."

"I won't." Unfolding her legs, Cass stood up and started for the door. "I won't have to because he's not going to dump me. In fact, I'm so sure he won't that I predict he'll ask me to the fall formal."

"Oh, Cass," Tabitha muttered as Cass stalked out of the room.

Cass thought Tabitha might've added more, but she was tired of listening to her stepsister's lectures so she headed to the bathroom to shower and prepare for her date.

The family had an early supper because Alex was coming at six. The moment the meal was finished, Cass dumped her dishes in the sink and hurried down the hall to finish dressing. She was ready with a few minutes to spare, so she returned to the living room to nervously wait for Alex.

Dad looked up from the newspaper when she appeared and whistled his appreciation. "Look at you! You're a sight for sore eyes, I tell you."

Cass ducked her head in embarrassed pleasure at the compliment. "Thank you."

"What time is your young man coming by?"

"Oh … Dad." Cass still hesitated sometimes when it came to calling Steve Dad. "Alex isn't my young man. That sounds so old-fashioned."

"Hey," Dad shrugged his unconcern, "I'm an old-fashioned kind of guy."

The doorbell rang before Cass could respond. Her mouth abruptly went dry and her stomach lurched, making her glad she hadn't eaten much at supper.

"I'll get it," Dad offered when Cass, rooted to her spot on the couch, didn't move toward the door.

As he got up, Mom came around the counter into the living room. Drying her hands on a towel, Tabitha followed close on her heels.

Oh, great, Cass thought sourly. *They're forming a welcoming committee. I'm sure Alex is greeted by the entire family every time he picks a girl up for a date. How humiliating.*

She couldn't keep Dad from answering the door, but she could keep the others from giving Alex the third degree if she moved fast enough. Springing into action, Cass swiftly crossed the room and was directly behind Dad when he opened the door. Peeking her head around her stepfather, she smiled nervously at Alex who winked and nodded. A flock of butterflies—or maybe it was a herd of buffalo—began bouncing off the walls of Cass' stomach.

"Hello, Mr. Spencer. Nice to see you again. How are things at the station?"

"Hi, Alex. Things are great. We miss you, though." Dad stepped aside to allow Alex entrance. "Why don't you come in for a few minutes? I understand you and my daughter have plans for the evening."

Confused, Alex looked at Tabitha before seeming to realize Dad was referring to Cass. Nodding, he walked into the house and shut the door behind himself.

"That's right. Cass and I are going to the movies." He waved to Mom and Tabitha. "Hi, Mrs. Spencer, Tabitha. I hope I'm not interrupting anything."

"Not a thing, unless you count doing dishes and that can wait," Mom said. "We finished dinner twenty minutes ago. I baked cookies for dessert, if you'd like some."

"Not right now, thanks." Alex smiled at Cass and moved to her side. For a moment she thought he'd take her hand, but he didn't. "It's such a pretty evening, I thought Cass and I would walk to the theater instead of riding our bikes." He glanced down at Cass. "If that's all right with you."

All right? she thought. *Are you kidding? It's better than all right. It's perfect! You can't hold hands when you're riding bikes. Plus, I love the idea of walking in the moonlight with you.*

Aloud, she replied casually, "That's fine."

"We'd better head on then," Alex said. "The movie starts at 6:30, and the place is bound to fill up fast since this is the first time it's being shown."

"Do you have any plans for afterwards?" Mom said, following them to the the door.

Cass glanced at Alex, curious about his response as well.

He raised his eyebrows at her. "What do you think? Would you like to stop in at the Yuk and get some dessert?"

Not wanting to appear too eager, Cass waited a couple of seconds before nodding. "Sounds good to me. I really like their ice cream sundaes." She turned to Mom. "Is that okay?"

"Sure, just be back by eleven." Mom smoothed Cass' hair, which she'd left loose, behind her shoulder. Her hand lingered a moment on Cass' back. "Have fun, you two."

Thinking she'd heard a note of uncertainty in Mom's voice, Cass looked at her. She was surprised to see a slight frown puckering her mother's forehead.

Doesn't she trust me? Cass wondered, then noticed Mom's eyes dart toward Alex, rest there a moment or two to study him, then move on. *Or maybe she doesn't trust Alex.*

Cass and Alex left the house and found themselves bathed in early evening sunshine. The sun was making its descent to the horizon, splashing the clouds with rose and gold. Cass paused on the edge of the lawn to slowly turn and take it all in.

"I think this is my favorite time of day around here," she murmured. "I wonder if I'll ever get tired of the sunsets."

Sliding his hands into his pockets, Alex grinned at Cass. "Probably not. You don't strike me as being like most people. You really pay attention to what's going on around you."

A shiver of delight tingled up Cass' spine. *He thinks I'm different*, she thought, not quite believing the possibility. *That's what I was trying to tell Tabitha before. Hah! Just wait till I tell her what he said.*

Alex's voice broke into her thoughts. "We can either stand here all night, and ooh and aah about the sunset, or we can head to the movie. It's your call. As long as I'm with you, I don't care what we do."

Tilting her head, Cass pretended to consider her options. "The movie," she finally decided. "I can always watch another sunset tomorrow night. And the night after that, and the night after—"

"Okay, I get the picture." Alex laughed. "The movie, it is."

They turned left toward the movie theater. Cass let her arms swing freely, in case Alex decided to take her hand. He didn't though, and she swallowed her disappointment.

After all, she reminded herself, *it's only our first date. I'm glad he's not rushing things*. She walked a few more steps before adding, *I think*.

The gentle breeze lifted her hair and sent it dancing across her face. When she went to brush the stray strands back into place, she bumped hands with Alex. Startled, she stopped walking and so did he.

"Sorry." With his laughing eyes, Alex looked anything but apologetic as he faced Cass. "You have such pretty hair. I thought I'd kill two birds with one stone. I'd help you fix it and get to touch it and see if it's as silky as it looks."

"Oh … uh …" Between the rushing in her ears and the pounding of her heart, Cass was at a complete loss as to how to respond. She licked her lips and tried again.

"Uh ... okay."

She stood perfectly still while Alex captured the errant strands and, taking his time, anchored them behind her right ear. If human beings were capable of melting, Cass was sure she would have done so on the spot.

"Hello, Cass. Alex."

The quiet greeting broke the spell for Cass, and she quickly stepped back from Alex as if they'd been caught doing something wrong. Logan had pulled up beside them and was leaning on his handlebars, staring. Resentment flared in Cass. *What's he doing—spying on us?* She finally broke the silence, saying, "Fancy meeting you here."

Logan didn't seem to notice Cass' frosty tone. "Yeah," he agreed cheerfully. "What are the odds?" He gave Alex a brief glance before turning to Cass. "Where are you two off to?"

"We're going to the movie at the Yuk theater. It's the new comedy that just came out."

"Oh, yeah?" Logan said. "What time does it start? Maybe Tabitha and I will join you."

Cass, who was about to urge Alex to resume walking, jerked her head around to gape at Logan. "What do you mean, you and Tabitha? Are y'all doing something tonight?"

Logan nodded. "Yup. You mean you didn't know?" Although he sounded innocent enough, Cass saw in his eyes that there was something else going on.

Drawing herself up as tall as she could, she squared her shoulders and looked Logan right in the eyes. "I'm sure Tabitha must have mentioned that the two of you had made plans, but," she paused and shot Alex a meaningful glance that Logan couldn't miss, "I've been a little distracted lately."

To Cass' satisfaction, it was Logan's turn to look disgruntled. He tried to smile and shrug, but couldn't quite pull it off. "That's okay. You're not your stepsister's keeper."

"And you are?" Cass blurted before she could stop herself.

"I'm her friend," Logan answered quietly. "Something she could really use right now."

Cass narrowed her eyes. "What are you implying?"

"Nothing." Logan shrugged. "Look, I'd better get going. Tabitha's probably wondering where I am. See you guys later."

Her mouth pursed, Cass briefly lifted a hand in farewell. Alex merely nodded.

The moment Logan took off, Alex turned to Cass with a look of amazement. "What's with you two? If I didn't know better, I'd say you hate each other's guts."

Cass resisted the impulse to glance back and make sure Logan actually turned in at the house. She found it hard to believe he and Tabitha really had a date—or perhaps she didn't want to believe it. The thought made her feel funny inside.

Alex nudged her. "Hey, did you hear what I said?"

Cass gave him an apologetic smile. "Sorry, I guess my mind wandered off for a few seconds. What did you say?"

After Alex repeated his remark, she chose to make light of the encounter. "That's how Logan and I treat each other all the time. It's almost like we're brother and sister."

Except a sister wouldn't be bothered at the thought of her brother taking somebody out, realized Cass. For just a moment she wished she could call off her date with Alex so she could go someplace and try to sort out her feelings about Logan and Tabitha. She gave herself a mental shake. *That's enough. You're where you want to be, on your way to the movies with Alex Johnson, the best looking guy in the junior class. You can think about Tabitha and Logan later. Right now, just enjoy this time with Alex.*

A short while later, Cass and Alex reached the theater and joined the line of people making their way inside. Like the other two theaters on the island, it didn't cost anything. Free movies were one of the benefits of living on Kwajalein, but the theater didn't look like any cinema Cass had ever been to. It was a large square building with a dirt floor and benches instead of individual seats.

Finding an empty row about halfway down the aisle, Cass and Logan walked to the end of the ten-foot bench and sat down. As Alex slid his arm along the back of the seat, Cass leaned slightly against him and decided maybe benches weren't such a bad idea after all.

CHAPTER 12

Mom and Dad were still up when Cass floated into the house a little before eleven. Even though Alex had neither held her hand nor kissed her, she'd had the time of her life that night. She was telling Mom and Dad about it—and trying to contain some excitement—when Tabitha arrived home.

Ignoring the fact that Cass was talking, Tabitha executed a twirl before collapsing onto the sofa next to Mom. She linked arms with Mom and rested her head on her shoulder. "I had such a great time tonight. I'm so glad I went."

Mom reached up to pat Tabitha's cheek. "I'm happy for you, sweetie. But you'll have to wait your turn. Cass was telling us about her date with Alex."

"Oops." Tabitha covered her mouth and giggled. "I completely forgot you went out." She assumed an interested expression. "So how did it go?"

Cass wasn't about to share the details of her evening with her stepsister. She folded her hands in her lap and nodded politely at Tabitha. "No, you go ahead. You look like you're about to burst."

Besides, she added silently, *I can't wait to hear what you and Logan did that got you so worked up.*

"Okay, if you're sure." Tabitha sat up, slipped off her sandals, and tucked her legs beneath her. "As Dad and Mom already know," she explained to Cass, "Logan and I went to watch Micah play baseball. Kira and Rianne were there but, lucky for me, Alison wasn't. The four of us had the best time watching the game. Rianne likes this guy, Josh, on the other team, and Kira was yelling and carrying on so he kept looking over in our direction. It was a riot. Rianne was dying of embarrassment."

Cass hated the huge smile Tabitha had on her face.

"Anyway, after the game—Micah's team won, by the way, thanks to his pitching—Kira marched right up to Josh and invited him to her house along with everybody else. By the time Micah was finished asking people, we wound up with fourteen people. Mrs. Alexander almost had a heart attack but she fixed us stuff to eat and everything. Micah put a bunch of CDs in the stereo, and we had a blast."

Cass frowned, annoyed both with Tabitha and the mounting feeling of envy she felt inside. "What happened with Rianne and Josh?" As much as she'd loved being with Alex, she found herself wishing she'd gone to the party at the Alexanders' instead.

Tabitha shrugged, then smiled. "Nothing much at first. You know Rianne. She's not exactly the pushiest person in the world. Then Kira decided to get involved. She somehow arranged things so Rianne and Josh ended up sitting next to each other when the food was brought out. They started talking, and he rode home with her. I can't wait to talk to her tomorrow and find out what went on after they left. She's liked Josh forever."

Cass stiffened. Rianne was her friend, and she wanted to be the first one to hear what happened between her and Josh.

I'll have to make sure I'm up before Tabitha in the morning so I can call Rianne first, she vowed to herself then laughed silently. *Yeah, like that'll be hard. Tabitha hardly ever rolls out of bed before ten o'clock on Saturdays. I can already be over at Rianne's by then, getting all the dirt.*

Tabitha continued, "Even better than the thing with Rianne and Josh is that I think I finally got Micah's attention tonight."

"What do you mean?" Cass wasn't sure she liked the calculating gleam in her stepsister's eyes.

Looking quite pleased with herself, Tabitha pulled a pillow onto her lap and leaned her forearms on it. "I could tell Micah didn't know what to do with the fact that Logan and I were there together. He had just come over to talk to me when the phone rang, and his mother said it was Alison. When he got back from talking to her, I made sure Logan and I were off in a corner by ourselves. We were just talking, but it was obvious Micah didn't like it. He kept following us around, trying to get me alone, but I stuck to Logan's side like glue." She clapped her hands in delight. "I gave Micah a taste of his own medicine, and it was the most fun I'd had in ages."

Cass couldn't believe it. "So you used Logan?" she demanded.

Tabitha rolled her eyes. "No, I didn't use him," she replied with overstated patience. "Logan knew what I was doing, and he willingly went along with it. Besides," she added, "what's it to you? You weren't there. You were out with Alex. If you care so much about Logan, how come you don't have time for him anymore?"

"Have time for him?" Cass could hear her voice rise. "What does that have to do with anything?"

"Face it, Cass," Tabitha almost spat out. "You don't want him, but you can't stand the thought of anyone else spending time with him."

Before Cass could say anything, Mom held up her hand. "No more. It's too late to get into this kind of discussion. You two can talk about it tomorrow."

"That's not fair!" protested Cass. "She gets to say what she wants, and I'm not allowed to respond?"

"Not tonight." Mom's firm tone brooked no further argument. "You can take it up again tomorrow if you're still upset."

"Fine." Cass pushed herself out of the recliner and spun on her heels. "In that case, I'm going to bed."

"Wait," Mom called after her. "I want to hear about your date."

"I don't feel like talking about it now," Cass snapped over her shoulder. "Maybe tomorrow." She stormed into her room and slammed the door.

Cass was up bright and early Saturday morning. Since it was too early to call Rianne, she showered and dressed and then headed to the kitchen for breakfast. She found Mom sitting at the dining room table, sipping coffee and gazing out the window at the ocean.

"Hey," Cass said hesitantly. She wasn't mad, but she wasn't quite sure how to act.

"Good morning." Mom set her coffee mug down on the table. "Would you like me to fix you some scrambled eggs and toast?"

Cass walked into the kitchen and opened a cupboard door. "No, thanks. Cereal will be fine." Selecting a box, she set it on the counter and retrieved a bowl and spoon.

"What are your plans for the day?"

Pouring the cereal into the bowl, Cass glanced over her shoulder at Mom. "For starters, I figured I'd go over to Rianne's for a while."

"Ah." Mom nodded. "I thought your nose looked a little out of joint last night when Tabitha was telling us about her and that boy. What was his name? Josh?"

"Yes, Josh," Cass acknowledged, hastening to add, "And my nose wasn't out of joint. I just want to spend some time with Rianne, that's all. It's been such a hectic week we've hardly had a chance to sit and talk."

"It seems to me Rianne isn't the only one you've been neglecting," Mom said quietly.

Cass carried her bowl to the table and set it down with a thump. Pulling up a chair, she settled herself across from Mom and glared at her. "Who is it you think I've been neglecting?" She spooned cereal into her mouth, suddenly not daring to look Mom in the eye.

"Tabitha, for one," Mom said evenly.

Cass almost choked on her cereal. She quickly swallowed then sputtered, "Tabitha? How can you say I've neglected her? We live in the same house."

"People can live in the same house and not talk to each other," Mom pointed out. "Which is what I think has happened to you girls. You've gotten so caught up in your own life that you haven't taken the time to find out what's going on in Tabitha's."

"So whatever is happening is my fault?" Cass frowned. "Naturally. It's always my fault."

"Stop the dramatics," Mom ordered. Although her tone was mild, her expression was stern. "Are you aware of how much she's hurting over this situation with Micah and Alison?"

Stung by Mom's implication, Cass replied hotly, "Of course I'm aware of how she's feeling."

"Do you care?"

"Yes!" Too upset to eat, Cass sat back in her chair and crossed her arms. "How can you even ask something like that? You know I care about Tabitha."

"I can ask it because you've been so self-absorbed this week that you've barely taken notice of anything else going on around you." Mom cupped her hands around the coffee mug, looking down at the table. "Tabitha could have used some support and encouragement from you. Instead, she's had to get it from other people."

"Has she been complaining to you about me?" Cass was so incensed she could hardly get the words out. It enraged her to think her mother and stepsister had been discussing her.

Mom reached over to pat her hand, but Cass jerked it away. "No," Mom said calmly. "She hasn't said anything. I've observed what's been going on and have come to my own conclusions. Tabitha needs someone to talk to about what to do about Micah. You're too busy. My guess is Tabitha finds it awkward to talk to Kira since Micah's her brother and she doesn't want to put Kira in the middle. So that leaves Logan, and I don't know how much help he is. It's not the same talking to a boy, plus he has problems of his own."

Cass frowned. "Is he someone else you think I'm neglecting? You said something about Tabitha being one of the people I'm not treating right. I suppose Logan's another one. How long is this list anyway?"

"Logan's the only other one." Mom hesitated, taking a sip of coffee. "Think about it, sweetie. You hardly ever talk to him anymore. As far as I know, you don't call him back when I tell you he's phoned. You haven't been to the lagoon or the pool with him all week. You used to go at least every other day."

"Perhaps you didn't notice, but school started this week." Cass shrugged, trying to push down the sick feeling in her stomach. "I've had homework. I couldn't be traipsing off every time I had a free moment."

"Hmm." Mom just looked at her, and Cass squirmed in her seat. "It seems to me you weren't too busy to go to Eamon with Dennis one afternoon or take a walk with Alex another day."

"Yes, but ..." Cass started, then abruptly clamped her mouth shut. Mom was right, and they both knew it.

"Sweetie, I'm not saying there's anything wrong with you spending time with Alex or Dennis or anyone else you want to be with." Cass refused to look at her. "But don't forget how kind Logan was to you this summer. He remembered what it was like to be new on Kwaj, and he tried to make the adjustment easier for you. He went out of his way to spend a great deal of time with you."

Cass darted a skeptical glance at Mom. "And you think he did it out of the goodness of his heart?" she drawled.

"I think," Mom replied softly, "he did it because he realized within a day or two of meeting you that he liked you. A lot."

"So what does that mean?" Cass challenged her. "That I owe it to Logan to spend more time with him?"

"It means you should be more sensitive to the needs of the people you say you care about."

Cass filled her spoon with cereal and let it dribble back into the bowl over and over again. "It's not like Tabitha and Logan have gone out of their way to ask me to do stuff with them, you know," she said finally. "Has it ever occurred to you that I go out with Alex and Dennis because they invite me? I can't remember the last time Logan or Tabitha included me in on any of their plans."

"You may have a point," Mom conceded. "But that doesn't relieve you of the responsibility to treat others the way you'd like them to treat you. Let's say Tabitha and Logan have been ignoring you. That doesn't give you an excuse to do the same thing to them."

Mixed up and discouraged, Cass stopped playing with her cereal and hung her head. "I'm not being dramatic this time. Somehow, though, I always seem to wind up in the wrong."

Mom got up and came around the table to hug Cass from behind. Resting her chin on top of Cass' head, she murmured, "Sweetie, I'm not blaming you. I just want you to think about your behavior. It appears both you and Tabitha could do a better job of being nice to each other."

Cass placed her hands over Mom's where they were loosely clasped around her neck. "Logan too," she reminded her mother. "Don't forget about him."

"Logan too," Mom agreed. "Except I'm not his mother so I can't tell him what to do." She straightened up and combed her fingers through Cass' hair. "Does it upset you when Tabitha and Logan go out?"

Cass shrugged. "I don't know." She picked at the fringe bordering her placemat. "Maybe a little bit." Tilting her head back, she peered up at Mom. "Do you think they're … you know … falling for each other?"

"I think they're drawn to each other right now because they have a lot in common," Mom said carefully. "Basically, though, what they have is a very strong friendship."

While Mom continued to play with her hair, Cass stared out the window at the never-ending procession of waves breaking on the beach. "I used to dream about Logan asking me out on a real date. Not just to the lagoon to go snorkeling, but to the movies like Alex did."

"And now?" Mom prompted when Cass fell silent.

"Now—" Cass sighed heavily. "I'm really confused. I like Alex and I had a great time with him last night. But the thought of Logan dating someone—not just Tabitha, anyone—gives me a sick feeling in my stomach. I don't know what it all means. Do I keep going out with Alex, provided he asks me? Do I try to find out how Logan feels about me? I don't know what to do."

"Have you tried praying?"

Cass laughed, although the sound lacked humor. "That's your answer to everything, isn't it?"

Mom gave Cass' hair a playful yank before moving back to her place across the table. "Yes, it is and don't you forget it. In my experience, no problem has ever been too big or too small to pray about. The Lord helps us with everything—we just have to wait for His response." She grinned at Cass. "Which isn't easy for a take-charge type like you."

"Tell me about it." Realizing her cereal was on the verge of becoming hopelessly soggy, Cass picked up her spoon. "Okay, I'll try to remember to pray. But, first, I'm going to finish breakfast then call Rianne and see if she's up for some company."

"When am I going to hear about your date?" Mom asked.

Her mouth full, Cass waved and mumbled, "Later."

Cass left the house twenty minutes later, retrieving her bike from the lanai. As she came around the fence that blocked the view of the ocean, she stopped.

The sight of the immense, ever-changing Pacific never failed to thrill her. The breeze coming in off the water tugged at her ponytail and caused stray tendrils to tickle her neck. Cass smiled. Despite everything, life was good, and Kwaj was a pretty incredible place to live.

"Oh Lord," she paused to whisper while marvelling at the beauty of His creation, "You really are in charge of everything. Please be with me in this whole thing with Tabitha, Logan, and Alex. Show me the right way to handle it—a way that's pleasing to You."

With one last look at the water, Cass turned to go on to Rianne's.

CHAPTER 13

For the third time in as many minutes, Cass stopped pacing long enough to peek out the front window for any sign of Alex. It was Sunday evening, and seventeen kids were scattered throughout the living and dining rooms, waiting for the youth group meeting to start. Alex had promised he'd be there, but it was one minute to six and he hadn't shown yet.

Out of the corner of her eye Cass saw Tabitha, Kira, and Rianne watching her with sympathetic expressions. She wanted to whirl around and screech, "He'll be here! Just you wait and see!" Of course she didn't. The situation was humiliating enough without her making a complete fool out of herself.

Why, oh, why, did I make such a big deal about Alex coming to the meeting? Cass berated herself.

At six, Dad called the meeting to order. With one last, longing look out the window, Cass crossed the room and sat down next to Rianne. Kira leaned around Rianne to arch her brows and shrug at Cass. Tabitha merely stared straight ahead.

While Dad opened the meeting with a prayer, Cass did her best to keep her mind on what he was saying.

But every other sentence she found herself wondering why Alex hadn't shown. Maybe he'd gotten sick or something unexpected had come up. Mainly, though, she suspected he'd either forgotten or had gotten a better offer.

She had just started to refocus on Dad's words when a squeak from the front door alerted her somebody had arrived. Trying not to get her hopes up, she lifted her head a fraction of an inch.

Her heart slammed against her chest. Alex was letting the door close silently behind him and glancing around the room, obviously pondering his next move. Before Cass could decide whether she should hurry over to help him, Mom realized he was there and beckoned to him to join her. Alex padded around the outside of the circle until he reached where she sat and perched on the arm of the sofa beside her.

As Mom resumed her prayerful position, Alex darted a furtive glance at Cass. When he caught her looking at him, he winked and lifted two fingers in greeting. Cass stifled the relieved laughter that threatened to spill out and contented herself with smiling before she closed her eyes again. She tried to concentrate, but her skin tingled with the awareness that Alex had made good on his word and sat a mere five feet away with his head bowed and his hands clasped loosely in his lap.

So there! she wanted to shout at Tabitha. *You were so sure he wouldn't show. What do you have to say for yourself now?*

The moment prayer time was over, everyone headed for the dining room table to fill their plates with the baked ham and potato salad one of the mothers had provided. Cass tried not to appear too obvious about wanting to wind up next to Alex in line, but as she chatted with friends, she kept an anxious eye on Alex, tracking his whereabouts in the room. When he got in line behind a girl named Tracy, Cass hastened to join him.

"Where are you going in such a rush?" Randy asked, suddenly angling his wheelchair across her path. "Are you that hungry?"

Cass swallowed the impatient response that leaped to the tip of her tongue. Pasting on a bright smile, she propped a hand on her hip and retorted, "I was trying to get to the food before you did. I figured there'd be nothing left once you went through the line."

"Very funny." Randy lightly bumped her with his chair. "How about you and I go through the line together?"

"You have to let me go first," Cass said brightly, although she sighed inwardly.

Randy assumed an injured expression. "Don't I always? You know I'm the perfect gentleman."

"You're the perfect something," Cass shot back. "Only I'm too much of a lady to say what."

Laughing, they got into line together. At one point Cass found herself across the table from Alex. She'd been talking with Randy when she glanced up and discovered Alex watching the two of them with a slight frown. As soon as he realized she was looking at him, however, he grinned at her. Cass returned his smile, although she wondered what his frown meant.

After heaping their plates with food, Cass and Randy joined the group that had migrated to the porch. Setting her supper and drink on the wicker coffee table, Cass sank cross-legged to the floor. Randy parked his chair next to the swing where Kira and Rianne sat.

"We have a good crowd tonight," Micah observed between bites of ham.

"Yeah, especially since—" Kira glanced around to see who else was in the room, then lowered her voice, "Alex showed up." She smirked at Cass. "Isn't that right, Cass?"

Cass popped a forkful of potato salad into her mouth and shrugged. She was uncomfortably aware of Logan leaning against the wall a couple of feet away.

Randy stopped with his fork midway to his mouth. "Don't tell me you like Alex Johnson."

Cass stiffened at the note of disapproval in his voice. "What do you have against Alex?"

"I ... uh ..." Randy stopped, then started again. "It's not that I have anything against him. I was surprised, that's all," he finished lamely. He shrugged. "I don't have anything in particular against Alex. I guess I'm jealous of him because he's everything I'm not."

Silence greeted Randy's admission. Cass fidgeted uneasily and noticed everyone was avoiding one another's eyes.

"You don't have anything—not a single, solitary thing—to be jealous about," Rianne said finally. Her gaze was fierce as it rested on Randy.

"That's right," Tabitha chimed in from her spot near Micah. "You're a terrific person and I won't let anybody—not even you—put you down."

Randy ducked his head in embarrassment. "I didn't say that so you guys would feel sorry for me," he mumbled.

Kira reached over and patted his knee. "We know that, silly." Her tone was affectionate. "You should know us well enough to know that if we thought you were fishing for compliments, you could wait from now until forever before we'd give you any."

Everyone laughed and the awkward moment passed. As the others resumed eating, Cass thought about how quickly they came to Randy's defense when he compared himself to Alex. She realized it took a special type of person to rally support like that. Although she didn't want to, she couldn't help wondering if Alex had friends who were as loyal.

At six-thirty, Mom and Dad announced that they had ten minutes to finish eating and reassemble in the living room. Struggling to her feet after nearly half an hour of sitting on the floor, Cass dug her fists into the small of her back and stretched. When she caught Logan watching her, she gave him a sheepish smile.

He smiled back and Cass' breath caught in her throat. She turned away in confusion. *How can my heart kick into overtime, the same way it does when I see Alex?* she wondered. *I'm not supposed to like more than one guy at a time … am I?*

She headed toward the living room and suddenly Alex seemed to appear out of nowhere. "Hey," he said, seeming half serious. "Have you been avoiding me?"

"Now why would I do that?" With a mischievous grin, she leaned close enough to Alex to confide, "To tell you the truth, I forgot you were here."

Instead of laughing, Alex just looked at her and Cass felt her stomach drop at the meaning behind his gaze. "Sure," he murmured in a tone that made Cass realize he saw right through her. "I can believe that." He touched her bottom lip with his fingertip.

Blushing, Cass jerked away from Alex's touch. She quickly glanced around to see if anybody had noticed their exchange, but all she saw was Logan's back as he headed for the living room. No one else was anywhere in the vicinity.

I hope Logan didn't see what Alex did. Cass studied the set of Logan's back, trying to figure out if he looked upset. *He seems okay*, she consoled herself. *He probably didn't see anything*.

She tried to tell by his face when she and Alex entered the living room, but he wouldn't look at her. In fact, as Cass looked around for a place for her and Alex to sit, none of her friends seemed to want to look at her.

If they weren't wanted, fine. She and Alex would find somewhere else to sit. Elbowing him, she indicated two empty places to their right and they sat down.

Once everyone quieted, Mom said a short prayer then launched into the evening's Bible study.

"Tonight we're going to look at Colossians 3, verse thirteen. Those of you who have your Bibles with you, I invite you to turn there and read along with me."

Although Cass had set her Bible on an end table in preparation for the meeting, she didn't go get it. She wasn't proud of herself, but she didn't want to look like a religious fanatic in front of Alex.

"Is everybody there?" Mom glanced around the room and Cass avoided meeting her eyes. "Great. Colossians 3:13 says, 'Bear with each other and forgive whatever grievances you may have against one another. Forgive as the Lord forgave you.' " Using a finger to keep her place, she closed her Bible and asked, "Can anybody tell me what it means to bear with each other?"

As usual, there was much clearing of throats and averting of eyes since nobody wanted to be the first to venture a guess. Cass felt Alex shift positions beside her.

"Does it mean to stick together?" he asked.

Mom turned to look at him. "You're on the right track. Now what do you mean by that?"

"Uh ..." Alex hesitated. "Stand by each other, no matter what?"

Mom nodded. "In one sense. What else can it mean?"

One girl raised her hand. "Staying friends with a person even if they aren't always nice to you?"

"For example?" Mom prompted when the girl fell silent.

"Well, let's say something is going on in her life and she doesn't want to talk about it—so when I ask her about it, she just sort-of snaps at me and walks away. I may want to say, 'Forget her' and find a new friend—but this verse says to stick with her until she wants to talk about it," she said in a rush.

Mom smiled. "That's an excellent example, Jennifer." She glanced around the room. "Anyone else?"

"I do what Jen does," Emily said. "If I can tell something's bothering one of my friends, I keep after her until she finally tells me what's wrong."

Her comment brought forth murmurs of agreement. Beside her, Cass felt Alex stir again.

"Aren't you being nosy when you keep pressuring somebody like that?" he challenged Jennifer and Emily.

The two girls exchanged uncomfortable looks. "I suppose that's one way of looking at it," Jennifer finally said, "but I prefer to think of it as being caring."

"Well, sure. Who wouldn't?" Alex laughed. "Caring sounds a lot better than nosy, especially when you're describing yourself."

Although she remained outwardly calm, inside Cass cringed at the sarcasm in his voice. She didn't dare look around since she was sure she'd discover Tabitha and the others glaring at Alex and, by association, her.

"Well, Alex," Mom said quickly, "you may have one point. Sometimes we can push too hard to show we care. But the girls are acting on a good principle; they don't give up on their friends."

"Yeah—until their friends say something mean about them," Alex replied.

There was stunned silence, then an uproar of protest. Cass felt herself turning beet red and wondered if it would be okay to move.

"Wait—I didn't mean specifically Emily or Jen," Alex said quickly. "I just meant that sometimes girls—and guys too—will stop being friends with each other for the stupidest reasons. And it's usually because someone has said something bad about someone else."

Mom waited until the voices quieted down a little. "That is true, Alex. It's a lot easier to 'bear with each other' when there isn't personal injury involved, right?"

"Well isn't that what the second part of the verse is saying?" Logan said over the other voices of agreement. "I mean, the part about forgiveness."

"Yes," Mom said, nodding. "Tabitha, can you read the verse again for us?"

"Sure. 'Bear with each other and forgive whatever grievances you may have against one another. Forgive as the Lord has forgiven you.' "

"What does he mean, 'Forgive as the Lord has forgiven you'?" Mom asked.

In the silence that followed, Cass knew Mom was waiting for her to answer. But still very conscious of Alex next to her, she couldn't bring herself to say anything.

Marcy finally raised her hand. "When Christ died on the cross and rose again, He forgave all our sins."

"Right," Micah jumped in. "Even though we weren't worthy of that forgiveness, just like sometimes in our relationships with each other we aren't exactly worthy of people forgiving us."

The group nodded in general assent, but Cass could tell Alex didn't agree. *Please don't say anything*, she said over and over in her head, *please don't say anything*.

"I guess I just don't understand how this all works," Alex said.

Cass inwardly groaned.

"I mean, we're just supposed to blindly accept that Jesus forgives us, and then blindly forgive everyone who wrongs us?" Alex gave a short laugh. "I don't know about anyone else, but I don't work like that."

Once again, there was stunned silence. Cass dropped

her head so her hair would hide her face, but she surreptitiously glanced around. Most of the other kids were also looking down—or anywhere other than at Mom and Dad or Alex. Mom looked like she was either about to yell or cry.

Before she could do either, Dad stepped in. "Well, Alex, you've voiced a concern many people have, and I'll try to answer you. See, we accept what Christ has done for us on faith. And yes, faith is blind. But the Holy Spirit works in our hearts to help us accept the grace given to us so freely, even when we don't deserve it. As for forgiving each other—that *is* a hard thing to do. We're human, so grace doesn't come as naturally for us as it does for God. But with God's help, as we grow in our faith and love for Him, we also develop a spirit of forgivness that allows us to share the grace and mercy of Christ." He paused. "Does that help at all?"

Alex shrugged. "Well it sounds good. But it also sounds pretty impossible."

Dad shrugged too and matched Alex's tone. "God specializes in what seems impossible to us humans."

They stared at each other for a moment. The room was filled with tense silence until Tabitha heaved a huge sigh. "Can I give Him my physics homework then?" she asked, and everyone around her burst out laughing. Cass desperately wished she were part of the group across the room. Instead, she was sure everyone saw her as being linked to Alex. It made her uneasy to think they probably assumed she agreed with his opinions, and she didn't know how to let them know she most definitely did not.

CHAPTER 14

Cass didn't say a word during the remainder of the discussion, which was unusual for her. To her relief, Alex also kept his mouth shut. She wondered if he'd run out of things to say or if Dad had said something that had caused him to rethink his positions. Not that she cared either way. She was just grateful he was quiet.

When the meeting ended, Alex asked Cass if she'd like to go for a walk. Since she and Tabitha always helped Mom and Dad clean up, she declined, secretly pleased that she had a valid reason to turn him down.

"Then how about walking me out to my bike?" Alex countered. He summoned up the mega-watt smile that once had turned Cass' knees to jelly. Now it left her cold. "Your folks can spare you for five minutes, can't they?"

Cass was tempted to say no again, then decided she'd like the chance to talk privately with Alex. "Hold on. I'll check to see if it's okay."

When Mom heard Cass' request, she frowned, but reluctantly agreed. "All right, but don't be any longer than ten minutes. It's your turn to vacuum."

As Cass exited with Alex, she was aware of Logan watching them. His disapproval was written all over his face, and Cass longed for a way to reassure him that it wasn't what it looked like. Her infatuation with Alex had taken a severe blow and she wasn't sure if their budding relationship could survive the damage. Even more importantly, she wasn't sure if she wanted it to. She'd seen a side of Alex tonight that was truly unattractive.

After locating his bike among the several scattered about the lawn, Alex wrapped his hands around the handlebars and turned to Cass. "I really liked the meeting. Thanks for inviting me."

Folding her arms, Cass looked at him coldly. "What did you like about it?"

Alex seemed completely oblivious to her frosty attitude as he leaned close to confide, "I liked shaking people up. You know, making them think. Everybody there was going along with the party line until I gave them another way of looking at things."

"I see." Cass nodded as if she concurred with Alex, while inside she seethed at his arrogance. "In other words, you saw us all—and that includes me, I guess—as too stupid to think for ourselves. If you hadn't spoken up, we'd have all sat there like robots, agreeing with whatever my parents said."

"Uh ..." Alex seemed to have suddenly caught on that Cass was angry. "No, I ... I thought people might appreciate hearing another point of view—something more realistic. You know, from somebody who doesn't go to church."

Cass wasn't buying his explanation. "Did you get anything out of what was said tonight, or was it a colossal waste of time?"

"It wasn't a waste of time at all," Alex said quickly. "I got a lot out of the discussion."

"Really?" Cass frowned. "Like what?"

"Well—" Alex hesitated. "It is good to forgive other people."

"Uh-huh." Cass' nod was accompanied by a knowing smirk. "And that's why you said what you did. Tell me," she plowed ahead when Alex opened his mouth to dispute her, "why did you even come tonight when you knew you wouldn't agree with what went on?"

Alex shrugged and as he flashed his engaging smile, reached out to gently touch her arm. "You invited me, remember? I thought it'd be a chance for us to spend some time together."

Not wanting to be touched again, Cass stepped back out of reach. "Are you interested at all in God?"

Alex kept his hands to himself, but he gave Cass a soulful look. "I'm interested in anything you're interested in."

She snorted. "Wow. How many times have you used that line? And please tell me no girl's actually fallen for it."

He frowned. "Why are you acting like this?"

"Because I don't like being embarrassed in front of my family and friends." Cass spun on her heels and started for the house.

"Wait!" He yelled, then dropped his voice. "Cass, please come back so we can talk."

Cass halted, hesitated a moment, then grudgingly turned and walked back to Alex. When she was a few feet away from him, she crossed her arms and said firmly, "We have nothing to say to each other."

"What if I apologize? Will that make things better? Come on," Alex coaxed. "I thought we had the start of something special."

Staring at his handsome face, Cass felt her resolve weakening and mentally shook herself. *I will not give in to him just because he's cute*, she vowed. *That's what he's counting on, but I won't be like all the other girls he's tried this with.*

She straightened and met Alex's imploring gaze straight on. "I need time to think things over. I'll talk to you tomorrow after I've had a chance to cool off."

Alex accepted her decision without argument, which Cass couldn't decide was a ploy or not. "Okay," he replied meekly. "We'll talk tomorrow." When Cass turned again to head back to the house, he called after her, "Don't forget what a good time we had Friday night."

Cass raised a hand in acknowledgement that she'd heard him and hoped no one else had. He made it sound as if they'd spent Friday engaged in one long make-out session.

Inside the house, Cass found her family putting the finishing touches on their clean-up efforts. All that remained for Cass was to vacuum. She started for the closet where the vacuum cleaner was kept but Dad's voice stopped her.

"Cass, could we talk a few minutes?"

Well, aren't I the popular one tonight? Cass drawled to herself as she went back to the living room.

Aloud, she chirped, "Sure thing. What's on your mind?"

"Alex," he said darkly. "I'm not sure it's a good idea for you to spend any more time with him."

Cass had just about reached the same conclusion herself, but it irritated her that Dad was telling her what to do. "Why not?" she demanded.

"Surely it's obvious after his performance here this evening."

"What? A person can't ask a few simple questions?" Cass knew that wasn't what Alex had done, but for some strange reason she felt compelled to defend him. "If he does, he's labeled a troublemaker or something?"

"Somebody who's honestly searching for answers could ask questions from sunup to sundown—he could even debate me on issues—and I'd be happy to talk to him. But someone who argues merely for the sake of arguing." He shook his head. "I won't allow myself to be drawn into a discussion with a person like that. That's what Alex was doing. He wasn't interested in anyone's responses. He was only trying to prove how clever he was. He not only doesn't share your beliefs, Cass. He doesn't even respect them."

Unable to withstand Dad's glare, Cass glanced at Tabitha, who pretended to study her nails. Cass resented the fact that her stepsister was present to witness the final humiliation of the evening.

"Do you have anything you'd like to say?" Dad asked quietly.

Cass shrugged. "Not really." She mustered a crooked smile. "When you're right, you're right."

"You realize we're not putting Alex down, don't you?" Mom said softly. "We're concerned about you. One of the most important things we can do to help us live correctly is to associate with people who share our beliefs and values."

"So we're supposed to completely shut everyone else out of our lives? Yeah, that's a good witness." Cass tugged at the hem of her T-shirt in order to avoid her parents' eyes. "Look, I know Alex acted like a jerk tonight, and I wound up looking like a complete idiot since everybody knows how much time we spent talking at school last week. They probably heard about our date too."

"Didn't I tell you it wasn't a good idea to go out with him?" Tabitha said quickly before Cass could finish.

Cass glared at her. "Thank you so much for the 'I told you so.' Way to 'bear with me.' "

"Oh, like you've gone out of your way to help me," retorted Tabitha.

Raising his hands, Dad stepped forward to put a stop to their bickering, but Cass beat him to the punch. "Don't worry. You don't have to listen to any more of our trash talking. I'm going to vacuum then I'm going out back to sit on the rocks awhile and think." She whipped her head around to glare at Tabitha. "And I want to be alone."

Tabitha just glared back.

Fifteen minutes later, Cass found herself sitting on one rock with her feet propped on another as she gazed out to sea. Phosphorescence glittered on the surface of the ocean like scattered stardust. She allowed the peaceful scene to gradually take control until slowly but surely the tension in her neck and shoulders eased.

"Okay, Jesus," she whispered, "I obviously made a huge mistake about Alex. I don't want to be with somebody who doesn't believe in You. But if You could maybe use me to teach Alex about You, I'd be willing to give it a try. And not just because he's so good-looking," she hastily added. "I'll do the same thing with Dennis too. It's up to You. I just need to know about Alex by tomorrow since that's when we're supposed to talk." She laughed softly. "Of course, You already knew that. Anyway, I really need Your guidance."

She stayed on the rock, just staring out at the ocean until she finally felt peace creeping into her heart as well. Then she got up, and with a quick, heartfelt thank You whispered to the sky, she went back inside.

CHAPTER 15

Cass and Tabitha didn't have much to say to each other the next morning during the ride to school. It helped when Kira and Micah caught up with them. The four of them could talk easily.

Once in school, Cass spent the time before homeroom avoiding Alex. She still wasn't sure what to say to him. She knew what she should say, but even after Alex's embarrasing behavior the night before, there was a part of her that rebelled againt cutting off all contact with a guy as good-looking and charming as he was.

God, she prayed as she walked into homeroom, *I'd really appreciate a sign here, and it can't be vague. I need something really obvious. Do I try to make it work with Alex or not?*

Rianne entered the class a couple of minutes after Cass. She hurried to take the seat near her friend, waving and returning greetings to the other students while weaving her way through the maze of desks.

After dropping her books on the desktop, Rianne slid into her chair and fixed Cass with a sympathetic gaze. "How are you this morning?" she asked in the hushed tone of a funeral director. She laid her hand on Cass' arm and gently squeezed it. "I meant to call you last night, but Randy and I got involved in a discussion and I forgot."

Cass frowned at Rianne's show of concern, not sure what had prompted it. "I'm fine. Why?"

"You know." Rianne glanced around. "That thing with Alex and the way he acted. You looked absolutely mortified every time he opened his mouth. Then you didn't say anything at the meeting, which isn't like you at all. I was worried about you. I could kick myself for not calling."

"Oh, that." Cass nodded grimly. "I *was* mortified. Alex went out of his way to stir things up. I told him that last night, and he wanted to know if it meant we couldn't be friends anymore. I said I'd let him know today."

"Randy and I thought he acted like a jerk." Rianne smoothed her silky blonde hair behind one ear. "Have you decided what you're going to say to him?"

"Pretty much. I just don't see how I can be friends with somebody I don't have anything in common with." Cass propped her chin on her hand and frowned. "The problem is he's so darn cute. Why didn't God put a great guy inside that terrific body?"

"Looks aren't everything," Rianne reminded her.

Cass made a face at her. "I know that," she said. "But they do count for something. I mean, look at who you like. Josh isn't exactly the Hunchback of Notre Dame."

"He's not a Greek god either," Rianne shot back. "He's nice-looking and all, but he's not drop-dead gorgeous like Alex. You know, sometimes I wonder," she mused, "if really great-looking people have it harder than ordinary people like us. From the ones I've met, it seems like they rely too much on their looks and don't spend enough time developing their personalities. When you think about it, it's kind of a curse."

"You're right. It's like me and basketball. I was always shorter than most of the girls on the teams back home, and I didn't have a natural shot, so I had to work harder than everyone else. I couldn't rely on my natural ability." Cass smiled proudly. "But I worked my tail off, and I made the starting team every year."

"Exactly. You couldn't count on your skills alone to get by." Rianne hesitated, then said softly, "I've never said this to anyone before, but I think in some ways Randy's accident was the best thing that ever happened to him. You know how good-looking he is. Before the accident, he stood a good chance of turning out to be really stuck on himself. Because of the accident, though, he was forced to make more of an effort to become the great guy he is today."

"Wow," Cass said. "So you're saying you think Randy's diving accident was a good thing?"

Rianne looked torn. "I'll always wish he weren't paralyzed. It would be wonderful to see him up and running around like he once was. But I also know good things came out of his being injured. I know it would do wonders for Robby's personality if he were stuck in a wheelchair for a couple of months. Maybe then he'd learn what's really important in life and stop being such a self-centered brat."

"In that case, I know quite a few people who could benefit from a little temporary paralysis," Cass said wryly. "Starting with me."

The conversation with Rianne stayed with Cass throughout the rest of the morning. She passed several acquaintances in the halls, Alex included, but was too preoccupied to do more than nod and smile, if she noticed them at all.

By lunchtime, she knew what she had to do—about both Alex and Logan. She would talk to Alex during lunch then catch Logan before he left school that afternoon. Pleased with herself, her stride was downright jaunty as she walked into the cafeteria.

Cass quickly ate her lunch with Rianne, Kira, and Tabitha. Although she didn't go into any details, she told them she'd made up her mind about Alex.

"Good," approved Kira. "I hope you're planning to tell him to take a long walk off a short pier."

"That wouldn't be very Christian, now would it?" scolded Cass. Her grin let Kira know she was teasing.

"Probably not," Kira said. "But it sure would be fun. I'd pay to see the look on Alex's face if you actually said something like that to him. It's about time somebody taught him a lesson."

"What in the world makes you think Cass is the one to do it?" Tabitha said sourly from her end of the table. "For all we know, she could be planning on pledging her undying love to Alex when she has this big talk of hers with him."

Kira turned worried eyes to Cass. "You're not going to do that, are you?" she asked.

"Hardly. If my stepsister knew me better," she shot Tabitha a withering look, then continued, "she'd know not to make such a ridiculous statement."

"If my stepsister hadn't acted like a jerk all last week," Tabitha retorted, "I wouldn't dream of making statements like that."

"Okay, ladies," Rianne broke in, "I'm trying to eat here, and I'd like to do it in peace, if you don't mind."

"Eat away," Cass said calmly. She crumpled up the bag Mom had packed her lunch in. "I'm going over to Alex's table to see if he feels like talking." Getting up, she pushed her chair back under the table. "Wish me luck."

Tabitha scowled up at her. "How can we do that

when we don't know what you're planning to say?"

Cass walked around the table to pat her stepsister on the head. "I guess you're just going to have to trust me, aren't you?"

Alex jumped up and hurried to greet her as she approached his table. His welcoming smile almost made Cass lose her nerve to say what she wanted.

"Hi, Cass." Alex intercepted her a few feet from the table. "I'd decided I'd give you five more minutes. If you didn't come over by then, I was coming to get you."

"What were you planning to do?" drawled Cass. "Lasso me and drag me out of the cafeteria?"

Alex laughed. "You're never at a loss for a comeback, are you?"

"I try not to be caught short." Cass inclined her head toward the doors leading outside to the courtyard. "Do you feel like talking?"

"I'm at your beck and call, fair lady. If a conversation is what you desire, then a conversation is what you shall have."

Oh, brother, Cass thought as they headed for the exit. *He's obviously decided he's not going to make this easy for me.*

Once outside, Cass and Alex made their way across the courtyard, away from the milling students to a more secluded spot. Reaching the lawn, they settled in the meager shade of a towering palm tree. The moment they sat down facing each other, Alex started talking.

"Before you say anything, I want you to know I thought it over after I got home last night, and I'm really sorry for the stuff I said. I was way out of line."

Hope flared in Cass. *Was it possible he'd actually seen the error of his ways?*

"What do you mean?" she asked cautiously.

Alex's smile was sheepish. "I wanted to impress you,

but I went about it the wrong way. I should've kept my mouth shut instead of spouting off the way I did."

"I see." That wasn't quite what Cass had hoped to hear. "Are you saying you realized that you agreed with at least some of the things people talked about during the meeting?"

Alex shook his head. "Nope. My opinions haven't changed. I just think I should have either expressed them nicer or not said anything at all."

The ember of hope in Cass flickered and died out. "Oh," she said in a small voice. She buried the intense disappointment suddenly flooding through her. "I'm sorry to hear that. I'd hoped you would tell me you'd rethought your position. Since that isn't the case, we don't have anything to talk about other than the fact that I won't be going out with you anymore."

Alex's head jerked up and his expression was stunned. "Why not?" he sputtered.

"We're too … different." Cass opted for the shortest explanation.

Alex's eyes narrowed with suspicion. "Did your parents tell you that you couldn't see me again?"

It was tempting to let them take the blame, but Cass couldn't bring herself to do it. "No, this is my decision."

"But why?" persisted Alex. "What do you mean 'we're too different'?"

All the reasons she'd rehearsed suddenly left her mind and Cass found herself floundering for a way to explain. "I don't know. It's complicated. We don't … think alike. I found out last night that the things that matter most to me aren't important to you."

"So we don't agree about religion. Big deal." Alex dismissed the issue with a wave. "That doesn't mean we can't go out and have a good time. We had fun Friday night, didn't we?"

"Yes," Cass was forced to concede. "But I didn't know then how you feel about my faith. Now that I know, it makes a huge difference, and I can't pretend it doesn't."

"Why? Do you think you're better than I am or something?" Alex asked stiffly.

"No!" Cass hoped she hadn't said anything to give him that impression. "That isn't it at all. Look," she went on, desperate for some way to explain her position. "What's your favorite thing in the world?"

Alex frowned. "What do you mean? Like my favorite thing to do or my favorite sport?"

"Either one."

Alex thought a moment. "I like football."

"Who's your favorite team?"

"The Pittsburgh Steelers," he said immediately.

"Okay. Let's say I don't like football, and I especially can't stand the Steelers."

Alex shrugged. "So? I wouldn't talk about them, that's all. Simple as that."

"It sounds simple, but I'll bet you it would turn into a problem after a while." Warming to her subject, Cass grew more animated as she talked. "What happens when football season rolls around and you want to talk about the games you've watched and how your team is doing? Sure, there are other people you could talk to, but you want to talk to me. Only you can't because I hate football and I don't want to hear anything about it. Do you see what I'm getting at?"

"Yeah, and it's stupid," muttered Alex. Irritated, he threw down the blades of grass he'd torn from the lawn.

"No, it's not," Cass insisted. "You'd want to be able to talk about something you care about, and it wouldn't be long before you found someone you could talk to. It's the same with me and the things I care about."

"I don't want to listen to this anymore." Alex stood

up, scowling down at Cass. "This is the most idiotic conversation I've ever had. You said when you started it that you didn't want to go out with me again. What made you think I was planning on asking you?" he sneered. "Did it ever occur to you that maybe I wasn't interested in a second date? That one date with you was one too many?"

Cass willed herself not to cry, although there wasn't much she could do about the flame of embarrassment she felt rushing to her cheeks. *He's only saying this stuff because I've hurt him and he wants to hurt me back*, she told herself.

"Then I guess it works out perfectly," Cass made herself say in as calm a voice as she could manage. Hoping she didn't look as shaky as she felt, she stood up.

"Not quite," Alex snapped. "I planned to drop you first, but you beat me to it."

Cass decided she was getting a little tired of his nastiness, particularly since it wasn't deserved. "Ah." She gave him a half-smile. "So it's an ego thing with you. You're used to being the dumper, not the dumpee. Okay." She shrugged amiably. "I don't mind you telling people you dumped me if it'll make you feel better."

She turned to go, but Alex grabbed her by the arm. She whirled around.

"Don't—" Cass pried his hand off her arm and flung it aside, "—touch me like that again. Otherwise, you'll have more than a damaged ego to deal with."

Spinning on her heels, Cass left Alex and stormed into the cafeteria. She marched to the table, snatched up her books, and stalked away without a word of explanation.

CHAPTER 16

After a stop in the bathroom to splash cold water on her face, Cass calmed down enough to make it through the rest of the school day. The afternoon dragged, though, as she thought about the conversation she planned to have with Logan. The clock couldn't move fast enough for her, and she practically leaped out of her seat when the final bell rang.

Without stopping at her locker, she jogged to the corridor where Logan's locker was located. He was opening the door when she skidded to a halt behind him.

"Hi, Cass," he said, sounding slightly startled. "Why are you in such a hurry?"

"I wanted to make sure I caught you before you left." She rubbed her palms against the sides of shorts.

"Oh, yeah?" Logan tossed some books into his locker, retrieved two others, and slammed the door. "Why?"

Cass suddenly found herself as uncomfortable with Logan as she had been the first day they'd met. "I was … uh … wondering if you'd like to … ah … to go to the lagoon with me," she stammered.

Logan only stared at her for a few seconds. "You

mean now? Today?"

Cass nodded. "If you're not busy."

"Oh, man," Logan said as he slumped against the locker, looking miserable. "I already have plans."

"That's okay," Cass said, swallowing her disappointment. "Maybe we can do it some other time."

How stupid can I get? she kicked herself. *Whatever made me think he'd want to spend time with me after the way I've treated him?*

Wanting nothing more than to end this humiliating episode, yet another in what seemed to be an unending series of them, Cass turned to go.

"Wait," Logan said quietly. "At least let me tell you what I'm doing this afternoon."

"You can if you want to." Cass' tone was as flat as her expression. "But you don't owe me any explanations."

"I do want to." Clutching his books in front of him, Logan continued to lean against the locker. "The thing is I asked Tabitha to come over to my house after school."

Oh, great, Cass thought sourly. *Thanks to my own stupidity, I've lost you to Tabitha of all people.*

"She's been a good friend, especially lately, so I decided to do something nice for her. We were talking last week, and she happened to mention that she's never had hot cocoa. I asked my mother if she'd make some—you know, the real stuff, not the kind from a mix—and she said yes. So I'm surprising Tabitha with hot cocoa this afternoon. I asked her about coming over between second and third periods."

Hot tears prickled behind Cass' eyelids and for the second time that day, she ordered herself not to cry. All she could think was, *Lucky Tabitha to be the one having Logan doing nice things for her. If I hadn't messed things up so badly, it could have been me.*

Cass smiled wanly. "That's really sweet of you. I know Tabitha will appreciate it." Seeing no reason to stick around and prolong her agony, she began to edge away. "I guess I should be going. Tell Tabitha if she hasn't already called Mom to let her know about going home with you, not to bother. I'll let Mom know."

"What about the lagoon?" Logan asked before Cass managed to escape.

She feigned a lack of interest. "Whenever you can make it will be fine. Just let me know." She didn't want to be rude, but if she didn't leave soon she'd wind up bawling right there in the middle of the hall, and that was the absolute last thing she needed.

"How does tomorrow sound?"

"Uh ..." Distracted by the sight of Tabitha coming down the hall, Cass couldn't think of anything to say for a moment. "That should work out fine. Let me check to make sure though, and I'll call you tonight."

"Better yet, let me call you," he said quickly. "Will you be home after supper?"

"As far as I know I will."

To Cass' dismay, she realized Tabitha had spotted her. Since it was too late to make her getaway, she resigned herself to putting up with her stepsister's gloating.

"Well, fancy meeting you here." Brushing by Cass, Tabitha leaned against the locker next to Logan's and mimicked the way he held his books. "What are you doing in this neighborhood?" Before Cass could reply, Tabitha smiled up at Logan. "Hello, Logan."

Looking ill-at-ease, he shifted his weight from one foot to the other. "Hi."

Tabitha's icy blue gaze returned to Cass. "What did you say you were doing here?"

"I didn't," was Cass' terse response. "You didn't give

me a chance to say anything." "Oops, sorry." Tabitha covered her mouth with a fluttery hand. "Go ahead."

"I stopped by to ask Logan something. He answered my question so—" Cass produced a bright, although false, smile, "—I'll be off. Have fun, y'all."

"We will," Tabitha assured her with an adoring glance at Logan. As Cass turned to leave, Tabitha asked, "By the way, would you tell Mom—"

Cass raised a hand in acknowledgment. "I already told Logan I'd clear it with her. Well—" not sure where to look, she settled on a spot midway between the pair. "Bye."

"See you."

"I'll call you tonight," Logan reminded her.

Cass nodded and kept walking. When she thought she was far enough away, she ducked into a doorway and looked back, watching as they jostled and joked their way out of the building. A knife of jealousy twisted in her stomach. What did Tabitha think she was doing, chasing after Logan like that? She knew Cass liked him.

Suddenly, a familiar figure cut across her line of vision. Before she had time to compose her features, the person halted in front of her and grinned.

"Wow!" Micah whistled. "I wouldn't want to be the reason you're looking so mad. What happened?"

Cass glanced at the doors through which Tabitha and Logan had disappeared and a thought—a deliciously wicked idea—popped into her head. *Two can play at this game*. She mentally stuck her tongue out at her stepsister. *Let's see how you like it when the shoe's on the other foot*.

Turning her attention to Micah, she smiled up at him. "I just thought about something that's been bugging me lately."

"Would you like to talk about it?" offered Micah.

Wow, this is turning out to be even easier than I hoped, Cass thought excitedly.

She gave him her most pleading expression. "Do you have the time?"

"Right now? Hold on. Let me check my schedule." Micah flipped open one of the notebooks he carried and pretended to study it with great care. Closing it, he laughed. "I'm free until—oh—the middle of November." He tousled Cass' hair, and she yelped in protest. "Of course I have the time, you dingbat. We're friends, and friends always have time for each other."

Gratitude warmed Cass' heart. "It's really nice of you to say that. Do you want to come over to the house and talk there?"

"That depends." Micah shifted his books to one arm and hefted Cass' backpack from the floor onto his shoulder. "Has your Mom baked anything lately?"

"There's strawberry pie and German chocolate cake left over from the meeting last night," Cass said.

Micah's eyes lit up. "Then it's your house for sure. Lead on. My mouth is watering already."

Cass obeyed, laughing. "You don't have to carry my books. I'm not helpless, you know."

"Hush up and keep walking," Micah growled good-naturedly. "The sooner we get out of here, the sooner we reach your house, and I get my hands—or better yet, my mouth—on a piece of your mother's strawberry pie."

When they reached the doors Cass sent up a quick, fervent prayer that Logan and Tabitha had delayed leaving for some reason. She'd forfeit an entire year's allowance to see Tabitha's expression when she realized Cass and Micah were together.

They emerged into the blinding sunslight and a hurried look around told Cass Tabitha and Logan weren't there. *That's all right*, she consoled herself. *I'll bring the subject up at supper and watch her have a fit.*

CHAPTER 17

"You'll never guess what Logan did for me this afternoon," Tabitha announced at dinner that night. She looked around the table at her family as if daring them to guess. Her gaze lingered a few extra seconds on Cass before moving on to Mom and Dad.

She knew it wasn't nice, but Cass couldn't resist the urge to wipe the smug smile off Tabitha's face. "Let's see." She thoughtfully chewed on a piece of cornbread. "Did he—oh, I don't know—surprise you with hot cocoa by any chance?"

Tabitha stared at her in amazement for several moments then her expression grew thunderous. "That was mean! You knew. I wanted to be the one to tell Dad and Mom." Crossing her arms, she flung herself back in her chair.

"But you asked us to guess," Cass pointed out in a reasonable tone designed to annoy Tabitha even further. She broke off another bite of cornbread and popped it into her mouth. Compared to Tabitha, she was the picture of serenity—which was just the way she wanted it.

"You didn't guess! You knew!" Tabitha fairly shrieked. "It's not the same thing."

Mom raised a placating hand. "Would someone please tell Steve and me what's going on? We're completely in the dark."

Although Cass politely waited for Tabitha to explain, her stepsister wasn't taken in by the charade. "You tell them," she ordered bitterly. "You've already ruined the story anyway."

Cass shrugged, then launched into an account of the surprise Logan had planned for Tabitha. After explaining to Mom and Dad about Tabitha never having tasted hot cocoa, Cass wrapped up the story by gushing, "So Logan—bless his heart—asked his mother to have some ready when he brought Tabitha by after school today. Isn't that the sweetest thing you've ever heard?" Pasting on a phony smile, she turned to Tabitha. "Was there whipped cream or marshmallows? Or, even better—" she trilled a fake laugh, "—both?"

Tabitha ignored her when she finished, but Mom gave her an odd look. "Did Cass get the story right?" Mom asked Tabitha.

Picking up her fork, Tabitha began pushing her baked beans around her plate. "I guess."

"Then it was very nice of Logan to arrange to do that for you," Mom said. She looked at Dad. "Wasn't that thoughtful of him, Steve?"

Dad nodded. "Extremely thoughtful." He frowned. "But I'm sure you've had hot cocoa at least once in your life, Tabitha. I seem to recall your Grandma making it for you when we visited her and Grandpa at Christmas one year."

Irritation tightened Tabitha's features. "If she did, I don't remember it so it doesn't count. Why are you trying to make what Logan did less special?"

Cass pretended to cough so she could cover her mouth and hide her smile. This was turning out even better than she'd anticipated. Dad had all but accused Tabitha of being a liar. *That'll teach her to keep her hands off other people's property*, she thought.

"I didn't mean to take away from Logan's kindness," Dad replied calmly. "What he did was very nice, regardless of whether or not you've ever had hot cocoa."

Tabitha merely sniffed and looked away.

This battle won, Cass scooped up a forkful of beans from her plate. Now she needed to decide when to drop the bombshell on Tabitha that she'd spent over an hour with Micah this afternoon.

"Why did you find it necessary to tell Tabitha's news, instead of letting her share it?" Mom asked quietly, breaking into her triumph.

"Uh ... uh ..." Cass' gaze darted from Mom to Tabitha to Dad then back to Mom. "Well ..."

"Yeah, why'd you do that?" No longer slouched in her chair, Tabitha leaned forward.

Cass wanted to come back with a snappy retort but she couldn't think of anything. "She asked us to guess. What was I supposed to do?"

"I'm not going to dignify that with a response." Mom gave Cass a stern look. "You knew exactly what you were doing and why. You should be ashamed of yourself."

Cass dropped her gaze to her plate. *This isn't turning out the way I'd planned*, she thought darkly. *Maybe I'd better wait until later, when Mom isn't around, to tell Tabitha about Micah*.

After dinner Mom and Dad left to visit friends, leaving Cass and Tabitha to clean up on their own. They warily eyed each other. Tabitha seemed a lot less cocky without Mom there to back her up, but Cass felt hesitant about bringing up her afternoon with Micah. The last thing she wanted was for Tabitha to go crying to Mom about how mean she'd been to her again.

Used to the routine they'd established over the past month, they worked in silence for several minutes. Tabitha busied herself filling the sink with soapy water while Cass traveled back and forth between the table and counter, carrying dishes and silverware. Tabitha finally caved in and broke the standoff.

"How come Logan told you about the hot cocoa?" she asked gruffly.

"I don't know." Cass set a bowl of cole slaw on the counter and went in search of plastic wrap to cover it. "We were talking at his locker, and he mentioned you were going over to his house and what he planned to do."

"What were you two talking about when I walked up?"

Cass occupied herself with the plastic wrap. "Didn't Logan tell you?"

"I asked him," Tabitha admitted, "and he gave me some song-and-dance about you wanting to go snorkeling or something." She snorted. "He's not a very good liar."

Cass hesitated, debating on whether or not to tell the truth, then shrugged. "He wasn't exactly lying. I did ask him if he'd go to the lagoon with me this afternoon, although I didn't say anything about snorkeling. Maybe that's why he thought I asked him."

"You've hardly paid any attention to him for a week, then out of the blue you invite him to Eamon." Suspicion was written all over Tabitha's face. "What gives? Wait a minute. I get it." She laughed sarcastically. "You gave Alex the old heave-ho at lunch and figured you could pick up where you'd left off with Logan. Except your scheme didn't work because he was busy with me."

Cass tried to wrestle her temper under control.

"Actually, everything worked out for the best," she blithely informed Tabitha. "Micah and I wound up coming here and spending some time together. I never realized how easy he is to talk to."

Tabitha whirled around to confront Cass, soapy water splashing across the counter and onto the floor. "What in the world did you and Micah have to talk about?"

"You." Cass gestured at the water dripping off the counter and puddling around Tabitha's feet. "There's water all over the place. You'd better clean it up before you slip and hurt yourself."

Tabitha paid no attention to her. "What do you mean you and Micah talked about me? What did you say? What did he say? Who started the discussion in the first place and why?"

Cass just smiled and reached around Tabitha for the roll of paper towels suspended above the sink. She ripped off a handful and, leaning down, began blotting up the water. "That was a lot of questions. Which one do you want me to begin with?"

"Who started the conversation?" Tabitha asked.

"I did." Cass tossed the soggy paper towels into the wastebasket, pointedly ignoring Tabitha.

"You? Why?"

"I wanted to know how Micah sees you," explained Cass. "As just a friend or as a potential girlfriend."

"You asked him that?" The face Tabitha turned toward Cass was horrified.

Cass rolled her eyes. "Oh, puh-leeze. Give me a little credit for having some common sense, will you? Of course I didn't ask him that, at least not in so many words."

Tabitha sighed impatiently. "In what words then?"

"Why are you acting so cranky?" complained Cass. "I was trying to do you a favor, you know." With an injured air, she picked up one of the plates Tabitha had set in the rack and began drying it.

"Would you cut out the dramatics and just answer the question?" Tabitha spat out through clenched teeth. "What did you say to Micah?"

Cass concentrated on making sure there wasn't a drop of moisture left on the plate, trying her best to keep her face blank. Things weren't going the way she'd imagined they would, and she desperately tried to think of a way to take back the upper hand.

"Cass—" Tabitha began warningly.

"I'm thinking!" she snapped. "We were talking about this and that and then I said something like, 'So, Micah, how would you feel if Logan and Tabitha started going out?' "

"You didn't!"

More water cascaded onto the floor, and Cass eyed it with irritation. "You're cleaning it up this time," she tartly informed Tabitha.

Tabitha ignored that. "What did Micah say when you asked him about Logan and me?"

A pleased smile curved Cass' lips. Now this was the way she liked things. She had information that Tabitha desperately wanted.

"Nothing for a few seconds. He was very surprised, to say the least."

"Then what?" Tabitha said when Cass didn't continue.

"When he finally got over the shock, he wanted to know why I'd ask something like that." Cass reached for another plate. "So I told him about you going over to Logan's house and the surprise Logan had waiting for you."

Tabitha sighed again. "Come on, tell me the whole story. Quit making me drag every little detail out of you."

Cass shrugged and picked up a third plate. "Micah didn't say anything about the hot cocoa thing, but I could tell he was upset. You know how he gets when he's mad. His eyes got all squinty, and his chin came out. Then he tried to act like it didn't bother him. He said, real casual-like, 'Tabitha's free to go out with anybody she wants to.' I just went, 'uh-huh,' like I agreed with him, and a couple of seconds later, he said, 'I always thought she and Logan were just friends. I can't believe she'd go out with him. He doesn't seem like her type at all.' "

"He actually said that?" Tabitha had given up all pretense of washing. She'd turned from the sink and stared at Cass.

Cass nodded. "Yup. So then I said, 'What do you care who's her type and who isn't? It's not like you're interested in dating her.' "

"Oh, my gosh." Tabitha clapped her wet hands to her burning cheeks. "What did Micah say to that? I mean, did he agree with you or did he put up some kind of an argument?"

"Neither. He clammed up, fast." Cass laughed. "You should have seen his face, though. He looked like he had about a million things he wanted to say, but he couldn't get them out. I figured, since we were on the subject, I'd ask him if Alison was his type. His eyes practically bugged out of his head."

Tabitha laughed. "You don't believe in holding back, do you?"

Cass just shrugged. "When I want to know something, I ask." Cass gave her a teasing look. "Be honest. Aren't you glad that's the way I am?"

"In this case, yes." Tabitha returned to her dishwashing. "What did Micah say about Alison?"

"He said she was okay." Cass shrugged. "He didn't seem all that taken with her. Whatever is going on between them, I'm convinced that 99 percent of it is coming from her."

Tabitha expelled a sigh of relief. "I could kiss you."

"Yuck! Please don't." Cass picked up another dish and backed away from her.

Tabitha didn't seem to notice. "Anyway, to get back to Micah, did he say anything else about Alison?"

Cass shook her head. "I tried a couple of different ways to get him to talk about her, but he's pretty close-mouthed when he wants to be. Every time I brought you up, though, he was happy to talk about you. It's obvious he likes you, so I don't know why he's never asked you out.

Tabitha repeated the reason she'd given Logan. "All I am to Micah is Kira's best friend. He doesn't see me as a real girl. You know, someone to date."

"That's where I think you're wrong." Cass paused in her drying. "A guy doesn't act as jealous as Micah did about you and Logan if he doesn't care."

Tabitha shrugged slightly. "I feel like I'm flying blind when it comes to Micah lately. I thought I knew him so well."

Cass resisted the impulse to pat Tabitha on the back. She was glad the tension between them had eased, but she was still uncomfortable about Tabitha's friendship with Logan. *If I just knew what was going on between them*, she thought darkly, then suddenly brightened. *But if she's focused on Micah, then Logan will be free for me*. She knew it wasn't the best of plans, but maybe—just maybe—it would work.

CHAPTER 18

Cass and Tabitha finished the dishes with a minimum of conversation, then went their seperate ways. Tabitha had homework she needed to get done. So did Cass, but her stomach kept churning at the thought of Logan calling. She wondered if she should call him and get it over with. Since finding out about his surprise for Tabitha, she didn't think they had anything to talk about so a trip together to the lagoon didn't make sense. Still, he'd acted like he was eager to spend time with her. Cass shook her head. It was all too bewildering. Maybe she'd just wait to see if he would call.

It was almost six-thirty when Cass went to her room to get her backpack. Too restless to stay cooped up in the house, she decided she'd tackle her homework assignments out back. She poked her head into Tabitha's room before she left.

"I'll be outside if anyone calls," she informed her stepsister.

"Huh?" Tabitha raised a distracted face from her trigonometry book. "Oh, okay." She gave a dismissive wave. "I got it."

Cass wasn't confident that she had gotten it, but she

didn't care to risk Tabitha's wrath by repeating the message. Shouldering the backpack, she headed for the back door.

After dragging a lounge chair from the patio across the lawn to the edge of the grass, Cass flopped onto it with a weary sigh. Squinting up at the sky, she figured there was about an hour of sunlight left. She unearthed her physics text and notebook from the backpack, along with a pencil, and arranged them in her lap.

No one will ever be able to convince me physics is fun, she thought as she turned to the page of problems the teacher had assigned, *but I can't complain about the setting I have to work in. Palm trees, warm tropical breezes, and the Pacific Ocean as far as the eye can see. It hardly gets better than this. Of course, Tennessee is still the best place on earth*, she hastened to remind herself. *But this*—Cass glanced around in genuine appreciation of Kwajalein's breathtaking beauty—*this isn't bad*.

She labored over physics for a full hour, not pausing for a single break. She was determined to find the key that would unlock the secret to understanding her homework assignment if it was the last thing she did. Only when she realized she was holding the book about an inch from her nose did she notice how dark it had gotten. Looking behind her to the west, she saw the sun sinking into the horizon amid ribbons of purple and orange clouds.

"I've been doing this way too long," Cass announced to herself and swung her legs off the chair.

As she stood and stretched her arms toward the twilight sky, it occurred to her that Tabitha hadn't come to tell her Logan had called. Cass frowned. *That's odd. I've never known Logan not to follow through on something like that*.

By the time she returned the lounge chair to its spot

on the lanai, Cass made up her mind that Tabitha was in her room with the stereo blasting and, therefore, wouldn't hear a bomb go off in the next room. She figured if she checked the answering machine, she'd find Logan had called and left a message.

Having constructed this likely scenario in her head, Cass skidded to an abrupt halt when she came through the door and discovered Tabitha happily chatting on the phone. Just to be on the safe side, Cass glanced at the answering machine on the kitchen counter. The message light stared back at her, unblinking. Nobody had called.

Cass hung around for several seconds, hoping Tabitha would take the hint and get off the phone. Other than a brief smile, however, Tabitha paid no attention to her. Irritated, Cass opened one of the kitchen drawers and retrieved a flashlight.

"I'm going to the Ten-Ten," she told Tabitha, who once again waved that she'd heard her.

It was close to eight-thirty when she returned home. Mom and Dad looked up from the couch where they were quietly conversing. Tabitha was nowhere to be seen.

"Hi." Mom interrupted her discussion with Dad. "Where have you been?"

Cass sank into the recliner opposite the couch. "Didn't Tabitha tell you?"

"All she said was that you'd left." Mom smiled wryly. "I started to get worried, then I told myself there was no reason to be concerned. Where could you possibly go?"

Cass laughed. "That was pretty much my reaction when I realized how late it was. Anyway, I went to the Ten-Ten." She held up a bag containing a candy bar and magazine and shook it. "Junk food for the body and the mind. I'm a happy girl." She made a show of looking around the room. "Where's Tabitha?"

Dad motioned toward the hall. "In her room, talking on the phone."

"Still?" Cass' eyebrows shot up, disappearing under her bangs. "She was on the phone when I left. I thought we had a fifteen-minute time limit."

"You do," Mom said calmly. "Tabitha was doing homework when we got in. She's been talking about five minutes."

"Oh." Cass toyed with the shopping bag. "Do you happen to know if Logan called?"

"She didn't mention it. Why don't you ask her?" Mom said.

I'd rather die, Cass silently retorted.

Aloud, she muttered, "I guess I'll do that." She stood up slowly. "I'm going to my room to read my magazine."

"Is your homework done?" Dad asked.

Cass made a face at him. "Of course. Ever since I started bringing assignments home, Mom's drilled it into my head that homework comes first. You can't imagine how much in life I've missed out on because of it."

"Oh, poor you." Mom played an imaginary violin. "Your life has been a nightmare and it's all my fault."

"That's right," Cass said impishly. "I hope you've got a lot of money stashed away because I'm going to need it for therapy someday. It's going to take years of counseling to help me get over my traumatic childhood. Or—" she tilted her head to one side and gave them both her most winsome smile, "—you can buy me a new car when I go back to the mainland for college, and we'll call it even."

As Mom and Dad laughed, Cass blew them each a kiss, turned, and sashayed off to her bedroom.

A short while later Cass was lying on her bed flipping through the magazine, when she heard Tabitha come out of her room. She was tempted to follow her stepsister down the hall and ask her about Logan, but squelched the impulse. Tabitha would tell her if he called. The fact that she didn't stop to knock at the door told Cass that he hadn't.

Two tears rolled down her cheeks and plopped onto the magazine page. The photos of the carefree models in their stylish clothes blurred as the tears continued to well in her eyes.

"I will not cry," she whispered angrily. "If Logan never talks to me again, I'll be getting exactly what I deserve. I treated him very badly. And why? Because I decided to choose someone like Alex. I don't know a good thing even when I trip over it."

Cass was still berating herself for her stupidity when there was a soft tap at the door. A second later, the door opened and Mom peeked inside. She held out the phone.

"It's for you."

Cass' heart lurched before settling into a beat approximately twice its normal rate. In one fluid motion, she turned over, rolled up to a sitting position, and reached for the phone.

"I think it's Randy," Mom said as she handed the receiver to her.

Her hopes dashed, Cass listlessly accepted the phone. "Oh ... all right." She waited for Mom to leave the room before putting the receiver to her ear. "Hello?"

Randy's amused voice came over the line. "Your mother was right. It is me."

"Hi, Randy."

"Gee, try to contain your excitment, will you?" teased Randy.

"Sorry," Cass apologized gruffly. "I have a lot on my mind."

"I know. That's why I called. Rianne told me about you telling Alex off." Randy paused. "Are you okay or do you need a shoulder to cry on?"

Cass was touched by his offer and the tears prickled behind her eyelids again. "Yes, to both questions," she replied in a voice thickened by the emotion clogging her throat. "I'm fine about Alex, but I could also use someone to talk to about a whole other situation."

"I'm your man if you feel like unloading on somebody."

Cass hesitated. "Thanks, but this is more of a girl thing. I hope you don't mind."

"Nah," Randy breezily assured her. "If it's a girl you need, I don't exactly meet the qualifications. Would you like me to put Rianne on, though?"

"No, that's all right." Cass realized she didn't feel like talking about Logan. She was too worn out to even think about him anymore tonight. "I have some reading to do." She glanced guiltily at the magazine, thinking, *Well, it's not really a lie*. "Tell Rianne I'll see her tomorrow. And Randy? Thanks for calling and checking up on me."

"Aw, what are friends for?" he said nonchalantly, then cleared his throat. "I'll see you at school tomorrow. I'll be the one in the spiffy set of wheels."

Cass laughed. "And I'll be the one with the long face and the lousy attitude."

"In that case, I'll steer my spiffy wheels clear of you," Randy said, quickly adding, "Bye," and hanging up before Cass could think of a comeback.

She pressed the off button and placed the phone on her nightstand. Leaning back against the headboard and folding her arms, she thought, *If I were in charge of the universe, the perfect guy would look like Alex, have Logan's sense of humor, and be as sweet as Randy. Of course, if I were in charge of the universe, I'd have a figure that would stop traffic and a face to match, plus I'd be as smart as Einstein.* Looking down at herself, Cass made a face. *Obviously I'm not in charge of the universe.*

Too tired to read anymore, Cass decided to get ready for bed. On her way to the bathroom, she detoured to return the phone to the living room. Dad and Mom still sat on the couch talking, and Tabitha was undoubtedly going deaf in her bedroom, if the volume of her music was any indication. Cass smiled in relief. She didn't want to talk to anyone. Well, she might make an exception if Logan called, but other than that she wasn't up for conversation.

As it turned out, she shouldn't have worried. He never called, and Cass wound up crying herself to sleep.

CHAPTER 19

"I'm so mad at you I could spit."

They were halfway to school the next morning when Tabitha made this announcement. Having been as rushed as usual in getting ready, Cass hadn't noticed anything unusual in Tabitha's attitude.

Now Cass stared at her in amazement. "Me? What did I do? I barely saw you last night."

"You saw me long enough that you could've told me about your conversation with Alex," Tabitha retorted. "Instead I had to hear about it from somebody else. You should have been the one to tell me."

"You could've asked me about our discussion," Cass said angrily, hating feeling like she was in the wrong when she knew she wasn't. "You knew Alex and I had talked."

"I shouldn't have to ask," Tabitha said. "You're my sister. I shouldn't have to hear about what's going on in your life secondhand."

Looking heavenward, Cass sent up a silent plea for patience. "Who told you anyway?"

"Rianne told Kira who told Logan who told me."

Cass almost ran off the road. "You … I … Logan

called?" she sputtered.

"Duh! How do you think he told me?" Tabitha rolled her eyes. "He didn't talk to Kira until after I left his house yesterday."

"When did he call?" Cass couldn't believe she'd spent the previous night in a state of misery when it could have been avoided.

"Actually, he called twice." Unaware of Cass' mounting fury and the reason for it, Tabitha blithely continued with her explanation. "The first call was while you were gone the first time, and the second one was a little while after you left the second time."

"What did you tell him?" Cass asked, so angry she was having trouble breathing.

Finally catching on that something was amiss, Tabitha shot her a curious glance. "That you were out and I didn't know when you'd be back. Why? What was I supposed to tell him?"

"The first time Logan called I was out back, you idiot! I told you I'd be outside doing my homework if anyone called for me. I was at the store the second time, which is where I told you I was going." She uttered a little scream. "I don't believe this!"

"Well, excuse me for getting it wrong." Tabitha raised her chin in a display of indignation. "I have more important things to do than keep track of your comings and goings."

"Why didn't you at least tell me he called?" Cass fairly shouted.

"I forgot!" Tabitha yelled back. "Besides, how was I supposed to know it was so important to you to talk to Logan, especially with the way you've been treating him lately?"

"Will you quit bringing up how I've supposedly mistreated Logan?" snapped Cass. "That's between him and me. You know what I think? I think you deliberately kept it from me that he called because you're trying to sink your claws into him. You can't have Micah so you're willing to settle for whoever you can get, even if it means using Logan."

"How dare you lecture me on using people?" said Tabitha, her eyes narrow and angry. "What about you and Micah?"

"At least when I talk to Micah, it's because I'm trying to get you two together," countered Cass. "I don't go around stabbing people in the back."

"That's what you said you talked about. How do I know that's what really happened?"

Cass opened her mouth to speak but nothing came out. She snapped it shut again, thinking, until the school loomed into view. "I refuse to stay here and listen to you accuse me of lying. I'm heading on."

With that, she bent low over the handle bars and pedaled as fast as her legs would go, ignoring the burn in her muscles. As she pulled up to the school, Cass saw Micah arriving from the other direction and smiled.

All right, Tabitha, you want war? Then you've got it. I'll teach you to mess with me.

Waving, Cass got Micah's attention and steered her bike toward him. Alison was also headed in his direction, but Cass wasn't about to let the other girl ruin her plan.

"Hey." Pulling alongside Micah, Cass braked and hopped off her bike.

"Hey, yourself."

"Are you busy this afternoon?" Cass said quickly.

Micah smiled down at her. "It depends. What do you have in mind?"

Before Cass could respond, Alison sidled up to Micah's other side. "Good morning, Mikey." She lifted her face to the sky. "It looks like it's going to be another gorgeous day in paradise. Don't you ever have bad weather around here?"

Mikey? Cass wondered. *He lets her call him Mikey? Uh-oh, this is even worse than I thought. I'd better warn Tabitha.* Remembering she was furious at her stepsister, she clenched her jaw. *Forget it. Let her find out on her own.*

"Do I know you?" Leaning around Micah, Alison fixed her incredible eyes on Cass.

Gosh, she's beautiful, Cass thought. *Her skin is perfect.* She felt as if the sunlight highlighted every freckle on her own less-than-perfect face.

Realizing Alison was waiting for an answer, Cass mentally shook herself. "We've met, but there's no reason you'd remember me. I'm Cass Devane."

"How long have you lived here?" Alison asked in her Texas twang.

"A little over six weeks." Cass wracked her brain for a graceful, but quick, way to end the conversation. The longer she stood near Alison, the worse she felt.

"Then you're a newcomer too," Alison said. "How do you like Kwaj?"

Cass shrugged. "I hated it at first, but it's starting to grow on me." Not wanting to seem rude, she asked, "What about you? Wasn't it hard leaving home, since it's your last year of high school?"

Alison's face tightened and a bleak look crept into her eyes. "I hate that I'm missing out on my senior year with all my friends. I'm sure I'll forgive my folks someday, but not for a long, long time." She suddenly smiled. "But I'm making friends here and that's what counts." She gave Micah a flirtatious smile. "I've met some really nice people."

"You mean like Mikey?" Cass said lightly, earning herself a scowl from Micah. "Yeah, he's a prince. We all think the world of him." She abruptly changed her tone.

"Speaking of which, I'll get back to you about this afternoon, Micah. Right now, I've got to go." She started to walk away to park her bike then turned back. "Alison, if you'd like to meet even more nice people, there's a youth group that meets at my house on Sunday nights. My parents lead it. We'd love for you to come."

Alison seemed both pleased and surprised by the invitation. "I just might do that."

"Great. Micah, why don't you tell her more about it?" Cass fluttered her fingers at them. "Bye, y'all."

The moment she turned her back, she broke out into a triumphant grin. *Hah! I can't wait to see the look on Tabitha's face when Alison shows up Sunday night. I know it's not the right reason for asking her, but it sure will be fun.*

After parking her bike, Cass headed for the building and her high spirits plummeted. Before the day was out, she'd have to face Logan, and she had no idea what she would say to him. He probably thought she couldn't be bothered calling him back. Then again, Tabitha hadn't made it clear who he'd called to talk to. Maybe both calls had been for Tabitha.

Cass groaned under her breath. It wasn't even eight o'clock and she already had a splitting headache. It promised to be a long day.

With careful planning, Cass made it to lunch without encountering Logan in the halls. It required a lot of ducking in and out of classrooms, but until she thought of what to say to him, she didn't want to risk running into him.

At lunch, Dennis waylaid her and asked her to eat with him. Cass gladly accepted. Even though she just liked Dennis as a friend, it was great to have an excuse not to eat with Tabitha. She almost changed her mind when she watched her friends out of the corner of her eye. Every time a gale of laughter erupted from the group, Cass would tense, sure Tabitha was telling them about her ill-fated efforts to link up with Logan. It set her teeth on edge to see her friends talking and giggling, and she had to force herself to pretend interest in what Dennis was saying. All she wanted to do was march over to the other table and demand to know what was so funny.

It occurred to Cass that lately no matter who she was with or what she was doing, she wished she were somewhere else doing something different. It frustrated her. *Why can't I just be content no matter what?* She thought, pretending to pay attention to some story Dennis was telling. Inwardly she sighed. *Maybe because I can't even remember what being content is like.*

The afternoon flew by in a blur of near-misses involving Logan. At one point, Cass saw him walking toward her as they changed classes. In desperation, she struck up a conversation with a perfect stranger who happened to be next to her, resulting in several puzzled looks from the girl. Her face blazing, Cass mumbled an excuse and hurried into the restroom the moment Logan passed by on the other side of the corridor.

This is ridiculous! Cass chided herself as she collapsed against the bathroom wall. The cool tile felt good through the T-shirt clinging to her sweaty back. *I've never walked away from a confrontation before. Why does this thing with Logan have me so spooked?* It took several seconds, but the answer finally came. *It's because I realize how self-centered I've been. All I've cared about since school started is me. I've been snotty to Tabitha, and I haven't thought twice about using Micah and Logan. I even used Dennis at lunch.* She closed her eyes and groaned. *I don't deserve to live.*

Moving on leaden feet, Cass shuffled to the sink, turned on the faucet, and splashed her face with cold water. As she reached for a paper towel, she caught sight of herself in the mirror. Her reflection returned her gaze without blinking.

"You, Cassandra Aileen Devane," she murmured to her image, "have a lot of making up to do. The way you're going to start is to quit playing games with people and their feelings." She fixed herself with a steely stare. "You got that?" Her reflection blanched, but nodded.

Cass barely made it to class before the bell rang. As she slipped into her seat at the last possible moment, she did so with a lighter heart. *Things will be better now,* she thought as the teacher started mumbling about last night's homework assignment. *Well, as long as everyone can find it in their hearts to forgive me.*

The odd thing was, now that Cass knew what she should do, Logan was nowhere to be found. She didn't see him either before or after her last class nor was he at his locker when she hastened there following a brief stop at her own.

She was heading outside to see if she could catch him before he left when she ran smack into Micah. Laughing, he grabbed her by the arms to steady her.

"Whoa! Are you okay?"

"Yeah—I was hoping to talk to Logan before he left. Have you seen him?"

Micah nodded. "He was out of here the minute the bell rang. A bunch of us guys decided at lunch to go golfing, so Logan high-tailed it home to call around and see if he could borrow some clubs. Is it important that you talk to him? I'm meeting him at his house, and I can tell him to call you."

"That's okay," Cass assured him. "It's nothing earth-shaking. I'll get a hold of him later." She flashed him a teasing smile. "I guess this means we won't be getting together this afternoon."

He hit his forehead with his palm. "I forgot you asked me if I was free. I feel like a heel."

Cass laughed. "It's all right. I was going to tell you something had come up anyway." *Like my conscience*, she added silently.

"So I'm off the hook?" Micah produced his most charming grin. "You're not mad at me?"

Gazing up at his kind face, Cass realized how special he was to her and shook her head. "Who could stay mad at you? You're too good a guy." She gave him a saucy smile. "And I'm not the only one who thinks that, you know."

Micah was instantly alert. "Who are you talking about?"

Cass figured it was time to start making amends to Tabitha. "Come on," she scoffed good-naturedly. "Surely you're bright enough to figure it out."

"I don't have time to stand around and play games," he said with irritation, but Cass could see right through it. "I have to get home, pick up my clubs, and meet the guys at Logan's before three. Either tell me who you mean or I'm out of here."

With an impish look, Cass glanced around, stepped close to Micah, stood on tiptoe, placed her mouth next to his ear, and whispered, "Have a good game."

His bark of laughter threatened to deafen her before she had a chance to back away. "You," he declared, "are a pain in the neck." He ruffled her hair. "But you're a cute pain in the neck, so I think I'll keep you as a friend."

With that, Micah turned and loped off down the hall. Smiling, Cass watched him go before turning to leave herself.

CHAPTER 20

Cass and Tabitha rode home separately, Cass accompanied part of the way by Rianne and Tabitha by Kira. They met up as they parked their bikes and headed for the back door. When Cass attempted to speak to Tabitha, her stepsister turned up her nose and stalked into the house. Rolling her eyes, Cass followed her.

Mom rose from the couch to greet them. "Hello, ladies. How was your day?"

"I've had better," Tabitha muttered.

"What happened?" Mom laid a hand on her arm, but Tabitha shook it off.

"Ask your daughter. She's the one who ruined it."

Mom looked at Cass. "What did you do?"

Cass shook her head in bewilderment. "Nothing. Honest." She put as much sincerity into her voice as she could muster. "Tabitha and I hardly talked all day."

Whirling on her, Tabitha sneered, "You know exactly what you did! You were all over Micah in the hall after school. I knew Alison was a threat, but I never expected to compete with my own sister."

Cass' stomach clenched as Tabitha burst into tears and fled down the hallway to her room. Turning to

Mom, she began to explain, but her mother held up her hand to silence her.

"I have had enough of this outlandish behavior between the two of you." Cass hated the way her mother spoke, pronouncing each word separately and distincly. "I'm calling Steve. He's going to have to handle this because I'm too exasperated."

Cass' stomach sank as she trailed Mom to the phone.

"Don't call St … uh … Dad," she implored. "Let me go talk to Tabitha. It's all a huge misunderstanding. I know we can work it out if I just explain to her what really happened."

"No. It's time we got this situation straightened out once and for all. Steve has a few things he wants to say to you girls, and now's as good a time as any to get them said."

Seeing that she wasn't going to change her mother's mind, Cass followed Tabitha's example and disappeared into her room. Whenever Dad showed up, he wasn't going to find her sitting in the living room, waiting for him like a naughty little girl. She'd use the time before he arrived to try to guess what he planned to lecture them about and to come up with arguments to refute him.

Cass hadn't gotten very far when Mom knocked on the door then opened it. "I talked with Steve. He wants you and Tabitha to meet him at the Yokwe Yuk at five."

Cass' eyebrows shot up in alarm. "Why? Is he planning to publicly humiliate us?"

Instead of smiling, Mom frowned. "Why do you always expect the worst from people? Surely Steve has proved to you by now that he only has your best interests at heart. You should know he would never do anything to deliberately embarrass you."

Cass frowned. "Excuse me for asking. I just thought it

was strange he wasn't going to talk to us here, that's all. I didn't realize I wasn't allowed to make comments."

Mom frowned, but closed the door without saying a word. A moment later, Cass heard a knock on Tabitha's door then the low murmur of voices. She threw herself on the bed and, folding her arms beneath her head, stared up at the ceiling.

Great. A date with Tabitha and her father. Math's not my best subject, but even I can figure out that makes it two against one. God, are You there? Could You send a couple of angels to the Yuk this evening at around five? Otherewise, I'm going to get creamed.

At ten to five Cass emerged from her room and discovered Tabitha sitting in the rocking chair, waiting for her. Her stepsister wore a green plaid sundress and had pulled her hair back with a matching scrunchy. Cass glanced down at the shorts and T-shirt she'd worn to school then over at her mother.

"Uh ... should I change?"

"You look fine," Mom assured her. "Besides, you don't want to keep Steve waiting."

Kicking herself for not thinking to dress up like Tabitha had, Cass wordlessly trailed her stepsister outside to their bikes. The meeting hadn't even started, and she already felt at a disadvantage.

"What do you think this is all about?" Tabitha asked as soon as they reached the road and turned left toward the restaurant.

Cass made a face. "My guess is our parents have had it with the fighting, and they've decided the only solution is to send me back to Tennessee."

"Would you like that?"

Cass could almost hear the hope in Tabitha's voice, but she didn't hesitate. "No."

"Oh."

"Actually, I figure Dad is going to get on me for giving you a hard time lately," Cass continued, as if Tabitha hadn't spoken. "Since you're always the one who acts upset, Mom and Dad wind up blaming me."

"What do you mean I act upset?" demanded Tabitha. "I'm not acting. I really am upset. You do some rotten things."

"Okay, okay." She glanced over at Tabitha, and the wind blew her hair across her face. "I'm not looking to start a fight. I'll admit I haven't been the nicest person the last week or so."

Tabitha's eyes narrowed with suspicion. "What are you trying to pull now?"

"Nothing." Cass expelled a frustrated sigh. "Just forget I said anything. I can't do anything right as far as you're concerned."

"You can't when you throw yourself at Micah the way you did this afternoon," retorted Tabitha. "And don't try to deny it. I saw you with my own two eyes."

"You didn't see what you think you saw." Cass struggled to keep her temper in check. "If you'd let me explain, you'll find out that what went on was entirely innocent."

"Hah!" Tabitha emitted a derisive snort. "Nothing you do is innocent. You're as sneaky as they come."

Cass knew if she didn't do something fast, she'd say something she would later regret. Muttering, "Forget it," she pulled ahead of Tabitha so they couldn't talk. They rode single file the rest of the way to the restaurant.

Dad was waiting patiently when they arrived. Tabitha kissed him on the cheek while Cass made do with a wan smile and a wave. She had a bad feeling about this get-together so she didn't see any reason to pretend she was happy to be there.

Linking arms with her father, Tabitha grinned up at

him. "It's not quite five. How did you get off early from work?"

Dad motioned Cass over to stand on his other side and she reluctantly obeyed.

"After Donna called, I called Ed Nishihara and told him there was a minor family crisis. I asked him if he'd mind coming in a few minutes early. He came right over."

Cass rolled her eyes. "Don't you think saying there's a crisis was a tad bit melodramatic?"

Instead of taking offense, Dad laughed. "Not after talking with your Mom. I would have told Ed it was a full-blown emergency, but I didn't want to worry him."

"Oh, Dad," Tabitha said, and tinkled the laugh that always made Cass want to smack her. "You're so funny."

Cass knew precisely what her stepsister was up to. She was using flattery in an effort to guarantee her father would take her side in the upcoming discussion. Although she didn't hold out much hope, Cass prayed Dad would see through Tabitha's attempts to manipulate him and be fair.

Because Dad had requested privacy, the trio was seated in a booth by a window. Cass worked the blinds so the sun no longer shone directly on them then looked around the room. It was early, so there was only one other table occupied. She decided she didn't have to worry about anyone overhearing their conversation.

When the waiter arrived to take their orders, Cass opted for her usual hamburger and fries. Tabitha waited until Dad ordered the grilled mahi-mahi then, with a wink at her father, chose the same thing.

Cass groaned to herself. *Oh, brother! I hope he's not falling for this stuff. If he is, I swear I'll never be able to respect him again.*

As soon as the waiter delivered their soft drinks and

a basket of rolls, Dad said, "So who wants to be the first one to fill me in on what's been going on?"

Tabitha concentrated on unwrapping her straw and placing it just so in her glass while Cass feigned great interest in selecting a roll.

"Come on," he urged. "You two hardly take a break from arguing with each other. Surely you have something to say to me."

"What do you expect us to talk about?" challenged Cass, choosing a roll and plopping it on her bread plate. "The weather? School? Politics? What?"

"How about the way you've been treating Micah and Logan, not to mention each other?" Dad suggested mildly.

"Oh." Cass' indignation evaporated, and she elbowed Tabitha. "Go ahead."

"Me?" Tabitha glared at Cass. "I haven't done anything wrong."

"Is that so?" Dad's soft voice was ominous and Tabitha suddenly looked wary. "What about the way you've been flaunting your relationship with Logan?"

Cass' jaw dropped. The last thing she'd expected was any kind of support from Dad.

"I haven't been flaunting anything," Tabitha protested in a sulky tone.

"I don't know what else you'd call it when you've gone out of your way to make sure both Cass and Micah were aware of how much time you've been spending with him."

Just as Cass began to privately gloat, Dad turned to her. "Of course, Tabitha's not the only guilty party here. You've done the same thing when it comes to Micah."

"But—" Cass started.

Dad silenced her protest with a stern look. "You girls have been behaving like two little bullies in a sandbox, not caring who else gets in the way while you kick sand all over each other. If you want to be mean and nasty to each other, that's one thing. But as I told Donna, I draw the line when you drag other people into the middle of these temper tantrums you're throwing because you're not getting your own way."

Feeling about two inches tall, Cass slid down in the booth and fixed her gaze on the basket of rolls. Beside her, Tabitha did the same thing.

"Correct me if I'm wrong," Dad continued, "but it appears to me you've been using Micah and Logan to get back at each other for some reason."

When Dad didn't go on, Cass risked a peek at him and realized he was waiting for a response. Since Tabitha sat as still as a stone, Cass figured it was up to her to offer an explanation.

"You're right," she conceded with a resigned sigh. She felt Tabitha's start of surprise. "I started thinking about it at school today and, even though it's embarrassing, I finally admitted to myself what a lowlife I've been the past couple of weeks." She raised uncertain eyes to Dad. "Do you want to know why or is it enough that I've confessed?"

"I think I know why, but perhaps Tabitha needs to hear your reasons," he replied.

"Well," Cass began and reached for her napkin, planning to shred it as she spoke. She realized it was cloth and folded her hands back in her lap. "I got caught up in the excitement of all the boys who paid attention to me when school started. I've never been that popular with guys, so it went to my head. I know I pretty much ignored Logan. Plus, I didn't have any time for Tabitha even though I knew she was upset about Micah and Alison. When I found out Logan and Tabitha were doing stuff together, I got mad, especially after I realized

I didn't like Alex and Dennis as much as I thought I did. So I decided to get back at Tabitha by acting like I was interested in Micah. I wasn't really, though," she hastened to assure Tabitha. "He's a friend, and that's all he'll ever be. Even today, when you saw us in the hall, I was teasing him about someone liking him. He wanted to know who it was, but I told him he was smart enough to figure it out for himself."

Although Tabitha looked like she wanted to believe Cass, the tone of her voice didn't indicate so. "You knew I was going through a rough time, but you acted like you couldn't care less," Tabitha accused her. "I needed you, and you weren't there for me."

"I know," Cass said glumly.

"Cass wasn't the only one behaving badly," Dad said. "You need to take your share of the responsibility for the situation, Tabitha."

Tabitha squirmed and crumpled the straw wrapper then smoothed it out to begin picking at it. "Okay, maybe I was a lowlife, too. I guess I got jealous when it looked like Cass could have any guy she wanted, and I couldn't get one boy, Micah, to notice me. Not as a potential girlfriend anyway. I said some things about Alex that weren't very nice. He's not as bad as I made him out to be. I also made a big deal about Logan and me, and it wasn't. Most of our conversations were about how he could get Cass to go out with him."

Cass mustered the courage to look Dad in the eyes. "We really messed up, huh?"

He shrugged. "Well, you certainly weren't 'bearing with each other,' like we talked about at youth group the other night. In fact, you both have behaved very selfishly. But at least you're admitting it and talking it out and—I dare say—forgiving each other?" He looked at them with raised eyebrows.

Cass hesitantly looked at Tabitha. *Lord, if You can forgive me …* She smiled, and surprisingly, Tabitha smiled back.

After a brief hesitation, Dad continued. "But that still leaves you with the problem of what to do about Logan and Micah."

Tabitha frowned. "What do you mean?"

The waiter chose that moment to bring their meals. Dad waited to answer until after the orders had been sorted out and the blessing had been said.

"I mean," he said finally, "that you girls need to look at things from their perspective. Being a former teenage boy myself—" He grinned and continued, "I can tell you that what's gone on the past couple of weeks has probably left them with their heads spinning. It's hard enough being boys their age without the girls around them acting crazy. They're so confused by now that they probably don't know which end is up."

Cass and Tabitha exchanged glances and laughed. Cass thought it was kind of nice knowing they had the power to bewilder guys when guys were so bewildering themselves.

"It's not funny." Dad tried to look stern, but failed miserably. "I've been worried about those boys. With all that's been happening, how are they supposed to keep straight who they like and who likes them?"

"I'm still crazy about Micah," Tabitha said.

"And I'm dying for Logan to ask me out on an official date," Cass added.

"So tell us, O wise man," Tabitha said, laughing, "how do we go about straightening things out?"

Dad pointed his fork at her. "Don't mock me," he warned in a voice that wouldn't frighten a mouse. "My advice is to stop playing games. Boys need all the help they can get when it comes to relationships. I speak for my gender when I say we're clueless. You want Micah and Logan to ask you out? Let them know."

Tabitha just stared at him. "How? Are we supposed to walk up to them and announce we like them and would give just about anything if only they'd ask us for dates?"

"You don't have to be quite that obvious," drawled Dad. "There are subtle ways to get the message across. Treat them differently so they know you don't think of them as just another friend. I can't give you specific examples. You'll need to ask your Mom for those. She's an expert in that department."

Cass set down her hamburger and acted like she was going to slide out of the booth. "Gotta go. The sooner I talk to Mom, the sooner I start putting Project Logan into action."

"I'm right behind you," Tabitha chimed in.

Dad laughed. "Finish your meals first, so you'll have the strength to follow through with your plans." He shook his head. "Those boys aren't going to know what hit them. Maybe I should warn them." He speared a piece of fish, then rested his fork on the edge of the plate to peer at them intently. "Take it from someone who knows. They like you, a lot. I don't know what's been holding them back from asking you out, but I guarantee you as soon as they know you're interested, they'll be camped out on the doorstep."

Cass and Tabitha grinned at each other. Cass was pretty sure Tabitha was thinking the same thing she was—*I can't wait!*

CHAPTER 21

"Have you thought about what you're going to do about Logan?"

After returning from dinner, Tabitha came into Cass' room and now, despite Cass' better judgement, they were painting their fingernails.

Cass laughed. "I haven't thought about anything else." Reaching for the nail polish remover, she uncapped it and poured some onto a cottonball to dab on her thumb. The pearly pink Tabitha had suggested was looking as bright as a neon sign. "Why? Have you decided what approach you're going to take with Micah?"

Tabitha snorted and began applying the candyapple red nail polish to her left hand. "Yeah, right. You're forgetting what I'm like when it comes to making decisions. I go back and forth until I eventually drive myself—and everybody else—nuts."

"You'd better not wait too long to do something," warned Cass. "Alison's on the prowl, and I don't know how long Micah will be able to resist her. Any guy she sets her sights on is almost a surefire goner."

"Thanks for the confidence booster." Tabitha made a

face. "Like I wasn't already worried enough."

"That's the thing," Cass earnestly pointed out. "You have to do more than worry. You need to take action."

"I'm not you," Tabitha reminded her. "You're a doer. I'm a thinker."

"Then think about how devastated you'll be if Micah and Alison do wind up going out." Cass deliberately set aside the pink polish and opened the clear. "If that doesn't light a fire under you, then nothing will."

"The fire was lit the first day Alison showed up at school," grumbled Tabitha. "The problem is I still don't know what I should do. I just can't see myself walking up to Micah and telling him I've been in love with him since eighth grade. I'd rather die first."

"Would you like me to talk to him for you?" offered Cass. "Tell me what you want me to say and I'll ride over to his house tonight if that's what you want."

For several seconds, alarm competed with acceptance in Tabitha's expression before alarm finally won out. "As much as I'd like to let you do that, I can't. Somehow I'm going to have to find the courage to talk to Micah myself."

"If talking to him is too scary, why don't you write him a letter?" Cass held out her left hand to examine her progress. Her shiny nails looked strange, but she forged ahead. "I've found that putting something down on paper is a lot easier sometimes than talking face to face."

"That's a thought," Tabitha said with a shrug. "Or maybe I could call him."

Cass immediately shook her head. "Calling seems like the chicken way out. Either write or talk to him in person."

"Well ... okay." Tabitha shrugged. "I'll sleep on it and see how I feel in the morning."

"Fine, but you only get one night to sleep on it—then

you have to make up your mind." Cass gave her a stern look. "I don't want to have this discussion two weeks from now when you're still trying to decide what to do."

Tabitha just smiled at her. "This is nice. I've missed talking with you. Kira's great, but it's—I don't know—different somehow with you."

Cass returned her smile. "I think it's because we survived the trauma of our parents getting married." She groaned as the tiny brush slipped and she ended up with a streak of polish on her finger. "How do you do this without making a mess?"

"Hold on. Let me finish my nails, then I'll do yours. Consider it my way of saying thank you for dropping a hint to Micah this afternoon."

Cass leaned back against the wall with a sigh of relief. "Thanks." She paused. "You know, Dad was really great tonight. Lecturing us without lecturing us. I was so nervous about getting a dad after all these years, but he's turned out to be such a fantastic one."

"That's how I feel about Mom." Tabitha looked up from the nail she was carefully laboring over. "We really lucked out, you know."

"Oh, I doubt luck had anything to do with it." Cass rolled her eyes heavenward. "I think God planned all along to get this family together."

"You're probably right. I'm still not used to thinking in terms of God instead of fate." Tabitha screwed the cap back on the bottle and began to alternately wave her hands in the air and blow on them. "I know I don't talk much about my mother, but I remember she was really into New Age stuff. She used to talk about karma and destiny. Dad did too, until he became a Christian."

Having been warned by Mom that Tabitha's mother was a painful subject, Cass had never asked about her. *But since she brought it up* ... She drew up her knees and loosely clasped her arms around them, then quietly asked, "Do you think about your mother a lot?"

Shrugging, Tabitha avoided Cass' eyes. "I try not to, but every now and then a memory pops into my head."

"When was the last time you saw her?"

Tabitha examined her nails. "Four years this December. She lives in Oregon. Dad and I stopped there for a couple of days on our way back to Tennessee to spend Christmas with his family. My grandmother lives about an hour from my mother. Gram had written and asked Dad if he could arrange for us to get together since she'd only seen me twice since the divorce. Dad was at the hotel, and I was at Gram's house when my mother unexpectedly showed up."

"You're kidding." Cass' jaw dropped at the thought of a mother who would voluntarily go for years without seeing a child. Her eyes narrowed with suspicion. "Wait a minute. That's way too coincidental. Do you think it's possible your grandmother might have told your mother you were coming?"

Tabitha vigorously shook her head. "I thought so at first, but Gram swore up and down she had nothing to do with it. She said my mother was always doing stuff like that. She'd go for months without getting in touch with Gram then, out of the blue, she'd drop in for a surprise visit. That's what Gram told Dad when he came to pick me up and he believed her, so I do."

"What happened when your mother came in?"

Tabitha's face tightened and several seconds passed before she answered in a low, strained voice, "She didn't recognize me. She walked in, said hi to Gram, and asked her who her little friend was."

"Oh, my." Cass was momentarily speechless. "What did you do?"

"I almost died." Tabitha's matter-of-fact tone couldn't

mask the lingering pain of that long-ago encounter. "My own mother didn't even know who I was. She hadn't seen me since she walked out when I was four, but Dad sent her pictures every few months or so. She should've recognized me." Her mouth twisted with resentment. "That's when it occurred to me that she probably couldn't be bothered looking at the pictures. I figured she threw them out without a second thought." She lifted her chin in a display of defiance. "But I didn't care. I still don't."

Cass doubted that, but didn't say anything. "When did she figure out who you were?"

"She didn't." Tabitha gave a brittle laugh. "Gram told her." For the first time, a ghost of a smile flitted across her lips. "You should have seen her face when Gram said it was me."

"I can imagine," Cass muttered, although she couldn't, really. "What happened then?"

"She started to cry and grabbed me in a big hug, but I refused to hug her back so she let me go." Tabitha gave a smirk of satisfaction before her expression grew bleak once again. "When she hugged me, though, I discovered she was pregnant. When she first came in, I thought she was just fat, but I felt the baby kick. I asked her, and she said she was six months along."

This whole thing just went from bad to worse as far as Cass was concerned. She didn't know how Tabitha had kept all the pain inside without exploding.

"So you have a half-brother or sister you've never seen?"

Tabitha nodded. "The baby was a boy. Gram wrote and told me after he was born. She's even sent a couple of pictures over the years. I'll show them to you later if you remind me. His name's Peace." She smiled wanly. "I told you my mother is kind of a hippy. He'll be four in

February." She hesitated a moment, then took a deep breath. "As if that's not bad enough, my mother had another baby in March, a girl. Gram wrote that she seems to have taken to motherhood this time around. Not that it does me any good," she added bitterly.

Cass wasn't sure what to say. "Uh ... what's this baby's name?"

Tabitha snorted. "Sunshine. Can you believe it? I have a brother named Peace and a sister named Sunshine."

"Do you wish you could see your mother?" Cass asked softly.

Tabitha's expression turned wistful. "Not really, but I would like to see her other kids. After all, they are related to me." Her face crumpled as she whispered, "I know I must've been really bad when I was little to make her leave me behind the way she did. I guess the kids she has now are more fun or better behaved or something."

Cass was next to Tabitha in an instant. She draped an arm across her stepsister's shoulders and pulled her close. "Don't you dare blame yourself," she ordered fiercely. "You didn't do anything wrong. Your mother did. Even if you were the brattiest kid in the world, that still didn't give your mother the right to walk out on you. Real mothers don't abandon their children. Mom's only been your Mom for a couple of months, but can you imagine her ever going away and leaving us behind?"

"Well, no," Tabitha admitted, although she continued to look troubled. "But I must have done something to make my mother leave. She hasn't walked out on Peace and Sunshine."

"So far," Cass reminded her. "Who's to say she's actually going to stick around this time? But let's say she does. All it'll mean is that she's finally grown up and has quit thinking only of herself."

Tabitha turned a cautiously hopeful face toward Cass. "You really think so? You honestly don't think her leaving was my fault?"

Cass' nod was vehement. "That's what I honestly and truly think." She removed her arm from Tabitha's shoulders, but remained next to her. "Haven't you ever talked this over with Dad?"

"Sure, but he's Dad. Whenever I bring it up, he always tells me I'm not to blame for my mother's treatment of me." Tabitha looked down at her nails again. "What else would he say?"

"The truth," Cass stated simply. "You know he doesn't lie. If he thought you did something to make your mother go away, he'd tell you."

"I know, but sometimes I can't help wondering about it." Abruptly, Tabitha stood up and went over to the window. "I'll probably talk to Mom about it again."

"Again?" Cass' head snapped up. "You've already talked to her about this? She never said anything to me."

"Well, duh." Tabitha turned around and smirked at Cass. "She doesn't tell me your private stuff. Why do you think she should tell you mine?"

"I don't really," Cass admitted. "I'm still not used to sharing Mom with you so it surprises me when I find out you two have things going on that don't include me. Actually, I'm glad to know she knows how to keep secrets." A wicked smile curved her lips. "I'd hate to think she tells you the things I say about you."

"Very funny." Tabitha walked over and playfully smacked the top of Cass' head. "Move over so I can do your nails. I have a ton of homework I need to get to."

Cass obliged by scooting over several inches. As Tabitha sat and reached for the bottle of clear polish, Cass suddenly asked, "What did you mean when you said at supper that Alex wasn't as bad as you made him out to be?"

Tabitha's eyebrows drew together in a frown. "Why?" she demanded warily.

Cass laughed at her worried expression. "I'm not looking to start back up with him again," she said. "I'm just curious about what wasn't quite accurate."

"I don't remember anything specific." Tabitha took Cass' hand and began applying the polish. "All I know is I tried to make it sound like he has a bigger reputation for playing the field than he actually has. I like Alex. He's always been nice to me. I didn't know he's as against religion as he is, but, other than that, he's basically a good guy. I said the things I did because I was mad at you for choosing Alex over Logan. Logan's one of the greatest people I've ever met, and it bugged me that you didn't seem to realize how terrific he is."

"You don't have to worry about that anymore." Cass' sigh was part blissful and part hopeful. "He's not about to get away if I can help it."

"Good." Tabitha squeezed Cass' hand for emphasis. "I'm glad you finally came to your senses. Now let's hope Micah comes to his and realizes I'm the only girl in the world for him."

"You have to do more than hope," Cass said. "You need to come up with a plan."

"I know." Tabitha frowned. "No matter what else we talk about, we always come back to that." She snapped her fingers. "Hey, I have an idea. You tell me how you're planning to let Logan know you like him, and I'll copy whatever you do."

They both laughed, but didn't come up with anything by the time Tabitha left to do her homework.

CHAPTER 22

Cass awoke early the next morning, not to the usual sunshine streaming into her room, but to the pearly light of an overcast day. After stretching, she folded her arms under her head and stared out the window.

Rain would be nice for a change, she thought. *If it lasts all day, I might ride over to the lagoon for a while after school. I like watching the rain on the water.* She bolted upright in bed. *That's it! That's how I'll let Logan know I'm interested. I'll invite him to a picnic at Eamon.*

Too excited to stay in bed, Cass flung off the covers and grabbed her robe off the bedpost. As she scrambled out of bed, she checked the time and hesitated.

Hmm, ten to six. Cass pushed her arms into the robe's sleeves and knotted the belt around her waist. *Too early to wake Tabitha and run the idea by her? Nah! She'd be mad if I didn't wake her up.*

Two seconds later, Cass was bouncing on Tabitha's bed, urging her to open her eyes because she had wonderful news.

They both hurried to get ready for school so they'd have more time to talk on the way. Unfortunately, the weather didn't cooperate. During breakfast, the light sprinkle turned into a deluge. Despite their ponchos, it was a constant struggle to stay dry in the face of the driving rain. They spent most of the ride to school with their heads down, glancing up only occasionally to make sure the road ahead was clear.

They attempted to resume their discussion at the lockers, but were cut short by Randy's arrival. Although water cascaded off him, he greeted the girls with a broad grin.

"Good morning. As my grandmother likes to say, isn't it a fine day for ducks?"

Cass eyed his yellow poncho, slick with rain. "You didn't wheel over here, did you? Surely you called a taxi to pick you up."

Randy feigned indignation as he made a show of wiping himself off. "Of course I drove myself," he said. "How many chances does a person get to hydroplane in a wheelchair?"

Cass laughed, shaking her head. "You're impossible. If I actually thought you could get up enough speed, I'd pay good money to see you hydroplane in that contraption."

"You want speed?" Randy asked, grinning. "I'm fixing to attach a turboprop to the back of this baby. Then you'll see speed."

"Yeah, but we'd only see it once because the last we'd see of you would be the splash you made as you zoomed right off the end of the island and landed in the ocean."

"Is he talking about outfitting his chair with a jet engine again?" Rianne showed up in time to hear the last of Cass' remarks. "Other guys dream of fancy sports cars. My brother—" she paused and affectionately rumpled Randy's hair, "dreams of having the world's fastest wheelchair."

Randy playfully batted away her hand and drew himself up with as much dignity as he could muster. "Who said, 'A man's reach should exceed his grasp or what's a heaven for'?"

"Somebody really short?" guessed Cass.

Rianne lifted a hand for Cass to high-five. "Very good," she said.

"I know when I'm not wanted," Randy grumbled, although not very convincingly. "I'm leaving." Turning his wheelchair, he added over his shoulder, "I'll be at my locker if anybody cares."

Rianne let him go a few feet before calling sweetly, "Oh, bro?"

"Yes?" Randy glanced back with a hopeful expression.

"No one cares." Rianne stuck out her tongue and laughed when, his shoulders slumping, he pretended great disappointment.

"You're so bad," Tabitha said, although she laughed along with the others. "Still, I'm glad he's gone. Listen to the idea Cass came up with to let Logan know she likes him."

Cass laid out the picnic plan she'd developed. Kira arrived in the middle of the discussion, so Cass had to go back over the details. She didn't mind, though. The more she talked about the idea, the better she liked it.

By the time they went their separate ways to their homerooms, the girls agreed Cass should make her move as soon as possible. Kira and Rianne thought she should aim for that afternoon even if it was still raining, but both Cass and Tabitha remained undecided about waiting for a pretty day. Cass promised the others she'd get a message to them the moment she made up her mind.

Unlike the previous day, Cass made no attempt to avoid Logan. Instead she did everything she could to make sure their paths crossed. Her efforts paid off after the first-period class when she found herself walking down the hall a couple of feet behind him. She hurried until she drew alongside him.

"Hey. Penny for your thoughts." Her light tone belied the butterflies tickling her stomach.

Logan looked down and his face lit up with a smile so dazzling that it chased away her nervousness and replaced it with something much more enjoyable. "Well, howdy, stranger. Long time, no see."

"I know. I'm afraid I let myself get sidetracked for a while there, but I'm back on the right track now." Cass hoped Logan understood what she was trying to say. His nod told her he did and she took it as a sign to continue. "I was wondering ..." Suddenly nervous again, she clutched her books tighter against a stomach lurching so violently that it threatened to erupt. "Would you like to meet me at Eamon this afternoon for a picnic supper?"

Logan raised his eyebrows, puzzlement filling his face. "Uh ... perhaps you haven't noticed, but it's raining cats and dogs."

Cass' heart sank. *He doesn't want to go. I've blown my chance with him.*

Trying to keep it light, she joked, "I figured we'd have the place to ourselves that way. Who else would be crazy enough to have a picnic in the rain? If you can't make it though, I understand. Maybe some other time." Somehow, though, she knew there wouldn't be another time.

"I'll be there," Logan said. "Tell me what time and what you want me to bring, and I'll be there. Picnicking in the rain is one of my favorite things to do."

Cass couldn't believe her ears. A feeling of weightlessness started in the pit of her stomach and spread upward until she couldn't contain the joyful grin that stretched from ear to ear.

"You mean it?" she asked, barely breathing. "You really want to go?"

Halting in the middle of the hall with the other students eddying around them, Logan grasped Cass' upper arm and stared into her eyes. "Nothing would make me happier than to spend a couple of hours with you."

A shiver shot up Cass' spine, and she dropped her gaze. "I … I don't know what to say."

"How about telling me what time you want me to come by and get you?" He sounded amused.

"No time." Cass smiled, coming back to earth. "I mean, just meet me at the lagoon at—uh, let me think—around five. I'll go early to get things ready."

"What should I bring?" Realizing they were causing a minor traffic jam, Logan released Cass' arm and nudged her to resume walking.

"Nothing. This is my treat." Cass smiled up at Logan. "All you have to do is show up."

"I think I can manage that." Logan reached his classroom and stopped. "I'm really looking forward to it."

"Me too." After what seemed like an eternity of staring at each other, Cass was the first one to look away. "I'd better get to class."

"Okay, see you later," Logan said, but didn't move.

"Yeah, see you." Cass didn't move either. "So how was your golf game with the guys yesterday?"

Logan made a face. "Don't ask. The only way it could have been worse—" He stopped and shook his head in disgust. "Actually, it was the pits. There's no way it could have been worse."

Cass tried to look sympathetic, but wound up laughing. "I'm sorry. I promise the picnic will be more fun."

Logan reached out and tucked a stray strand of hair behind her ear. "I'm counting on it."

After saying goodbye, Cass floated to her class. A heartfelt sigh escaped her lips as she settled into the desk behind Rianne, who immediatately swiveled around in her seat.

"I saw you and Logan talking in the hall. I take it things went well?"

"They went wonderfully." Cass heaved another sigh. "We're having the picnic this afternoon."

"Way to go!" Rianne said. "I'll see Kira next period and spread the news."

"Thanks." The bell rang, and Cass quickly finished, "We'll talk more at lunch."

Cass did her best to concentrate on school, but she wasn't very successful. Thoughts of the picnic with Logan kept intruding as she remembered one more thing to bring or one more thing she wanted to say to him.

On her way to the cafeteria at the beginning of the lunch period, she stopped to phone Mom to ask her to boil eggs for egg salad sandwiches and to bake a pan of brownies. That done, Cass crossed those items off her mental list and headed for the lunchroom.

"Aren't you even going to say hello?"

Lost in her thoughts, Cass was caught up short by this teasing demand. Her eyes narrowed when she recognized Alex lounging in the cafeteria doorway. "Hi," she said tersely and attempted to pass him.

He shot out an arm to stop her. "Hey! Can't you spare a couple of minutes for a friend?"

"Sure." Cass took a leisurely look around. "Unfortunately, I don't see one."

Although Alex laughed, his face tightened with annoyance. "Ouch." He clutched the left side of his chest. "You hit the target with that one." Seeing that Cass wasn't going anywhere, he dropped his arm. "I waited out here for you because I wanted you to know I've thought a lot about what happened the other day. We both said some things we shouldn't have, and I think it would be a good idea if we cleared the air. How about we get together this afternoon?"

Cass didn't even bother trying to sound regretful. "No can do. I'm busy." She began to walk away, then paused and added, "But I appreciate the apology. You were way out of line Monday."

"What apology? I didn't apologize. All I said—"

Cass walked away without turning around, making her way through the tables to where her friends waited for her. Tabitha just stared at her as she slid into an empty seat.

"Wow, what did you say to Alex? He looks totally ticked."

Dumping the contents of her lunch bag onto the table, Cass recounted their brief exchange.

Kira laughed. "You go, girl! Poor old Alex probably doesn't know what hit him. He's used to having everything go his way. He'd be a much better person if he weren't so spoiled."

"Amen to that," Rianne agreed fervently. "It's too bad that good looks like his are wasted on somebody so stuck on himself. Imagine how perfect he'd be if only he were a nice guy."

"He'd be too good to be true," Tabitha said, and the rest laughed.

The conversation turned to Cass' picnic. Her head swam with all their suggestions, but she appreciated their interest and support.

I haven't been here very long, she thought at one point, *but I've sure made some great friends*. As her gaze swept around the table, it lingered an extra second or two on Tabitha. *I've also acquired a pretty terrific stepsister.* She hesitated, then smiled slightly. *Or maybe it's time to start thinking of her as my sister.*

CHAPTER 23

Throughout the afternoon, the sun made a valiant effort to put in an appearance. As Cass and Tabitha rode home, it played peek-a-boo with the clouds until finally vanishing once and for all. They made a mad dash for the house as the heavens unleashed an impressive downpour.

Once inside the porch, Cass shook herself and shrugged. "Oh, well. At least it didn't rain on the way home. Going to school this morning was like riding through a monsoon."

"That was nothing. Just wait until the rainy season hits," Tabitha said darkly. "After a while, you think you'll never be dry again. Mold starts growing between your toes." She gave a delicate shudder.

"Please tell me you're kidding," Cass said, following her into the house.

Tabitha just shrugged. "Wait and see. You'll find out soon enough how bad it gets."

The aroma of fresh brownies welcomed them when they came into the kitchen. Mom stood at the sink shelling hard-boiled eggs. Going up behind her, Cass slipped her arms around Mom's waist and squeezed.

"Thank you!" she said. "You're the best mother in the world."

Mom reached around to pat Cass' cheek. "I appreciate it, sweetie. I'm going to remind you of that the next time you get angry at me."

Propping her elbows on the counter next to the sink, Cass leaned back on them and laughed. "When do I ever get mad at you?" she said.

"Hmm, let me think." Mom cocked her head to one side. "That would be—what?—every other day? If I'm lucky, that is. If we're having a bad week, I can usually find something irritating to say or do every day."

"Not that you ever go out of your way to deliberately bug me," Cass drawled.

"Me?" Mom gave her an innocent look. "Never! Have you already forgotten I'm the best mother in the world? I'd never do something like that."

"Uh-huh." Cass wasn't convinced.

From her position at the other counter where the brownies sat, Tabitha exhaled an impatient sigh. "While you two amuse yourselves, is it okay if I cut myself a brownie? You're not planning on taking the whole pan, are you, Cass?"

Cass shook her head while Mom replied, "Half the pan should be enough for their picnic. The rest is ours."

"Oh, goody." Tabitha leaned over to open the silverware drawer and retrieve a knife. "Does anybody else want a piece?"

"I'll have a tiny one." Cass walked around Mom to the refrigerator. "You want milk, Tabitha?"

"Yes, please." Tabitha held the knife over the pan, ready to cut.

"Do you want one, Mom?"

"No thanks, sweetie. You guys enjoy them."

Cass hurriedly washed down her brownie with a glass

of milk. She had almost two hours before she needed to leave for the lagoon, but there was a lot she had to get done.

"Are you going to make the egg salad or do you want me to do it?" Mom asked as Cass headed to the sink to rinse her glass.

Cass turned to her with a hopeful expression. "You don't think it'd be cheating if I let you make it? I planned to do everything myself so Logan would know how special I think he is."

"I already baked the brownies," Mom said. "So what difference does it make now? The important thing is the thought you've put into planning the picnic."

"Okay. You talked me into it." Cass' grin was tinged with relief. "I'm going to my room to tape a bunch of Logan's favorite songs off CDs. I want to have them playing in the background while we eat."

Mom arched an eyebrow at her. "Exactly how romantic is this dinner going to get? Will there be candlelight and flowers?"

Cass and Tabitha exchanged wary glances. "Uh ... now that you mention it," confessed Cass, "Tabitha and I did discuss having a couple of candles burning. Do you think it would be too much?"

Mom reached into the cabinet for a bowl and set it on the counter. "No, it should be fine. Just don't overdo things."

Cass felt the heat rise to her cheeks. "Honestly, Mom! We'll be out in the open at the lagoon, even if we do wind up in the pavilion on account of the rain. Anybody could show up. It's not like anything is going to happen. Not," she added quickly, "that I'm planning on something happening." She turned away quickly so she wouldn't have to see more of Mom's knowing smile. "I'm going to my room now. The taping shouldn't take more than thirty minutes or so. Then I'll be back out to start packing stuff up."

"You want me to help you tape?" Tabitha said. "I can find the songs you want while you do the actual taping."

"Would you?" Cass turned a grateful face to her stepsister. "I'd really appreciate it."

"You get started, and I'll be right there." Tabitha picked up the knife she'd left in the brownie pan. "I want to cut myself another piece."

Cass had just placed the first CD in the player and pressed the record button when Tabitha sauntered into the room. She nudged the door closed with her hip, her hands full with the plate and glass she carried. Setting them on the nightstand, she sank down next to Cass.

"Good choice," Tabitha approved as the opening notes of the song began to play. "I like this one too." Looking down, she started rummaging through the CDs scattered across the floor. "Let's see what you have here."

Cass named several titles she wanted, and Tabitha rapidly located them for her, stacking them in order on the floor beside the stereo. Before she started on the next batch, she plucked the brownie and milk from the nightstand and set them down next to her.

"I need a little something to keep me going," she explained when Cass glanced over at her. "You're working me to death here."

Cass made a face, but otherwise refrained from comment. As soon as one song finished, she snatched the CD out of the player, handed it to Tabitha, and replaced it with another one.

"Are you nervous about the picnic?" Tabitha asked after several minutes of silence.

"Sort of." Cass looked up from the CD cover she'd been studying. "Why?"

"You're strung as tight as a drum, that's why," drawled Tabitha. "I've never seen you like this. Relax." She gave Cass' shoulders a quick massage. "It's a picnic. You're supposed to have fun, remember?"

"But so much is riding on tonight," Cass said.

"Don't do this to yourself." Tabitha took the CD from Cass and set it aside. "The fate of the world doesn't hinge on what happens between you and Logan at the lagoon. Try to remember it's just a simple picnic. Sure, you have an ulterior motive, but don't forget Logan's your friend and he's already halfway in love with you as it is. All you have to do this evening is give him a little shove and push him over the edge."

Although it was somewhat shaky, Cass managed to grin. "You really think it's going to be that easy?"

Tabitha gave an airy wave. "Like taking candy from a baby. A walk in the park. A piece of cake. A—"

"Okay, okay." This time Cass erupted in a full-blown laugh. "I get the picture."

The song ended. Leaning around Cass, Tabitha pressed the pause button, took out the CD, slipped in the next one, and released pause.

"I don't want to raise your stress level again, but has it occurred to you, if you play your cards right, you might wind up with a date to the fall formal before the night is out?" Tabitha gave Cass a sly look.

Leaning forward, Cass clamped her hands over her ears. "Don't say that. I'm antsy enough as it is. If I start thinking about the fall formal, I'll fall apart."

Smiling, Tabitha pried one of Cass' hands off an ear. "Fall formal, fall formal," she singsonged over her stepsister's moans.

"Well, why don't you go call Micah and ask him on a picnic? You can set it up for tomorrow."

That stopped Tabitha in midchant. Her mouth

remained open, but no sound came out.

Cass pressed her advantage. "Go on. Call him," she urged. "Since you have such a good feeling about Logan's and my picnic, maybe that's a sign you should set one up with Micah."

"I'm not doing the same thing as you," protested Tabitha. "How would that make Micah feel to know I couldn't be bothered coming up with an original idea for a way for the two of us to spend time together? Logan must have told him by now about your picnic. You expect me to call Micah up and invite him on one too?"

"Maybe not," Cass said.

"Besides," Tabitha continued, "Micah and I aren't you and Logan. You two are the sporty, outdoors type. Micah and I are—"

"Classier, more refined?" suggested Cass.

"No." Tabitha shot her a look that said she knew Cass was teasing her. "We're more the dinner-at-a-restaurant type."

"That's it!" Cass sat up straight. "Ask Micah to have supper with you at the Yokwe Yuk. You can get all dressed up, and he can wear one of his wild Hawaiian shirts. It'll be great."

"I don't know," Tabitha hedged. "I don't think I'm brave enough to ask any guy, let alone Micah, on a date."

"Don't think of it as a date," advised Cass. "Think of it as a couple of friends spending a few pleasant hours together."

Tabitha shook her head. "We shouldn't be talking about Micah and me right now. You and Logan are the ones who matter. How many more songs do you want?"

"All right, I can take a hint." Cass reached around Tabitha to break off a piece of her brownie. "I think eight or ten songs should be enough, don't you?"

CHAPTER 24

Cass was dressed and ready to go early. Too keyed up to sit down while she waited to leave, Cass prowled around the kitchen, checking and rechecking the picnic basket every few minutes. Unable to wait until four-thirty, Cass lifted the basket off the counter at twenty after.

"I think I'm going to head out," she announced.

She loaded up her bike and made it to the lagoon minutes ahead of the next rain shower. Parking in the shelter of the pavilion, she took a few moments to look around and calm her jangling nerves before beginning the process of unloading the items she'd brought.

Fortunately, there was no one else there, and Cass doubted anybody would show up. That meant she and Logan would be able to talk without worrying about eavesdroppers. If things didn't go as she hoped, at least she'd be spared public humiliation.

Choosing a table closest to a sheltering wall, Cass spread out the royal blue tablecloth Mom had chosen for her. On top of that she placed a pair of pale blue ceramic candleholders and inserted matching candles. Stepping back, Cass studied the placement of the candles for several seconds before nudging them a fraction of an inch closer together. Satisfied so far, she reached back into the basket and took out two plastic plates and cups. She placed them side by side then, across the table from each other, then side by side again.

Uh-oh, Cass realized, *I didn't think about this part, and it's too late to ride home and ask Tabitha what I should do*.

Rubbing her temples, she closed her eyes and tried to visualize her stepsister standing next to her. Almost immediately Cass knew what to do. She reached for a plate and cup, and moved them across the table. *That way you and Logan can look at each other while you eat*, she heard Tabitha's voice adivse her.

The plastic utensils had been laid out atop the linen napkins that matched the tablecloth and the food had been arranged; all that remained was to light the candles and turn on the music. Cass planned to do both the moment she heard Logan approaching.

She didn't have to wait long. Only a few minutes passed before the sounds of a bicycle splashing through puddles reached her.

Jumping up, Cass grabbed the matches off the table. Despite her fumbling fingers, she managed to slide open the box and retrieve one of the tiny sticks. Her hands refused to stop shaking long enough to allow her to light it, however. Cass was about to scream with frustration when the match finally struck. She finished lighting the second candle just as Logan rode into the pavilion.

Surveying the scene, Logan braked and slowly dismounted from his bike. With one hand, he pushed back the hood of his poncho while, with the other, he reached out to touch the edge of the cloth that hung off the end of the table.

"You did all this?" he asked in a hushed tone.

Rendered temporarily speechless by nerves, Cass nodded.

"This is amazing." His gaze swept across the table before coming to rest on Cass. "You're amazing. I don't know what I expected, but it sure wasn't this."

Cass finally found her voice. "So you like it?" she asked shyly.

"Like it?" echoed Logan. "I'm blown away. Noboody's ever done anything like this for me."

"I'm glad."

An uneasy silence descended between them during which Cass realized she could hear the rain pattering on the tin roof. She turned stricken eyes to Logan.

"I forgot to turn on the music," she wailed. "I put together a tape, but I forgot to turn it on. It was supposed to be playing when you got here." Her voice trailed off, and she felt like she was about to cry.

"It's okay," Logan assured her. "I like the way the rain sounds. We can listen to the music later."

With that, the awkward moment passed, and Cass found herself more comfortable with Logan than she'd ever been. As they talked about school and friends, they helped themselves to egg salad sandwiches, dill pickles, barbecue chips, and baked beans. They said a quick blessing, then Logan grinned at Cass as he popped the tab on a can of cola.

"Is this just a lucky coincidence or did you plan to have all my favorites?"

"What do you think?" countered Cass.

"I think you planned it, but I don't know why you'd go to so much trouble." Logan sounded genuinely curious.

Taking a deep breath, Cass replied in a rush, "Because I wanted to show you what a great guy I think you are and to let you know I'm sorry for acting like such an idiot this past week."

Logan, caught in the act of taking a drink of his cola, gulped and plunked the can back down on the table.

"Wow!" he sputtered. "Do you ever not say what you're thinking?"

"Sometimes with my Mom," Cass admitted. "It's safer that way." She stared down at her plate, unable to meet Logan's eyes. "Did what I said upset you?"

"Heck no!" His response was instantaneous and heartfelt. "I've been wanting to let you know how I feel about you for several weeks, but I couldn't get up the courage. Then it seemed like I'd lost my chance. When you asked me to come on this picnic, I promised myself I'd tell you how I feel, even if it took all night to get the words out."

"Really?" Cass folded her hands in her lap and gazed across the table at Logan. "Of course, you haven't actually told me how you feel yet."

Logan swallowed hard, started to speak, stopped, and motioned to Cass. "Ladies first. After all, the picnic was your idea."

"How do I feel about you?" Picking up her fork, Cass traced a pattern on the tablecloth. After several seconds, she decided she had tortured him long enough, looked up at him, and stated matter-of-factly, "I like you. You're one of the nicest people I've ever met, and I'd like to get to know you better."

Logan expelled his breath in a whoosh, making the flames of the candles flutter. "I ... uh ... I like you too. The night you went out with Alex was the worst night of my life. I kicked myself from here to kingdom come for not asking you out first."

Not being the giggly sort, Cass was amazed to hear one come out of her mouth. "You were jealous." She sat up straighter and beamed. "Cool. I don't think a boy's ever been jealous over me before."

Logan groaned. "I was beyond jealous. I was ready to beat Alex to a pulp. Me, the guy who's never been in a fight in his life. I was so mad I scared myself."

Cass laughed. "My hero," she purred.

"Knock it off," Logan growled before giving in to the smile twitching at the corners of his mouth. "You don't need to act like somebody else to impress me. I like you just the way you are."

"I know." Cass dropped the pose. "That's one of the reasons why I like spending time with you. I can be myself and not worry about it."

"I know exactly what you mean." Logan smiled, and Cass suddenly had to remind herself to breathe.

Halfway through the meal, Cass remembered the tape she'd brought. After asking Logan if he'd like to hear it, she switched on the player. Music filled the pavilion, accompanying the sound of the rain. When the third selection began, Logan shot Cass a puzzled look.

"How do you know what my favorite songs are? I don't remember us talking about the music I like."

"We never sat down and went over a list or anything," Cass said. "But with some of them, I remembered them coming on the radio and you saying how much you liked them. When it came to the rest, I asked Tabitha what songs you like."

Logan shook his head in astonishment. "I don't think I could do something like this for you."

"I don't expect you to." Done eating for the moment, Cass pushed her plate to the side and folded her arms along the edge of the table. "It's not a competition or a test. I put this picnic together as a gift, sort of a combination 'apology and I hope you still like me' meal. You don't have to do anything in return. Honest."

"I would like to ask you something, though." Logan's gaze anxiously flickered between Cass and something over her shoulder. "Not because I feel like I have to, but because I want to."

Cass' breath caught in her throat as she allowed herself to hope he might bring up the fall formal.

"I was wondering—" Logan's voice squeaked so he coughed and started again. "I was wondering, if you're not busy Friday night, would you like to go bowling and get something to eat? The snack stand at the bowling alley sells pizza and stuff like that."

It wasn't an invitation to the fall formal, but it was a genuine date and that was good enough for Cass. She struggled to contain her grin so she didn't look like a complete fool.

"Bowling and pizza sound great." She fixed Logan with a challenging look. "I hope you don't mind losing to a girl. I'm pretty good, if I do say so myself."

Logan snorted, but laughed as well. "You may know your way around the basketball court, little lady, but I'm king of the bowling alley."

"We'll see." Cass permitted herself a smug smile. *This is going to be fun.*

By the time they finished dessert, the rain had stopped and a steady breeze was sending the remaining clouds on their way. Cass and Logan slipped off their sandals and walked through the wet sand down to the water's edge to wade in the warm Pacific.

One by one, the stars began to wink in the inky sky as the wind continued to sweep away the clouds. The only sounds were the steady drip of water on leaves and the ocean lapping at their feet. The combination of heat and moisture intensified the fragrances of the nearby flowers, and Cass felt almost heady from the mingled aromas.

This is the most perfect night I've ever experienced, she decided. *I'm here on a tropical island with a guy I like who—wonder of wonders!—likes me, and we're walking in the Pacific Ocean. It doesn't get any better than this.*

Then it did. Without saying a word, Logan took Cass' hand. An electric shock shot up her arm. She glanced up at Logan and found him smiling down at her.

"Thanks for asking me here tonight," he said softly. "I've had the best time. We'll have to do it again, only next time I'll be in charge."

"I'd like that." Cass grinned impishly. "Just so you know, hot dogs and potato salad are my favorite picnic meal."

Logan squeezed her hand and pulled her closer so that their arms brushed as they splashed through the surf. "I'll file that away for future reference." He heaved a regretful sigh. "I hate to say it, but I have to be going soon. My mother said to be home no later than eight-thirty since it's a school night. It's probably close to eight now."

"Yeah, that's when Mom told me to be back too." Cass cast a longing glance at the beach stretching ahead of them. "I guess we'll have to save our moonlit stroll for another night."

"Like one when the moon is actually out?" teased Logan.

"Honestly, boys are so unromantic," Cass complained good-naturedly. "Fine, if you're going to be picky about it, then I guess you could say a moon is required for a moonlit stroll."

"Actually," Logan murmured as they turned to head back to the pavilion, "I'd stroll with you any time of the day or night."

Grinning, Cass squeezed his hand. "Okay, maybe you're not completely lacking in the romance department. There may be hope for you yet."

Since there wasn't much left to pack, they finished cleaning up the picnic things in no time. Logan insisted on toting the picnic basket and tape player back to Cass' house and stowed them in his bicycle carrier. Despite pedaling as slowly as they could without losing their balance, the ride to the house went by too quickly.

Almost before they knew it, Logan was walking Cass to the porch door. He set down the basket and player and took Cass' hands.

"I hope this doesn't sound weird," he said quietly, "but it's something I read in a Christian teen magazine a few months ago, and I've wanted to try it ever since. I just haven't had a chance to until tonight. Would it be all right if we … uh … prayed together before you went in?"

A feeling of incredible happiness surged through Cass. Too moved to say anything, all she could do was nod.

Together they bowed their heads as he prayed, "Lord, thank You for our time together this evening. Thank You for our friendship. Help us to grow closer to You and, if it's Your will, closer to each other. Watch over us tonight and bless us. In Jesus' name, amen."

"Amen," echoed Cass. She knew she must be beaming when she gazed up at him. "That was really special. The perfect way to end a perfect evening." She bent down and picked up the tape player and basket while Logan held the door open for her. "I'll see you tomorrow. Be careful riding home."

"I will," Logan assured her. "Thanks again for the picnic. It was the nicest thing anybody's ever done for me."

"My pleasure." Cass walked through the door then turned to smile at Logan. "Good night."

He blew her a kiss. "Sweet dreams."

Cass felt as though she were floating three feet off the ground as she sailed into the house. She found Mom and Dad sitting at the table, drinking coffee and talking. Tabitha was nowhere to be seen.

Placing the basket on the counter, Cass glanced into

the living room. "Where's Tabitha?"

"Hello to you too," teased Mom.

"Oh, yeah. Hi. Where is she?"

Mom shook her head and smiled. "She's in her room. Did you have a nice time?"

Cass' rapturous sigh told it all. "It was wonderful." She took off for Tabitha's room, adding over her shoulder, "I'll put away the picnic stuff after I talk to Tabitha."

Tabitha was curled up on her bed when Cass burst into her room. "Whatever it takes for you to get up the nerve to ask Micah out," she said fervently as a greeting, "do it. If your time together goes half as well as Logan's and my picnic did tonight—" she stopped, rolled her eyes, and fanned herself. "Believe me, you won't be sorry."

CHAPTER 25

This is the day I finally do it, Tabitha thought as soon as she woke up the next morning. *This is the day I ask Micah out*.

After much agonizing and prompting from Cass, she finally decided late last night that today would be the day she talked to Micah.

Although her heart beat in nervous anticipation of inviting Micah to dinner at the Yuk, Tabitha also felt right, even peaceful, about the decision she'd reached. It was time for her to make her move and find out where she stood with Micah. Not knowing was driving her crazy.

Tabitha dressed with special care, left her curls loose to bounce around her shoulders, and even applied a touch of lipstick, something she seldom bothered to do for school.

Calling goodbye to their parents, Tabitha and Cass exited the house to find Logan waiting on the lanai. He greeted both of them with smiles, although the one he gave Cass held a bit more warmth. Tabitha didn't mind. If all went according to plan, it wouldn't be long before Micah was smiling at her like that. A shiver of delight tingled through her at the thought. She couldn't wait.

Then again, maybe she could. The closer the threesome got to the school, the more leaden Tabitha's legs felt and the slower she pedaled.

Maybe I'm not as ready for this as I thought I was. She felt panic rising in her chest. *Maybe it would be better if I talked to him later, like sometime around Christmas. That would give me more than three months to really think about what I want to say and practice. Yeah, that's what I should do.*

As if reading her mind, Cass asked, "You're not thinking of backing out, are you?"

Before Tabitha could reply, Logan glanced curiously from one to the other. "Backing out of what?"

Tabitha raised her eyebrows in warning at Cass. They'd agreed at breakfast that Cass wouldn't say anything to Logan until Tabitha had spoken to Micah.

"I'll tell you what's going on when we go bowling tonight," Cass answered Logan, making Tabitha sigh in relief. "Tabitha made me swear on a stack of Bibles that I wouldn't say anything before then."

"Okay. You don't have to tell me." Logan's shrug was amiable. "But am I allowed to know if she's backing out of whatever it is?"

Cass considered his request. "Sure, why not?" She glanced over at Tabitha. "Well, are you?"

Although she still struggled with her fears, Tabitha slowly shook her head. "No, I'm going through with it." She set her lips in a thin, determined line. "I may be violently ill, but I'll do it."

"Man, I wish I knew what was going on." Logan said. "It must be something really important if just thinking about it is enough to make you sick, Tabitha."

She flashed him a wry smile. "You can drop all the hints you want to try to get me to tell you what's going on, pal. But my lips are sealed."

"So are mine," Cass declared loyally.

"Honestly, do sisters always stick together like this?" complained Logan.

Tabitha and Cass exchanged pleased smiles. It was nice that Logan recognized how far they'd come in their relationship.

"I don't know how other sisters operate," replied Tabitha, "but Cass and I definitely stick together. We're a team."

"I think I liked it better when you two couldn't stand each other," grumbled Logan.

"Those days are long gone." Cass winked at Tabitha. "Right, sis?"

"Absolutely."

They laughed when Logan let out a disgusted groan.

As if Tabitha weren't anxious enough, a very upset Kira was waiting for them at the bike racks when they arrived at the school. She distractedly acknowledged Cass and Logan before turning her attention to Tabitha.

"We need to talk."

"Can it wait?" Accustomed to Kira's dramatics, Tabitha took her friend's urgent request in stride. "I was planning to talk to somebody else this morning before school started."

"No, it can't wait." Kira clamped a hand around Tabitha's wrist and glanced at Cass. "Maybe you should come and hear this too."

"Me? Why?" Cass looked concerned

Kira started tugging on Tabitha's arm. "I'll tell you in a minute. Come on—it's an emergency."

Still not convinced Kira wasn't exaggerating the importance of her news, Tabitha shrugged and allowed herself to be dragged away from her bike. "I'm coming. Now let go." She shook free of Kira's grasp.

"What about you?" Kira turned to Cass.

Cass sighed. "I guess I'm coming too." She gave Logan a crooked smile. "I'll come by your locker if this doesn't take too long. Otherwise, I'll see you around school."

"Sounds good. I'll park your bikes," he said.

Instead of heading into the building, Kira led them to a secluded section of the courtyard outside the cafeteria. Her agitation kept her pacing while Tabitha and Cass hoisted themselves onto the cement wall.

"All right." Tabitha knew she probably shouldn't sound so amused. "You have us where you want us. I'm assuming you have some terrible crisis to report. What is it?"

Kira planted herself in front of her friend. "There's no easy way to say this, so I'm just going to give it to you straight. Micah asked Alison out last night. I'd have called you, but I didn't know about it until this morning when he mentioned to Mom that he was going out tonight."

Tabitha's world suddenly stopped. The chattering of the nearby students was drowned out by the blood pounding in her ears. The breeze abruptly ceased and sweat immediately prickled her scalp and broke out between her shoulder blades. Out of the corner of her eye, she saw Cass turn to her, but her stepsister appeared to be moving in slow motion. Cass' lips moved, but no sound came out.

Just as Tabitha was beginning to wonder if she might be about to pass out, everything suddenly clicked back into place. Somebody's laugh reached her. The wind lifted and tossed her hair, and she understood what Cass was saying.

"Tabitha, are you all right? You look like you're about to throw up."

Tabitha realized she was clutching her stomach as if

she'd been punched. Letting go, she raised a hand to her forehead and discovered it was clammy with perspiration. The brief nausea passed, but she still felt miserable.

"I'm okay." When she noticed how badly her hands shook, she produced a wan smile. "Or I will be once I get over the shock. I can't believe it. Micah actually asked her out." She swung tear-filled eyes to Kira. "Are you sure? Could it be some kind of mistake maybe?"

Kira shook her head. "It's not a mistake," she replied flatly. "Micah's exact words were, 'Mom, I won't be here for supper. I'm taking Alison to the Yuk. It's her birthday.' I don't think it gets much clearer than that."

"No, it doesn't," Tabitha agreed. She wanted to howl at the unfairness of it all, but she was so calm it scared her. "All these years he never pays a lick of attention to me. Then Alison Ross shows up, and it takes him less than two weeks to ask her out. It's pretty obvious I've been kidding myself. Micah was never interested in me. I was nothing more than a friend." Her face contorted with pain. "Thank God you talked to me before I made a complete fool out of myself, Kira."

With that, Tabitha burst into tears. She dropped her face into her hands so that no one would see.

"She decided last night that today was the day she was going to ask Micah to the Yuk," Cass said as she put her arm around Tabitha's shoulders. "She was on her way to find him when you caught her."

"I could kill my brother for being so stupid," Kira said. "Why would he ask Alison out when there's someone as great as Tabitha around to date? I don't get it."

Even though Tabitha knew Kira meant well, her comment only made the tears come harder.

When she finally felt like she could cry no more, she raised her head and stared blankly ahead. "I'd better get to the restroom and see if I can repair the damage," she said, her voice raspy from crying. "I don't want to go to class looking like I just lost my best friend." She shrugged sadly. "I can't even use the excuse I lost my boyfriend since Micah was never really mine."

Suddenly, Cass jumped down from the wall and stood in front of her. "Okay, that's enough crying," she said firmly. "If Micah doesn't recognize quality when he sees it then he's not worth crying over anyway. So—" Cass took Tabitha's elbow to coax her off the wall. "Let's get this show on the road. We'll go to the restroom with you and help you get fixed up."

"But you'll be late for class," Tabitha protested weakly.

"It won't be the first time." Kira dismissed her concern with a wave.

"And it probably won't be the last," added Cass. "Come on. I'll carry your backpack." She lifted it off the ground and hefted it onto her shoulder.

"I wish I had some sunglasses." Bowing her head, Tabitha shielded her eyes with her hand. "I hate for people to see me like this."

Kira rummaged in her purse and produced a pair. "Here you go."

Tabitha put them on and immediately felt better. "Thanks. You guys are so great for sticking by me like this."

"Aw, what are friends for?" Kira said.

"Not just friends, but sisters too." Cass nudged Tabitha in the ribs and Tabitha smiled.

It didn't take as long as Tabitha thought it would to cover up the evidence of her tears, so they made it to their homerooms a full ten seconds before the bell rang.

CHAPTER 26

At lunch, Cass, Kira, and Rianne formed a protective shield around Tabitha as they entered the cafeteria. Tabitha's emotions were still raw, and Cass knew nobody was sure what, if anything, might set her off.

Shortly after they sat down, Alex hesitantly approached the table. Cass noticed his unusually subdued attitude but told herself not to be taken in by it.

"Uh … hi." Alex smiled briefly.

"Hello," Cass responded coolly while the others nodded and went back eating.

"Could I talk to you?" Alex asked her.

"Sure." Cass bit into her peanut butter and jelly sandwich. "What's on your mind?"

Alex's face tightened. "I'd like to talk to you alone if you don't mind."

"I don't mind," Cass assured him, "but now's not a good time. We—" she indicated her tablemates, "have a few things we need to discuss."

Alex frowned. "When then?"

"I'm kind of busy the rest of the day." Cass met Alex's stormy gaze. "Why don't you call me tomorrow?"

"Any particular time?" he responded with a hint of a

sneer in his voice.

"After eleven would be good. Saturday morning's the only chance we get to sleep in." Cass made a face at Tabitha, who responded with one of her own. "Mom makes sure we're up by ten though, so, if you wait till after eleven, that will give me a chance to eat and stuff."

"I'll call you sometime tomorrow then." Alex gave a small wave and left.

"Why do you think he keeps coming around?" Cass asked the moment he was out of earshot.

"That's easy." Kira shrugged, eating a potato chip. "You walked away from him, and his ego is crushed. That's not how the script is supposed to go."

"You mean he's trying to get me back so he can dump me?"

Nodding, Kira crunched into another chip. "I do believe that's the plan."

"But that's ... sick," sputtered Cass.

"Uh-huh. So what's your point? Alex is one of those guys who's into playing games when it comes to relationships—and he plays to win."

"Not this time he won't," Cass said. "He didn't know what he was getting himself into when he took me on."

"No, he didn't." Tabitha shook her head in mock sympathy. "I almost feel sorry for him."

"I don't," declared Rianne. "He deserves whatever he gets, and I'm glad Cass is the one giving it to him. He broke my heart three years ago when I was too young to realize what a phony he is. I've forgiven him, but I haven't forgotten. It's about time he got paid back."

"Honestly, you're making me sound like the Terminator or something," Cass protested with a laugh. "I'm not out to destroy Alex. I'm just not interested in playing his little games. Now can we quit talking about him, please, and maybe discuss something cheerful?"

"How about you and Logan?" Tabitha asked, arching an eyebrow at her stepsister.

"No, we've talked that topic to death. I won't have anything new to report until after our date tonight." Cass grinned at Rianne. "We haven't heard much about you and Josh lately. What's up with y'all?"

Rianne's blush said it all. "Things are coming along quite nicely, thank you. He ate supper with my family last night, and we're going to the movies tonight."

"Do you think he'll ask you to the formal?" Kira asked.

Rianne glanced uncomfortably at Tabitha. "Maybe we shouldn't be talking about this right now."

Tabitha just smiled at her. "It's okay. I'm not self-centered enough to think the world revolves around me and my problems. I promise I can listen to you talk about Josh without weeping and wailing."

The rest of lunch and the remainder of the afternoon passed quickly. After the final bell rang, Cass joined Tabitha at her locker. From the look on her stepsister's face, Cass concluded she was having a rough time. "Hey, are you okay?"

"Give me a couple of minutes and I will be." Tabitha took a deep breath. "I was listening to everybody make weekend plans and decided to throw myself a pity party. Sitting home while Micah takes Alison out to dinner is the last thing I expected to be doing this weekend."

From her locker next to Tabitha's, Kira peeked around the open locker door. "You don't have to sit at your house. Why don't you come home with me?"

Tabitha rolled her eyes at her friend. "Oh, that's a swell idea. I can watch Micah get ready for his date with Alison. That should cheer me up."

Kira looked stricken. "I'm sorry. I wasn't thinking." She frowned. "You know, I don't want to watch that either. I'm going over to your house," she said.

"Great." Tabitha slammed her locker shut. "The more the merrier."

When they walked outside, they found Logan waiting for them by their bikes. After saying hello, Tabitha and Kira went on while Cass and Logan took their time.

Cass had gotten Tabitha's permission to tell Logan what had happened with Micah, and she did so as they loaded their backpacks into their bicycle baskets. When Cass was done, Logan threw his hands up in disgust and expelled a whoosh of breath.

"Man, I figured Micah had more sense than to fall for Alison's lines. I noticed she was hanging on him more than usual today, so I guess this explains why. It bugs me that he didn't tell me he asked her out. We're supposed to be friends. Did he think I wouldn't find out?"

"I think I know why Micah asked Alison out instead of Tabitha," Cass said when Logan finally calmed down.

"Oh, yeah? Why?"

"Because he's an idiot! He's certifiably nuts!" Cass allowed herself to say the things she'd wanted to say since the morning. "Someone ought to sit him down and give him a good talking to, and I'd like to be the one to do it. I'd like to hear him just try to explain why he chose Alison over Tabitha. He wouldn't get three words out before I blasted him."

Laughing, Logan leaned over his bike to give Cass a brief hug. "You're really something. Is there anybody you're not afraid to take on?"

"Not when it comes to the people I care about," she replied fiercely.

"I hope you count me in that group." Logan released her with obvious reluctance.

Cass gave him a teasing look. "What do you think?"

"I think," Logan said as he backed his bike out of the

rack, "I'd better not push my luck."

"Smart boy," Cass said and grinned.

They had just turned off the school grounds when Logan snapped his fingers. "I just had an idea. How about asking Tabitha to go bowling with us tonight?"

"Have you been reading my mind?" Cass looked at him in amazement. "I thought about that earlier. I hate the idea of her sitting home moping. I wasn't sure if I should ask you though. Plus, this was going to be our first official date. I want to help Tabitha out, but a part of me doesn't want to share our time tonight with her," she confessed. "That sounds awful, doesn't it?"

"It sounds honest. Besides, I feel the same way." Logan's face suddenly lit up. "I know. If Tabitha goes with us tonight, that gives me a legitimate excuse to take you out tomorrow night. I've thought about asking you, but I figured your parents might object to us going out two nights in a row. How can they, though, if we do a good deed and let Tabitha tag along on tonight's date?"

"Ooh, you're sneaky." Cass grinned. "I like that in a guy. Okay, that settles it. We tell Tabitha she's coming bowling with us. She'll try to argue, but we'll just tell her we're not taking no for an answer."

"Then tomorrow we do something by ourselves." Logan nodded in satisfaction. "Sounds like a plan."

As expected, Tabitha protested when Cass and Logan presented their proposal to her. She insisted she didn't need a baby-sitter and that she wasn't about to ruin their evening by agreeing to be a fifth wheel. When she was done, she turned to Kira to back her up.

"Tell them how silly their idea is," she said. "You can keep me company just as well as they can."

Kira looked uncomfortable. "Actually, I can't. I'm baby-sitting tonight, remember?"

"So?" Tabitha gave a careless shrug. "I'll go with you."

"I'm baby-sitting for the Feldmans. You know Mrs. Feldman doesn't like me to have anyone over." Kira made a face. "She's afraid I'll be distracted and not pay enough attention to her precious twins."

Tabitha's face blanched, but when she spoke, she sounded unconcerned. "No problem. I'll just stay in tonight and get my homework done. That way I'll have the rest of the weekend free."

"Go ahead. Ruin our evening." Cass plopped down onto the couch and crossed her arms.

Tabitha shot her a puzzled look. "What are you talking about?"

"If you're staying here, then so are we. Right, Logan?" When he nodded, Cass continued in a mournful tone, "And I was really looking forward to bowling."

"Don't be ridiculous. Of course you'll still go." Tabitha frowned. "Won't you?"

"Nope." Logan sat down beside Cass. "We decided on the way here that we weren't going if you weren't. We can play cards or maybe Monopoly. I like Monopoly."

"Me too." Cass heaved a gusty sigh. "Not as much as I like bowling, but I do like it."

"Oh, brother!" Tabitha raked her fingers through her hair. "You're making me feel like a heel."

"Sorry. We don't mean to." Cass tried to look pitiful.

"Yeah, we're just trying to help." Logan hung his head in apparent misery.

"Okay, you win." Tabitha threw her arms up in defeat. "You two look so pathetic sitting there, acting all hurt. What can I say? I'll go with you."

While Tabitha stomped off to the kitchen, Cass and Logan exchanged smug smiles. Kira flashed them a thumbs up before hurrying after Tabitha.

CHAPTER 27

Since she was fixing dinner for the Feldman twins, Kira left to baby-sit. Tabitha was still reluctant, but propelled by Cass and Logan, she got on her bike and followed them to the bowling alley.

It didn't take long for her to relax and have a good time. Cass and Logan went out of their way to include her in everything they said and did. Instead of feeling like an intruder, she wound up enjoying herself more than she thought possible.

After bowling four games, they decided to take a break. While they waited for their pizza, Logan gloated about winning three out of the four games. Cass promptly challenged him to a rematch the following Friday. Tabitha, who'd barely broken a hundred in her games, opted to stay out of their discussion and tortured herself instead by wondering what Micah and Alison were doing.

"Hey, earth to Tabitha." Cass snapped her fingers in front of Tabitha's nose. "What in the world are you thinking about? I've been trying to get your attention for five minutes."

Tabitha frowned. "I doubt that. We haven't even

been sitting here for five minutes."

"It's just a figure of speech. You take everything so literally," complained Cass. "Anyway, what were you thinking about?"

Reluctant to admit the truth, Tabitha shrugged and swished the ice in her drink. "It wasn't anything important. You know, school, friends, stuff like that."

"Alison and Micah?" guessed Cass.

Tabitha concentrated on coiling the straw wrapper around her finger. "Maybe."

"You want me to run over to the Yuk and spy on them?" Cass asked, grinning and looking like she was about to get up and run out.

"No!" Tabitha pretended to be horrified by the suggestion, even though, deep down, she wished she could take Cass up on it. "If they saw you, they'd probably think I'd sent you to do my dirty work for me."

"Hmm. That wouldn't be good." Cass sipped her Coke. "Okay, here's another idea. Don't think about them. You'll only make yourself more miserable. Every time they pop into your head, make yourself think about something else."

Tabitha shrugged. "That's easier said than done, but I'll try." Anything had to be better than the sick feeling she got in the pit of her stomach whenever she imagined Micah and Alison enjoying a romantic dinner for two.

Their pizza order came up, and Logan went to the snack counter to get it, along with a handful of napkins. Cass' gaze followed him.

"He's so great," Cass sighed, then turned toward Tabitha. "The only way I could be any happier right now would be if you and Micah were together."

"Yeah, well, that's not going to happen." Tabitha clenched her teeth and ordered herself not to cry. "He made his choice, and I wasn't it. Oh well, I guess I'll have to find someone else."

"Alex is available," Cass said lightly.

Tabitha shuddered. "And he can stay available. I'd have to be a whole lot more desperate than I am at the moment to go out with him."

Cass raised an eyebrow. "I thought you said you liked him."

"I do, but strictly as a friend. I can't ever imagine having romantic feelings for him." Tabitha smiled up at Logan as he set the pizza down in the middle of the table. "He's had more girlfriends than Eamon Beach has grains of sand."

"Are you talking about me?" Logan puffed out his chest in an exaggerated display of masculine pride.

Cass made a face at him. "Yeah, in your dreams." She slid a slice of pizza onto a napkin and handed it to Logan. "Tell the truth—counting me, how many girlfriends have you had?"

"Counting you?" Logan thought a few moments. "One and a half."

Laughing, Cass passed a piece of pizza to Tabitha. "What do you mean one and a half? How can you have half a girlfriend? You liked her, but she didn't like you?"

"Or maybe she was really short?" suggested Tabitha.

"You mean there are actually girls out there shorter than Cass?" Logan shook his head in amazement. "I didn't think that was possible."

"Very funny," drawled Cass. "Explain what a half girlfriend is."

Logan waited until they had all taken a slice and said a silent blessing. "Okay, here's the deal," Logan explained between bites. "When I was a freshman back in my old high school, I had a huge crush on a senior. But you know how it is. It's okay for older guys to date younger girls, but older girls hardly ever give younger guys the time of day. Anyway, Lisa and I were in band together, and we started talking and kidding around. After a while, we got to be pretty good friends. She told me about the boys she liked and how she could never get them to notice her and she gave me rides home from school. Finally, with one month of school left, I got up the nerve to ask her out."

Logan stopped, and Tabitha and Cass exchanged a knowing glance.

"What happened then?" Cass asked.

"She laughed at me." Logan picked a pepperoni off his pizza and popped it into his mouth. "In fact, she laughed so hard she almost had to pull the car over."

"That's awful," murmured Tabitha. "What did you do?"

Logan shrugged. "What could I do? I pretended it was a joke. I told her I was glad she knew me well enough to know I was just kidding."

"But inside, your heart was breaking, wasn't it?" Cass said and Tabitha almost gagged at the syrupy tone of her voice.

He devoured the rest of his pizza before replying, "Not really. I was more ticked off than anything else." A mischievous smile curved his lips. "Besides, I got my first kiss out of it, so it wasn't a total bummer."

"She kissed you after that?" Cass asked in surprise.

Logan nodded. "Yup. When she pulled into the drive-way to let me out, she turned to me and said no one made her laugh the way I did and kissed me right on the mouth."

"No way!" exclaimed Tabitha, outraged on Cass' behalf.

"Yeah, she was kind of forward, but I wasn't about to complain. I got my first kiss from a senior girl." Logan helped himself to another piece of pizza. "So that's the story of my half girlfriend."

"I'm sorry I asked," Cass muttered.

Tabitha could see the jealousy in her stepsister's eyes. "I have an idea. Don't think about it," Tabitha said sweetly. She smiled innocently when Cass glowered at her. "If it works for me, it should work for you too."

Cass just made a face at her before returning her attention to her food.

By the time they finished eating, everyone had lost their enthusiasm for bowling. Leaving the noisy building, they stepped out into the warm, fragrant evening. They retrieved their bikes and pushed them to the road.

"What do you want to do now?" asked Logan.

"Anything but go home," Cass said. "It's so beautiful out here tonight."

Tabitha's discomfort returned and she started to edge away from the other two. "You guys have been really nice, but I've imposed on you long enough. I'm heading back to the house."

Before she could get on her bike, Cass caught her by the back of the shirt. "You're not going anywhere, missy. You agreed to go out with us tonight, and the night's not over."

"But—" Tabitha protested.

"But nothing," Logan broke in. "Cass is right. Tonight we're a package deal. Where one goes, we all go."

"You make it sound like we're the Three Musketeers." Tabitha couldn't help laughing.

"Speaking of Three Musketeers," Cass said, "we didn't have dessert. I could use a candy bar or two. How about y'all?"

"I'm game." Logan tapped Tabitha on the shoulder. "What about you? Are you hungry?"

"A candy bar sounds good." She hesitated. "I'm not sure I want to go into the Ten-Ten, though. What if Micah and Alison happen to come in?"

"Wow, that'd be an exciting birthday celebration for old Al." Cass snorted. "Dinner at the Yuk and a visit to the Ten-Ten to top off the evening. It would probably take her weeks to get over a date like that."

Tabitha wasn't amused. "I'm serious. I don't want to risk running into them. I'll wait on Macy's porch while you and Logan get the stuff."

"I have a better suggestion. We can wait together while Cass buys what we need." Logan glanced at Cass, who nodded in agreement.

Tabitha shot him a wry look. "Are you scared I'll run away if you don't keep an eye on me?" she asked.

"Partly," Logan admitted. "But mainly I don't like the thought of you sitting alone in the dark."

"This is Kwaj," drawled Tabitha. "It's not exactly a hotbed of criminal activity. I'll be perfectly fine staying by myself for a few minutes."

"I know, but I'll feel better if I stay with you." Logan flashed her his most charming smile. "So humor me, okay?"

Tabitha heaved an exasperated sigh. "Your boyfriend is a pain in the neck," she grumbled good-naturedly to Cass.

"Yeah, but he's a protective pain in the neck." Cass smiled. "Do me a favor and let him sit with you. Otherwise, he'll sulk the rest of the night."

Shaking her head in mock irritation, Tabitha motioned to Logan. "Oh, all right. Come on." To Cass, she added, "We'll be on the porch. I'd like a Baby Ruth bar, the biggest one you can find."

"I'll take a Snickers bar and a bag of M&M's." Logan dug in his pocket, pulled out several wadded-up dollar bills, and handed them to Cass. "Here you go."

Tabitha's expression turned mischievous. "I didn't know Logan was buying. In that case, throw in a can of soda for me."

Logan laughed. "Get whatever that will buy. Knowing us, we won't have any problem eating it all."

While Cass disappeared into the Ten-Ten, Tabitha and Logan parked their bikes in front of Macy's and climbed the steps to the porch to sit on the railing. The store was closed, but several people came and went as they checked their post office boxes.

"I've had fun tonight," Tabitha said. "Thanks for letting me tag along."

"I'm glad you decided to come with us."

"What choice did I have?" Tabitha laughed softly. "You and Cass can be pretty persuasive when you put your minds to it."

"We wanted to make sure you knew it was okay for you to join us."

"You convinced me all right." For some reason—perhaps because of Cass and Logan's kindness—Tabitha suddenly found herself on the verge of tears. To hide the fact, she joked, "So what are we doing tomorrow night?"

Logan laughed and draped a friendly arm around her shoulders. "Sorry, sweetheart. You're on your own tomorrow night. I'm counting on having a real, honest-to-goodness date with Cass, and that doesn't include any third parties. I'm looking forward to being alone with my girlfriend."

"Oh, yeah?" Tabitha grinned up at him. "What have you got planned?"

"We'll start with—"

"Tabitha? Logan? Is that you?" a voice called from the yard, interrupting him.

The pair turned together and squinted into the darkness.

"Micah?" asked Logan.

Climbing off his bike, Micah took the flashlight out of his handlebar basket and shone it on his face. "Yeah, it's me." He looked as grim as he sounded.

"Hey, buddy." Logan slid off of the porch railing and spun around. "Talk about it being a small world. What are you doing here?"

Sure Alison was lurking somewhere out there in the dark, Tabitha was loathe to take more than the quick peek she'd already allowed herself. Moving as slowly as she could, she climbed off the railing and stood up.

"I was just about to ask you the same thing." Micah paused a couple of beats then added, "Hello, Tabitha."

This is absolutely my worst nightmare come to life, she groaned silently.

She forced herself to turn around and almost collapsed with relief when she saw Micah was alone. "Hello." Tabitha amazed herself with how calm she sounded.

Micah's gaze lasered in on Tabitha as if Logan weren't there. "I called your house a little while ago, and your Mom said you'd gone bowling with Cass and Logan. I was on my way to the bowling alley to see if I could find you. But what do I discover instead?" His bark of laughter was short and humorless. "You and Logan all cozied up on Macy's porch. Where's Cass? Did you ditch her?"

Beside her, Tabitha felt Logan tense, and she laid a quieting hand on his arm. Micah's scowl told her he hadn't missed the gesture.

"Cass is in the Ten-Ten buying us some snacks," Tabitha explained, struggling to keep her own temper in check.

"So while she was busy, you and Logan came out here to steal a few minutes by yourselves?" sneered Micah.

Logan started to jerk forward so Tabitha tightened her hold on his arm, although she wouldn't have minded if he had beat Micah to a pulp. "That's a terrible thing to say!" she blazed. "You should know us better than that! For your information," she went on, raising her voice to drown out Micah's protest, "Cass volunteered to get the snacks while Logan sat out here with me. I didn't want to accidentally run into you and Alison. I was afraid you might decide to drop in at the Ten-Ten after your date."

"What date?"

Tabitha put as much scorn into her snort as she could muster. "Don't play dumb with me. When a guy takes a girl out to eat for her birthday, most people consider that a date."

"Who says I took Alison out?" Micah asked.

"Your sister, so don't try to weasel out of this by pretending it didn't happen."

"You mean like you're trying to weasel out of me catching you and Logan hugging?" Micah taunted her. "Even though I saw you two with my own eyes?"

"That's it!" Logan roared. "I've had enough of this!"

Breaking away from Tabitha, Logan launched himself down the stairs and ran smack into Cass. She grabbed his arms to keep from falling then looked at him, Tabitha, and Micah in turn.

"What's going on?" she demanded. "I could hear you guys yelling and carrying on all the way over at the Ten-Ten."

"Micah accused Tabitha and me of sneaking around behind your back," Logan said, spitting out the words.

"Honestly, Micah," Cass said, "you know better than that. Why in the world would you say something so ridiculous?" She glanced around. "What are you doing here anyway? Where's Alison?"

"Why does everybody keep bringing Alison into it?" Micah asked. "How should I know where she is? Home, I guess." He thrust his chin out at a defiant angle. "I'm here because I came looking for Tabitha."

"So you could yell at her?" Cass demanded.

Micah threw his hands up in exasperation. "I was looking for Tabitha because I wanted to talk to her."

Tabitha's heart jumped, but she couldn't think of anything to say.

Cass responded instead. "Oh. Well in that case, what's stopping you? She's standing right up there."

Digging the toe of his sandal into the grass, Micah avoided looking at anyone as he muttered, "I'm going home. I don't feel like talking anymore." He grabbed his bike, then paused before getting on. "I was way out of line just now with the things I said," he apologized gruffly. "Sorry." He quickly pedaled away.

After a few seconds, Tabitha joined Cass and Logan on the steps.

"What was that all about?" she murmured.

"If you want my opinion, I think he's gone off his rocker." Logan looked at Cass, who was grinning.

"Tabitha, what just happened here?" she asked.

Tabitha gave a twitch of irritation. "What do you mean? You heard most of what went on. I was just sitting there, minding my own business, when all of a sudden Micah showed up and started ranting and raving about Logan and me. It was bizarre."

Handing the bag of food she'd bought to Logan, Cass took Tabitha by the shoulders and gently shook her. "Think about it," she ordered. "Micah came looking for you. When he found you and Logan together, he immediately jumped to the wrong conclusion and went berserk. What does that tell you?"

"That I should be grateful someone as unstable and unpredictable as he is prefers Alison over me?" Tabitha asked.

Cass gave her a harder shake then released her. "For someone who's usually so smart, sometimes you can be incredibly dense."

Tabitha stiffened. "Excuse me?"

"Now don't get all huffy with me." Cass smiled at Logan, who had moved off to one side. "Here's the plan. Logan and I are going back to the Ten-Ten to get my bike. Then we're going to go home and sit out on the rocks and talk about Micah's strange behavior."

"And eat candy bars?" Logan asked.

Walking over to him, Cass patted his hand. "Yes, and eat candy bars. Wait here," she said to Tabitha. "We'll be right back."

Logan and Cass had only gone a couple of feet when Tabitha stopped them. "Cass?"

Her stepsister looked back. "Yes?"

"Are you thinking what I'm thinking about Micah?"

"Probably. We'll know for sure when we talk."

Tabitha sighed, feeling optimistic for the first time since her talk that morning with Kira. "I hope so."

"Me, too, Sis. Me, too."

CHAPTER 28

Cass and Tabitha reached the same conclusion regarding Micah. It was clear to both of them that he felt more than mere friendship for Tabitha. The problem was that they differed on what she should do about it. The debate raged on for two more hours after Logan left at ten.

As usual, Cass was in favor of Tabitha taking immediate action. She was all for Tabitha calling up Micah and asking him to come right over so they could get to the bottom of what was going on.

Tabitha, on the other hand, announced she was adopting a wait and see attitude. Since Micah had taken Alison out, it was up to him to seek out Tabitha and initiate a discussion.

"But that's what he was trying to do when he went looking for you tonight," argued Cass.

It was almost midnight, and she was in Tabitha's room sprawled across the bed. Her stepsister sat at the desk with her feet propped on the books scattered across its top.

"Then he can do it again." Tabitha rasped a file across her left pinky fingernail. "He's the one who made a scene so he can be the one to set things straight."

"Has anyone ever told you you're as stubborn as—"

"You are?" Tabitha completed Cass' question for her. Cass made a face and she laughed. "I was really easygoing until you came along. But I've had a couple of months to learn from the best. Now I'm as hardheaded as they come."

"Flattery will get you nowhere," Cass said. "You're not going to sweet talk me into agreeing with you that waiting for Micah to make the first move is the right thing to do."

"It doesn't matter whether you agree with me or not." Tabitha yawned. "I've made up my mind, and nothing you say will make me change it."

We'll just see about that, Cass thought. She didn't appreciate Tabitha ignoring her advice, especially when it seemed so logical to her.

Tabitha removed her feet from the desk and slowly got up. "I can tell you're not happy with me for standing up to you. If you had your way, everyone would do what you told them to, no questions asked."

"Would that be so bad?" countered Cass. "I happen to think most of my ideas are pretty good. If people would just listen to me, the world would be a much better place."

"You're hopeless." Tabitha stood over the bed. "Come on—I'm tired and I want to go to sleep."

"Party pooper," griped Cass. She took her time rolling over and sitting up. "Can't we talk a few more minutes?" she wheedled. "I promise I won't mention Micah."

"Yeah. You might not mean to, but sooner or later you know you'll bring him up." Tabitha pushed Cass off the bed and toward the door. "Come on. Out of here."

"Gee, and I thought having a sister would be fun," Cass whined jokingly as she moved toward the door. "Sort of like living in one, long slumber party where we'd stay up all night and do each other's hair and talk about guys."

"Life sure can be disappointing sometimes, huh?" Tabitha waggled her fingers at Cass. "Ta-ta. Sweet dreams."

Cass' sulky expression brightened. "They will be because I intend to dream about Logan." She gave Tabitha a sly look. "What are you going to dream about?"

"What life used to be like before Dad married Mom," Tabitha retorted. "How simple it used to be. How happy I was."

Pausing at the door, Cass flashed her a knowing smile. "Somehow, I doubt that's what you're going to be thinking about when you fall asleep. Not after that episode with Micah."

"You're probably right," Tabitha conceded happily. "I tell you what. If I do start dreaming about Micah, I'll wake myself up, sneak into your room, and get you up so you'll know your prediction came true. How's that?"

"Don't you dare!" Cass exclaimed, opening the door. "I don't want to be disturbed if I'm dreaming about Logan. Wait and tell me in the morning."

Tabitha shrugged. "Have it your way. Good night, Cass."

" 'Night, Tabitha." About to leave, Cass suddenly turned and jogged back to her. Taking Tabitha by surprise, she flung her arms around her stepsister. "I really love you."

Tabitha seemed shocked at first, but then returned her hug. "I love you too, and I'm glad we're related."

"Me too." Before she got overly emotional, Cass let go and stepped back. A little embarrassed by her impulsive display of affection, she didn't quite meet Tabitha's eyes. "Well ... uh ... goodnight again."

Tabitha busied herself gathering up her robe and pajamas from the end of her bed. "Sleep tight."

Before falling asleep, Cass plotted how to get Tabitha

and Micah talking before the weekend was out. She resolved to talk to Logan first thing in the morning to see if he had any suggestions.

Cass rolled out of bed on her own early the next morning, eager to begin scheming with Logan about how to get their friends together. Since she decided it would be inconsiderate to call him before nine on a Saturday morning, she hopped into the shower first. After that, she carried a bowl of cereal out to the rocks so she could sit and watch the waves and let the breeze dry her hair while she ate breakfast.

Mom was in the kitchen when Cass returned to the house shortly after nine.

"What are you doing up so early?" she asked as Cass washed her dishes.

"I couldn't sleep." Cass placed the bowl, juice glass, and spoon in the dishrack. "I have a lot on my mind."

"Good things or bad things?"

"Definitely good. I'm trying to think of a way to get Tabitha and Micah to talk to each other before the day is over. I'm going to call Logan and see if he has any ideas." Cass' eyes lit up when she turned and spotted the griddle Mom had just put on the counter. "What are you making?"

"French toast." Mom retrieved eggs, milk, and butter from the refrigerator. "Want some?"

Cass thought a moment then regretfully shook her head. "No, I just ate."

Mom set a bowl on the counter. "What does Tabitha think about you meddling in her and Micah's business?"

"You know Tabitha." Cass waved her dismissal of her

stepsister's feelings. "She's not happy about it, but she'll thank me once things get worked out between them."

"I think perhaps you ought to leave the two of them alone to handle the situation as they see fit." Cracking eggs into the bowl, Mom peered over her shoulder at Cass.

Cass crossed her arms and glared at her. "Is that an order?"

Mom smiled, probably recognizing the stubbornness in Cass' tone. "In this case, it's only a suggestion. Since you know Micah, and probably Tabitha, better than I do, I'll leave the decision up to you."

Cass' face brightened. "Do you really think I know Tabitha better than you do?"

"In all likelihood, yes." Mom beat the eggs with a whisk. "She's opened up to me quite a bit, but the two of you talk more than she and I do."

Sliding her hands into the pockets of her shorts, Cass leaned back against the counter and watched Mom work. "She told me a little bit about her mother the other day, about the last time she saw her."

Mom smiled grimly. "The situation with her mother is very sad. For the life of me, I don't understand how a mother can abandon her child the way that woman did."

"Tabitha said she can't imagine you ever doing that to us."

"She did?" Her smile brightened. "I'm glad. I want Tabitha to feel secure about my love for her. She still struggles with thinking she did something to make her mother leave. Steve says it's gotten better, but she used to be terrified he'd leave her too."

"What a horrible way to live," murmured Cass, her heart swelling with sympathy for her stepsister. "Somebody should string Tabitha's mother up by her thumbs."

"I can certainly understand how you might feel that way," Mom admitted. "After some of the things Steve's told me, I have to confess I've been tempted to call the woman up and give her a piece of my mind. I have to remind myself the matter is between God and her—not me and her."

"Even when you want to so badly you can almost taste it?" Cass arched an eyebrow at Mom.

"Especially then," Mom replied with a chuckle. She gave the jar of cinnamon she held an enticing shake. "Are you sure you don't want some French toast?"

"Of course I'd like some. But I'm trying to exercise self-discipline so please stop tempting me." Cass checked the clock. "It's ten after nine. Time to call Logan and enlist his help."

Logan's mother answered the phone and informed Cass that he was still asleep. "Do you want to call back later or have me wake him up?"

"Definitely wake him up," Cass decided with a touch of malicious glee. "It's too pretty outside to waste the day sleeping."

Mrs. Russell laughed. "I'll tell him you said that. Hold on a second." She set down the receiver with a thud.

Several moments later, the phone was picked up and Logan's sleep-hoarsened voice inquired, "Hello? Cass?"

"Rise and shine," she chirped. "What are you still doing in bed?"

"Sleeping," Logan croaked. "What time is it?"

"Ten after nine. I've been up since before eight-thirty," Cass said brightly.

"Goody for you." Logan paused. "Are you always this cheerful this early in the morning?"

"I am when I'm talking to my favorite people in the world."

"Are you saying I'm one of your favorite people?"

"One of about two or three hundred," teased Cass. "You're definitely in the top fifty, though."

"Gee, thanks," drawled Logan. "I really feel special now. Did you call for a reason or just to talk?"

"For a reason, a really good one." Cass paused for dramatic effect. "I want you to help me find a way to get Micah and Tabitha together."

Logan laughed. "I'm two steps ahead of you. I called Micah when I got home last night."

"You did?" Her voice almost squeaked. "What did he say?"

"He was pretty bummed about what happened. He must have apologized twenty times for accusing Tabitha and me of sneaking around on you."

"Good," Cass said. "He should have apologized twenty more times. Did he say anything about Tabitha?"

"He told me he doesn't know what to do now. He said he figures she'll never want to have anything to do with him again."

"Did you tell him he's wrong?"

"Sure, but he's convinced he blew it with her."

"Hmm." Cass stared out the dining room window at the ocean as she pondered the situation. "Do you have any suggestions?"

Logan yawned before answering, "How about we leave it up to them to work things out?"

Cass sniffed her disdain for his reply. "Typical male response. What kind of world would this be if people didn't care about one another's problems?"

"A less nosy one?" Logan said lightly.

"Don't start acting all superior with me," Cass said. "You called Micah last night, remember?"

He laughed. "Okay, you made your point. Since you're the one who's all fired up about helping them, what ideas do you have?"

"None that seem workable so far. That's why I thought we could put our heads together and see what we come up with." Glancing up at the cloudless blue sky gave Cass an idea. "Would you like to meet me at the pool to talk about it?"

"That'd be great. Give me about thirty minutes, and I'll be there."

"Good. See you in a little bit."

Hanging up, Cass realized Mom was watching her with a faint scowl. "Oops, I should've asked first if it was all right to go swimming."

"Yes, you should have." Mom plugged in the griddle and adjusted the dial to the desired temperature setting. "Just because Kwajalein's so safe, and we know and trust Logan, doesn't mean you can come and go as you please without checking with one of us."

"I know. Sorry." Cass had the grace to look chastened. "Can I meet Logan at the pool?"

"Yes, you may." While the griddle heated, Mom got the bread out of the refrigerator. "How long do you think you'll be?"

"I don't know. Probably a couple of hours. He's supposed to meet me there in about a half-hour, but I'd like to go on over now, if that's okay."

"That'll be fine." Mom sliced off a pat of butter onto the hot griddle. "Since you're going down the hall, would you knock on our door and tell Steve breakfast is almost ready? He was awake when I got up, so you don't have to wake him."

After carrying out Mom's request, Cass changed into her swimsuit, donned an oversized T-shirt, and headed next door to the pool. To her surprise, she met Randy coming from the opposite direction.

"Hey!" Cass returned his grin with one of her own. "What are you doing out so early?"

"Some people jog in the morning. I ride." Randy held up his gloved hands. "Since I use my electric wheels so much, I like to get out in my old hand-powered chariot to keep in shape. It helps work my upper body muscles."

Cass looked at his sculpted muscles, gleaming with perspiration, and had to agree. "How long do you ride?"

"I've mapped out a two-mile course up and down different streets, and I usually go around twice." Randy wiped the sweat off his forehead with the back of his hand. "I try to go early in the morning before it gets too hot, but I got a late start today."

"I won't keep you then. I don't want to be the reason for you getting all flabby," teased Cass.

"Actually, I'm glad I ran into you. I have something I want to ask you."

Randy, who was always the picture of calm, suddenly appeared nervous. He rolled his chair back and forth a few inches each way.

His edginess was contagious. Cass found herself tensing. "Ask away." She hoped she didn't sound as wary as she felt.

"Okay, here goes." Randy took a deep breath, expelled it, swallowed twice, and blurted, "Would you go to the fall formal with me?"

Cass was glad she had on sunglasses so he couldn't read the shock in her eyes. If she'd listed all the possible questions he might have asked her, that one wouldn't even have been on the list.

"I—I—" she stammered.

After an awkward pause, Randy gave her a sickly smile. "Don't worry about trying to find a nice way to let me down. I can tell by your expression the answer is no." He swallowed. "It was a shot in the dark anyway. I figured Logan or somebody had already asked you."

Slowly regaining her composure, Cass shook her head. "No, no one's asked me."

"But you're hoping Logan will." It was a statement, not a question.

Believing honesty is the best policy, Cass nodded.

"Man, I can't believe I beat old Logan to the punch." A satisfied grin briefly lit up Randy's face before his expression dimmed once more. "Not that it does me any good. I guess you'd rather wait for Logan to ask you, huh?"

In the few moments since Randy had issued his invitation, Cass had gone from being stunned to considering taking him up on his offer. The fact was she wanted to go to the formal and he had asked first. Could she call herself his friend if she turned him down because he wasn't her first choice? Or, even worse, because he was in a wheelchair?

Sliding her glasses down her nose, Cass peered at Randy over them. "Are you withdrawing your invitation?"

Randy looked confused. "I am if you want me to."

Snorting, Cass threw her hands up in disgust. "Great, just great. I get asked to my first formal then, two minutes later, the guy takes it back."

Randy hesitated. "Are you saying you want the offer to stand?"

"I'm saying I at least want the opportunity to accept it or turn it down without you—" Cass gave Randy her most scathing glare, "—making my mind up for me."

Raking his wheat-colored hair back from his sweaty forehead, Randy fixed Cass with a steady gaze. "Why are you thinking about going with me?"

Although Cass knew what he was getting at, she chose to give him a straightforward answer. "Because you asked."

"It's not because you feel sorry for me? That you think of it as your good deed for the month or something?"

Cass' heart went out to Randy for even considering such a possibility. She decided to set the record straight once and for all. "I don't know who you just insulted more, me or yourself. I hate to break this to you, but I don't feel sorry for you at all. Chair or no chair, you're a terrific person, and you have a lot going for you. Any girl in her right mind would be honored to be your date for the formal. Since I like to think of myself as being in my right mind, I guess that means you've got yourself a date, mister."

Randy's eyes widened in astonishment. "You mean it? You'll really go with me?" A smile slowly spread across his face until it stretched from ear to ear.

Cass responded with a broad grin of her own. "Do you see anybody else standing here?" she teased.

Randy made a show of scanning the surrounding area. "Nope. It looks like you're it." His smile lost some of its brilliance. "What about Logan?"

"I really don't know. You'll have to check with him." Shrugging, Cass pushed her sunglasses back into place. "But I don't think he'll go with you, seeing as how you already have a date. He'll think you're being greedy."

A shout of laughter burst from Randy. "I can't wait until the dance. We're going to have a blast." Still laughing, he added, "To get back to Logan though, you know what I meant. You know him better than I do. Do you think he's going to be mad that I asked you?"

"I have no idea. I'm meeting him at the pool in a few minutes. I'll run it by him and see what he says." Cass swept back the hair the wind had blown across her face.

"Remind him there's always the winter formal." Randy flashed her a wicked grin. "But he'd better not wait until the last minute again. I'll be lurking in the shadows. I'd love to have the pleasure of your company at that dance too."

Cass clasped her hands together in the middle of her chest and pretended to heave a rapturous sigh. "I feel so wanted. I must be the luckiest girl in the world. Maybe somebody should pinch me so I'll know I'm awake."

"Don't tempt me," drawled Randy, causing Cass to blush when she realized what she'd said. He gripped the wheels of his chair and prepared to leave. "I'm off again. Since I'll be escorting the prettiest girl on the island to the dance, I've got to make sure I'm worthy of the honor."

"Hey—" Cass propped a hand on her hip and feigned indignation. "What's this about escorting the prettiest girl on Kwaj? I thought you were taking me."

Although Randy smiled, his eyes were serious as he reached out to briefly touch her arm. "You have no idea how beautiful you are, inside and out."

Too taken aback to respond, Cass could only gape at him.

Randy tipped an imaginary hat in farewell. "Talk to you later." He rolled a few feet, stopped, and added, "Thanks for saying yes, Cass. It means more to me than you'll ever know."

With tears clogging her throat, all Cass could do was nod and wave. As she turned to climb the steps to the swimming pool, happiness flooded her heart.

Thank You, Jesus, for giving me the right words to say to Randy. If I'd had my way, I'd be going to the formal with Logan, but You had a better plan and I'm glad. Maybe one of these days, I'll finally get it through my thick skull that Your will is perfect.

CHAPTER 29

Cass was stretched out on a lounge chair, her red hair bleaching to copper in the sun, when Logan arrived.

"Quit standing there gawking at me and get over here," she said, laughing, when she noticed he had paused at the gate. She patted the lounge chair she'd dragged next to hers.

"I didn't mean for you to catch me staring. I thought you were asleep," Logan said as he dropped his towel and lotion beside the chair and sat down.

"I'm wearing sunglasses," she replied wryly. "How could you tell whether or not my eyes were open?"

"I hate it when you're logical," Logan grumbled. "I thought girls were supposed to be illogical."

"That's just another of life's many myths." Cass laughed. "Like the one that says guys don't make passes at girls who wear glasses. I'm wearing these sunglasses and so far, I've had a very successful day."

"Some guy made a pass at you?" Logan glared around the pool as if to spot the culprit. The only males present, however, were three toddlers in the kiddie pool, several grade schoolers, and a couple of husbands with their wives. He turned back to Cass with a puzzled frown.

"Nobody made a pass at me," she assured him. "But thanks for thinking someone might. Actually," she continued, "I met Randy on my way here, and he invited me to the fall formal."

Logan's face fell. "No way! I was going to ask you when we went out tonight." A glimmer of hope brightened his otherwise disappointed expression. "You didn't say yes, did you?"

Sitting up, Cass reached over to place her hand on his arm. "I really wish you'd asked me first, but you didn't. If anyone else had invited me, I'd have said no so I could wait for you. But it's different with Randy and, in case you're wondering, it's not a pity thing. I like him, and I know how much courage it took for him to invite me. No matter how much I wanted to go with you, I couldn't tell him no."

Cass watched as frustration and understanding warred on Logan's face before understanding finally won out. Taking Cass' hand, he nodded. "You did the right thing. I really mean that. I was looking forward to going with you, but there'll be other dances." His eyes narrowed with a brief flash of irritation, but he covered it with humor. "I'll have to remember to tell Randy to find his own girl next time. Otherwise, we might have to arm wrestle for you."

"Guys." Behind her sunglasses, Cass rolled her eyes. "Does everything have to be a competition?"

"Not everything." Logan played with Cass' fingers, making her shiver despite the heat. "But it sure makes life more interesting."

"I'm glad I'm not a guy," Cass observed.

"So am I," Logan agreed. "Believe me, so am I."

After going for a quick swim, they settled back into their chairs to discuss Tabitha and Micah. They proposed and discarded several schemes to get them together until Cass finally groaned with exasperation.

"I think we're making this harder than it needs to be. Can't we come up with an easy plan?"

"How about you go back to your house and get Tabitha while I run over to Micah's and drag him back here?" suggested Logan. "It doesn't get any easier than that."

"You know, that's not a bad idea." Warming to the possibility, Cass sat up and swung her legs around so she faced Logan. "Once they're both here, we can leave them alone to talk." She stood up and grabbed her towel. "I like it. Let's do it."

They parted at the gate with promises to meet back at the pool in half an hour. Crossing her fingers, Cass hurried home. She had no idea how she was going to talk Tabitha into returning with her. She only knew she had to.

Cass found Tabitha lounging on the porch, talking with Mom. She was dressed, which Cass took to be a good sign. If Tabitha were still in her pajamas, Cass doubted she'd be able to convince her stepsister to leave the house without showering first. She sighed in relief. *One hurdle down, a couple more to go.*

Mom smiled as Cass approached them. "Back already?"

Since her suit was dry, Cass perched on the other end of the couch from Tabitha. "I came back to get you. Get your suit on, and let's go."

"Wait a minute." Tabitha frowned. "Mom said you were at the pool with Logan. I don't want to barge in on you two again."

"He's not there anymore. He left." Cass was glad to be able to tell the truth. "I want to stay a little longer, but I don't want to be by myself. Please come and keep me company. We haven't gone to the pool together in a couple of weeks." She tried to assume her most earnest expression.

Tabitha continued to glare at her. "Are you going to badger me about talking to Micah?"

Cass shook her head. "I won't say a word. I promise."

Leaning back, Tabitha studied her for several moments. "I think you're up to something, but I'll go with you. I'm warning you, though. If you say a word about Micah, I'm leaving."

Mom waited until Tabitha left the porch to change into her suit before she whispered, "You and Logan have cooked something up, haven't you?"

"Yup, we—" Cass began.

Vigorously shaking her head, Mom stopped her. "Don't tell me. That way, if Tabitha asks, I can truthfully say you never said a word."

"Okay." Cass shrugged agreeably. "My lips are sealed." Her eyes sparkled with mischief as she added, "But I predict our plan is going to work."

"I hope so." Mom smiled. "I think Micah and Tabitha are good for each other."

"As good as Logan and I are?" Cass asked.

Mom laughed. "No. You two are in a class by yourselves."

"Thanks." Cass frowned. "I think. I'm not sure how to take that."

Mom just shrugged.

Tabitha was ready in ten minutes, and they left the house talking and laughing. A hasty check of the pool area told Cass that Logan hadn't returned with Micah and she relaxed. She was afraid Tabitha might head straight back to the house if she spotted him right off.

Tabitha had just finished applying lotion when the squeak of the gate announced someone's entrance. She glanced over her shoulder and froze when she saw it was Micah.

Whirling around to confront Cass, she hissed, "You

lied! Micah and Logan just walked in."

Cass bristled. "How did I lie?"

"You didn't tell me Micah would be here."

"You didn't ask," retorted Cass.

"You set me up."

Grinning, Cass didn't look the least bit repentant. "So? What's your point?"

"You shouldn't have done it."

"Oh, well. Too late now." Seeing the boys headed in their direction, Cass gathered up her belongings. "See you later. Have fun."

"You're leaving?" Panic flared in Tabitha's eyes.

Cass gave her a look of exaggerated patience. "How do you expect to talk to Micah with Logan and me hanging around? Honestly."

"Who said I even want to talk to him?" demanded Tabitha, but Cass walked away without a response.

Passing Micah on her way out, Cass gave him to a bright smile. "Fancy meeting you here."

"Yeah, what are the odds?" he muttered.

"Ooh, somebody woke up on the wrong side of the bed," she said brightly. "I hope something—or someone—manages to put you in a good mood."

Logan linked hands with her and together they exited the pool. They waited until they were sure they were out of sight before congratulating each other with exuberant high-fives.

CHAPTER 30

Tabitha watched as Micah hesitantly approached her. When he got close enough for her to see the worry in his eyes, she gave him a wry smile.

"Looks like we both had one pulled on us this morning." Tabitha shook her head. "Those two need to find a hobby—other than meddling in our lives, that is," she added in a sarcastic drawl.

"I don't know." Micah spread his towel on the concrete beside Tabitha's chair and sat down. "I'm kind of glad they decided to poke their noses into our business."

Tabitha wished he wasn't wearing sunglasses so she could read the expression in his eyes. "Really? Why?"

"Number one, because it shows they care."

"Wondering if Cass cares has never been an issue," Tabitha assured Micah. "The problem is that sometimes she cares too much." Leaning her elbow on her knee, she propped her chin on her hand and gazed down at him. "Why else are you happy that they meddled?"

Micah hesitated, then took a deep breath. "Because they succeeded in getting us together. I've been wanting to talk to you for a long time, but especially since last night."

"You could have talked to me any time," Tabitha said. "You didn't have to wait for Cass and Logan to cook up a scheme."

Micah grimaced. "I know. But sometimes it's not that easy to do what you want to do without a push from somebody."

Tabitha allowed the silence that settled between them to stretch before saying anything. "We're here now and we have all the time in the world. What do you want to talk about?"

A self-mocking grin twisted Micah's mouth. "There's so much I have to say, I don't know where to start."

"Start anywhere, but just start," Tabitha said in a rush. "My heart is about to explode. Tell me something. Anything has to be better than sitting here, not knowing what's on your mind."

"Okay, but could you sit down here beside me?" Micah patted the oversized towel. "It'll be easier to talk if we're on eye level with each other."

Tabitha slid off the lounge chair and settled down next to Micah, taking care that they didn't touch. He took off his sunglasses, which made her smile.

"The first—and most important—thing I want to tell you is that I'm crazy about you," Micah said quietly. "I have been for almost six months. I remember the exact day I looked at you and saw you for the first time as a person, not just Kira's friend. It was March 30th."

Tabitha was so rattled by Micah's revelation that she had to remind herself to breathe. "I don't remember March 30th. Did something unusual happen that day?"

"Nope." Micah picked up her hand and began gently bending her fingers, one by one. "I was sitting on the couch, and you walked into the house like you had a thousand times before. For some reason though, when I looked up that time to say hi, it hit me like a ton of bricks that you were the most wonderful, best-looking girl I'd ever met. I felt like jumping up and grabbing you and asking you out right on the spot."

"Oh, my." Tabitha swallowed. "Why didn't you?"

"How could I?" Releasing her hand for a moment, Micah spread his in a gesture of helplessness. "You're my sister's best friend. What if you didn't feel the same way, and I messed things up between you and Kira? I couldn't risk it."

Tabitha narrowed her eyes. "I don't think you're being completely honest with me. I've had a crush on you for years and I haven't done a very good job of hiding it. You must have known I'd jump at the chance to go out with you. There's some other reason why you didn't say anything."

Picking up her hand again, Micah threaded his fingers through hers. "Look at our hands," he told Tabitha. When she did, he continued, "You're a blue-eyed blonde and I'm half black. The racial thing might not mean anything to you or even to most of the people on the island. But Kwaj isn't like the rest of the world. There are lots of people who have a real problem with interracial dating."

"So what? Who cares what people think?" Tabitha was astonished that Micah was uncomfortable about something she'd never thought twice about. "Besides, you're just as much white as you are black."

"That doesn't matter to people who are prejudiced." For the first time, a hint of bitterness crept into Micah's voice. "If you have one drop of black blood in you, then as far as they're concerned, you're black."

"But you know I don't think like that," protested Tabitha. "Neither does my father. Even if you were all black, it wouldn't matter. The only thing that counts is what kind of person you are. That's what Dad raised me to believe, and I do."

"I know *you* do," Micah said softly. "But when I realized how I felt about you, it was right before you and your father were going back to the mainland for vacation. I asked myself, what if we started dating and you told your relatives about me, and they objected because I'm mixed? It would kill me if you came back and broke up with me because they made you see the light."

Tabitha snatched her hand back from Micah and glowered at him. "I can't believe you just insulted me like that. As if I'd go along with anyone who told me you're not good enough for me because of the color of your skin. Please! You know what I think?" Her voice grew ominously soft. "You weren't as worried about me and how my relatives might react as you were about getting your precious feelings hurt. You say you were looking out for me, but I think you acted like a coward."

Micah straightened as if she'd slapped him. "Talk about insults," he growled.

Tabitha was on a roll and had no intention of backing down. "If the racial issue were really such a big deal, why did you take Alison out? She's white."

"She's mixed like me," Micah said softly. "Well, not exactly like me. Her mother's Mexican and her father's white, but it's the same principle."

Too furious to speak, Tabitha could only stare at Micah for several seconds. When she finally found her voice, it shook with rage. "You accuse other people of being prejudiced, but you're the real racist. Without anything to go on, you decided how my family would react if we went out. You also assumed Alison's family would be just fine with the two of you dating. If you can't see how downright unfair that is, I feel sorry for you."

Micah didn't say anything for a while. "You're right," he finally admitted. "I was wrong to assume your family back home wouldn't like you dating me because I'm mixed. You're also right about me putting my feelings ahead of you. I was so worried about what it would do to me if you dumped me that I didn't take into account how it made you feel when I practically ignored you."

"Thank you." Tabitha was partially mollified by Micah's concession.

"But," he went on, "you're wrong about believing I ever took Alison out. She's been after me since the first day of school. I don't know why she singled me out, but she did, and I'll confess it was flattering at first. Plus, I thought if I could make myself get interested in her, maybe I'd get over my feelings for you. I invited her to the house after school one day, but that was enough to let me know we had nothing in common."

"I remember Kira telling me you'd asked her over," Tabitha said softly. "I wanted to crawl into a hole and die."

Micah covered her hand where it lay on the towel between them. When she didn't resist, he picked it up and sandwiched it between his. "I was kidding myself when I thought Alison could take your place. After that day at my house I did my best to avoid her, but she never got the hint. Or, if she did, she ignored it. Anyway, she called Thursday and mentioned her birthday was the next day. I made the mistake of asking her what she wanted, and she said for me to take her out to eat. I didn't say anything so she asked me what the problem was since I wasn't dating anybody and it would be her treat. Other than coming right out and telling her I didn't like her, I didn't have an answer so I wound up saying fine, we'd go."

"When Kira told me yesterday morning you were taking her out, it was the worst moment of my life." Tabitha frowned. "I'd decided I was going to invite you to the Yuk for supper so I could tell you how I feel about you, then Kira announced you had a date with Alison. I felt like I'd been punched in the stomach."

"I know. I'm sorry." Micah rubbed his thumb over Tabitha's palm. "I was sitting in the restaurant with Alison when it finally dawned on me you'd probably heard about our so-called date. All I could think about after that was finding you and explaining what had happened before I blew any chance at all of you ever going out with me. The minute I got home I called your house and your mom said you were bowling with Cass and Logan, so I went straight over there."

"Then, on the way, you found Logan and me on Macy's front porch." Tabitha's voice was rich with laughter.

"It's not funny," Micah chided her. "I was ready to grab Logan and beat him to a pulp. You have to admit you two have spent a lot of time together lately."

"All we did was talk about you and Cass. He was a good friend when I needed one. Plus, he had the added benefit of giving me a guy's perspective on things, which was something Kira couldn't do."

"I know all that now. But the only thing that mattered last night was that Logan was with you and I wasn't." Micah's expression was sheepish. "I made a fool out of myself."

"Yes, you did," Tabitha said and laughed. "But then I figured, if you got that worked up over seeing Logan and me together, you must like me. I was pretty happy by the time I got home."

"And I was completely miserable. I decided you were never going to talk to me again."

"Hah! Fooled you, didn't I?" With her free hand, Tabitha wiped a bead of perspiration trickling down Micah's cheek.

He sat very still under her touch, his dark eyes searching her face. "Tabitha, I'd be the happiest guy in the world if you'd agree to go to dinner and a movie with me tonight."

"Then prepare to start celebrating," she teased, "because my answer is yes."

"All right!" Micah squeezed her hand so hard it almost hurt. Then, seeming to realize what he was doing, he loosened his grip but didn't let go. "Should we go find Cass and Logan and let them know their plan worked?"

Tabitha grinned. "Nah. Let's keep them wondering a little while longer. Cass especially thinks she knows what's best for everybody. It would do her a world of good if we made her sweat it out."

"And you call yourself her sister."

Tabitha's shrug was unconcerned. "If you can't bug your family, who can you bug?"

Standing, Micah pulled her to her feet. "How about your friends?" He scooped her up in his arms and acted as if he was about to dump her into the pool.

The lifeguard blew her whistle and Micah reluctantly set Tabitha back on her feet. "Honestly," he pretended to grumble, "a guy can't have any fun around here."

Tabitha reached out to flick his chin. "Oh, you think so, huh? You don't think spending time with me is fun?"

Capturing her finger, Micah lightly kissed it before releasing it. "Since you put it that way, maybe I can figure out some way to enjoy myself."

"How about this?" Tabitha broke away from him and jumped into the pool. Surfacing, she slicked the hair out of her eyes and taunted, "Last one in is a rotten egg."

Micah cannonballed into the water beside her with a bloodcurdling yell. When he came up, he started a water fight that soon had them both breathless with laughter.

CHAPTER 31

After Logan left to do some yard work for his mother, Cass took another quick shower to rinse off the chlorine. Not sure what to do with herself while she waited for a report from Tabitha, she went in search of her parents.

"What are y'all up to?" she asked after she found them in the back yard.

"Your mom and I were just discussing heading over to Macy's to see about some new sandals for me." Dad lifted his foot to display the sorry condition of his current pair. "You feel like tagging along?"

"No thanks. I want to be here when Tabitha gets back." Cass glanced over at the pool, wishing she could see through the concrete wall. "I'm really anxious to hear how things turned out."

"I'm assuming it's a good sign she's not back yet," Mom said.

"That's what I've been thinking," Cass said, smiling. "I figure, the longer she stays at the pool, the better things are going. At least they're probably talking."

"I've been praying they would work it out." Mom smiled up at Dad. "I have a sneaking suspicion Steve's been praying they don't."

"No I haven't," he protested, adding with a sheepish grin, "Not exactly anyway. What I've done is tell God that I'm a dad and my heart breaks a little bit every time I think about my girls falling in love."

"Oh, Dad," Cass scolded in an affectionate tone, "Tabitha and I are way too young to fall in love. All we're looking for is to be in like."

Dad laughed and gave her a quick hug. "Thanks, sweetie. I needed that."

After seeing them off, Cass turned and walked back inside. It wasn't often she wound up home alone, and she found herself appreciating the quiet.

Cass had just settled down with her book and a glass of lemonade when the phone rang. Scowling, she thought about letting the answering machine pick up, but then the possbility that it might be Logan occured to her, so she leaped up and sprinted across the floor.

"Hello?"

"You're out of breath. It's amazing how often I have that effect on girls."

Too late, Cass remembered Alex had said he'd call. "Hi, Alex." She made her voice as flat as possible.

Alex didn't seem to notice. "What are you doing?"

"Not much. I'd just sat down and started reading."

"You're going to stay inside and read on a beautiful day like this?" he asked incredulously.

Cass bristled at his tone. "I've already been out this morning. I was at the pool earlier."

"Oh." Alex sounded surprised. "Did you go by yourself?"

"No." Cass didn't feel the need to say anything further.

He sighed, then asked, "Are you in a bad mood?"

I wasn't until you called, Cass wanted to retort. Aloud, she replied, "I don't think so."

There was a brief pause. "Do you remember I said yesterday that I wanted to talk to you?"

Cass couldn't help laughing slightly. "Uh ... yeah. Exactly how bad do you think my memory is?"

"Aren't you curious about what it is I want to talk to you about?"

Actually, Cass was. "Yeah, but I figure you'll tell me when you're ready to tell me."

"I'm ready now." Alex paused dramatically. "Technically speaking, it's not something I'm going to tell you, but something I need to ask you. Will you go to the fall formal with me?"

Fortunately Cass managed to not laugh out loud. *What are the odds*, she marveled, *of having three boys ask me to the formal on the same day?*

In the midst of her amazement, she remembered Alex was awaiting a response. "I'm sorry. Somebody else already asked me and I told him yes. Thanks for the invite, though."

"Who?" he demanded after a stunned silence, adding hastily, "No, don't tell me. It's Logan, isn't it?"

"Nope." Cass couldn't recall the last time she'd enjoyed a phone conversation this much. "Randy."

"Randy?" echoed Alex. "Randy Thayer?"

Hearing Alex's shock secretly pleased Cass. "That's the one."

"But he's a ... cripple!" sputtered Alex. "You can't dance with a cripple."

If Cass could have reached through the phone and throttled him, she would have. "Randy is a terrific guy who just happens to be in a wheelchair. I plan to have a great time with him at the formal, whether we dance or not, although I wouldn't put it past him to figure something out."

"Does Logan know you're going to the dance with Randy?"

"Not that it's any of your business," snapped Cass, "but as a matter of fact, he does. What's more, he's fine with it. The thought of me going out with a disabled person doesn't bother him the way it does you."

"Then he ought to have his head examined," muttered Alex. "I can't believe I was ever interested in a girl who thinks dating cripples is a good idea."

"Yeah, well, I can't believe I was ever interested in somebody as shallow as you," Cass shot back.

"Temper, temper," Alex scolded nastily. "I give up. I've tried to be nice to you but it doesn't work. This was my last-ditch effort for us to have a relationship. As of this moment, I'm washing my hands of the whole thing."

"Okay." Cass couldn't help grinning.

"Is that all you have to say?"

"Okay." Cass thought a moment, then added, "Thanks?"

"You think you're funny, don't you?" sneered Alex.

"Actually, I know I am." Cass stifled a giggle, knowing it would only further enrage him. "I'm sorry things turned out the way they did, but no hard feelings, okay?"

"I'll think about it and get back to you," he retorted cooly.

Cass just shrugged, wishing he could see her. "Don't wait too long," she cautioned, "or I might not remember what you're talking about."

She hung up before he could say anything. She felt great for being able to put him off—but also slightly guilty.

Lord, please be with that boy, she prayed as she headed back to the sofa. *Help him realize someday how much You love him and how much he needs You.*

She fell asleep on the couch and was abruptly awakened when Tabitha plopped down beside her. "Wh … what?" She bolted upright, blinking the sleep out of her eyes.

"Wake up, sleepyhead," sang Tabitha. "I have the best, most fantastic news to share with you. Your plan worked! Micah and I are officially a couple!"

Cass clapped her hands in delight. "Hooray! Only it wasn't really my plan," she confessed. "Logan's the one who actually came up with it."

"I don't care who thought of it." Tabitha got up and twirled around, her arms out and her face lifted to the ceiling. "The important thing is it worked."

"So you got everything straightened out? The situation with Alison? Everything?"

"Every last little thing," Tabitha said, grinning. "Plus, we're going out tonight. He's taking me to the Yokwe Yuk then to a movie."

"That's what Logan and I decided to do!" squealed Cass.

Tabitha's eyes lit up. "You want to double-date? Wouldn't that be great, the two of us going out together with our guys?"

"Mom would definitely consider it a Kodak moment." Cass laughed. "If Logan and Micah are agreeable, let's do it."

"You're on. I'll call Micah then you call Logan." Tabitha collapsed onto the couch again. "I'm so happy I could burst. Thanks for helping to make it happen."

Cass leaned over and patted her arm. "We're family. That's what family's supposed to do, help and support each other."

"How about love one another?" Tabitha turned her head where it rested on the sofa cushion to gaze at Cass.

"That too." Cass smiled. "Especially that."

CHAPTER 32

"What are you and Micah doing tonight?"

It was two weeks later and Cass and Tabitha were relaxing on the lanai. The sun shone as brightly as usual, although storm clouds were gathering on the horizon. They'd brought their schoolbooks out with them, intending to tackle their homework, but so far their books remained stacked beside their lawn chairs.

"We decided we'd eat at his house." Tabitha stretched. "Then get a movie. I'm pushing for a romantic comedy. But of course—" she wrinkled her nose, "—he wants something with a little more action."

"Maybe you could find a romance where the guy blows up his girlfriend at the end," suggested Cass.

"That's awful." Tabitha tried to look disapproving, but wound up laughing. "Although I'm sure a movie like that would be right up Micah's alley. Why are boys so unromantic?"

Cass pursed her lips as she pretended to ponder Tabitha's question. "I think it has something to do with biology. They're missing some essential gene."

"I'm so glad I'm a girl." Lifting her face, Tabitha sniffed the air. "It smells like rain. I hope we get a good storm. Dad said the water level in the tank is so low we might have to start rationing."

Cass glanced over her shoulder at the clouds growing darker and closer with each passing moment. "I've gotten used to just about everything about life here. But I don't know if I'll ever get used to worrying about something as basic as water. Have you ever run out?"

"Not since I've been here," Tabitha said, shrugging. "We've always had enough to see us through to the rainy season."

"That's good to know." Cass wasn't entirely reassured, but she decided to drop the subject. "Did you hear Josh finally asked Rianne to the formal?"

"When? Last night?" When Cass nodded, Tabitha clapped her hands. "Yay! With Kira going with Logan, that means the eight of us can quadruple-date."

"Mom's almost finished with my dress, so she'll be starting yours in the next day or two."

"Good," Tabitha sighed, then grinned. "Not that I've been worrying about her getting it done in time." At Cass' snort, she admitted, "Okay, maybe I've been a little concerned. But the blue Mom decided on for you is gorgeous. And the lilac she chose for me—" Tabitha sighed, "—is absolutely perfect."

"Not that you're conceited or anything," teased Cass.

Pretending to take offense, Tabitha gave a little flounce. "If you have it, flaunt it. That's my motto."

Cass laughed. "In my case, if you don't have it, act like you do and maybe you'll be lucky enough to fool at least a few people."

Tabitha made a face at her. "I hate it when you put yourself down, even if you do mean it as a joke. I wish you knew how pretty you are."

"I'm okay. At least people don't run away screaming at the sight of me." Cass shrugged. "I'm not you, though.

The first time I saw you, I thought, 'Oh great, I'm going to be spending the evening with somebody who makes me look like one of Cinderella's ugly stepsisters.' "

Although Tabitha laughed, she still scolded, "Don't say things like that. You know what Mom says—if you go around comparing yourself to others, you usually don't wind up feeling any better about things. You can always find people you're better than, but then again, there are always the ones you don't measure up to." Suddenly, she frowned. "Like Alison Ross."

"Give it up, will you?" Cass said impatiently. "She's out of the picture. Micah has pledged his undying devotion to you. What more do you want?"

"For Alison to drop off the face of the earth?" Tabitha suggested hopefully.

"Why is that even necessary? You know she's already set her sights on some other guy," Cass reminded her. "Patrick what's-his-name. The senior with the blonde ponytail."

"Patrick Sanders. I've seen them around school, and they seem really tight. Still, I'd sleep better if Alison would somehow magically disappear."

Cass fixed her with a stern gaze. "Don't you trust Micah?"

"Of course I trust him," Tabitha said. "It's Alison I don't trust."

Cass shook her head. "You can't have it both ways. Either Micah's the honest, dependable guy you think he is, which means you can trust him even if Alison decides to throw herself at him again. Or he's not, in which case you're better off without him. Why waste your time with someone you don't trust?"

Tabith frowned in thought. She was quiet for a while, then said firmly, "I trust Micah completely. He's always been straight with me. Actually, I've never known him to lie to anyone. He's the best guy I know."

Cass gave her a mischievous look. "He can't be, because Logan is. But Micah can be second-best."

"Gee, thanks," drawled Tabitha. "Anyway, let's not fight about it. I know what the truth is. You—" she stuck her tongue out at Cass, "just think you do."

Before she could respond, a gust of wind lifted Cass' hair, tangling it about her face. Glancing up, she saw a line of ominous clouds bearing down on the island.

"Maybe we should move this party indoors before we wind up getting drenched."

"I'm right behind you." Gathering her books, Tabitha stood up. "Looks like we won't have to worry about rationing water for a little while longer."

Once inside, Tabitha disappeared into her room to do homework. Cass sat on the porch swing for a few minutes and made a halfhearted attempt at studying before going in search of Mom. She found her in the living room, hemming her formal.

"Almost done?" Cass longed to take the dress from her mother and hold it up in front of herself the way she had at least a dozen times in the last week.

"Ten more minutes, and it'll be finished." Mom smiled up at her. "I don't suppose you'll have any objections to trying it on to make sure it fits."

"None at all," breathed Cass. She managed to keep herself from jumping up and down and clapping.

"I don't believe I've ever seen you this excited about an article of clothing," Mom said wryly.

Cass sank down onto the opposite end of the couch from Mom and tucked her legs beneath her. "Don't start thinking I'm turning over a new leaf. I'm only excited because it's a special occasion. Plus, it's my first formal."

"And here I thought you were finally turning into a girl," Mom teased.

"That's what you have Tabitha for," Cass shot back. "Too bad you didn't marry Steve ten years ago so you could have had a little girl who liked to dress in ruffles and lace, instead of denim."

"Well, better late than never." Mom glanced up from her sewing, and her expression suddenly sobered. "I've been wondering about something. Since you're looking forward so much to the dance, is there a part of you that wishes you weren't going with Randy?"

Cass bristled, ready to defend her decision, then honesty replaced her initial reaction. "Yes," she admitted in a voice barely above a whisper. "Mostly I'm glad I said yes to Randy, especially when I'm talking with Rianne and she tells me how excited he is about the dance. Sometimes, though, I get to thinking about how much more fun it would be to go with Logan, not just because we could actually dance and stuff, but because we're dating. Then I start to feel sorry for myself. I even—" she hesitated, not sure she wanted to confess her deep, dark secret, "resent Randy for asking me first."

Mom momentarily set aside her sewing. "I thought you might be feeling that way, sweetie."

A tiny frown puckered Cass' forehead. "What gave me away?"

"Every now and then you get a look on your face when you and Tabitha are talking about the formal that lets me know there's something about the evening that bothers you," explained Mom. "I decided it was probably related to going with Randy."

Cass nibbled at her thumbnail. "I hope nobody else has picked up on the signals I've been sending, especially not Randy. I wouldn't hurt him for the world."

"I doubt he's noticed anything out of the ordinary," Mom said. She retrieved the dress from the arm of the sofa and went back to her stitching. "Don't forget I'm your mother. I'm paid to keep an eye on you and figure out what's going on in your life."

Instead of laughing, Cass asked quietly, "Are you disappointed in me for not being a hundred percent happy about going with Randy?"

"Absolutely not. If anything, I'm prouder than ever of you that you're going anyway, even though your heart's not entirely in it."

"Thank you." Cass ducked her head in embarrassed pleasure at the compliment. "While I'm on a roll, I guess I should also tell you I'm sort of jealous of Kira being Logan's date. The other day, he asked me what color flowers he should get to go with her dress, and for a few seconds I saw red. Or I guess I should say, green," she added in a self-mocking tone.

"A little jealousy is perfectly understandable, as long as it's not affecting your friendship with Kira." Mom arched an eyebrow in Cass' direction. "It's not, is it?"

Cass shook her head. "Nope. Kira and I are cool. She's been great through this whole thing. When Logan asked her, she checked with me to make sure it was okay to say yes before she gave him an answer. And of course, he asked me if it was all right to invite her. Any problems I have are of my own making."

"Are you worried Logan and Kira might suddenly discover they're meant for each other as a result of their date?" Mom asked, eerily reading Cass' thoughts.

Cass shrugged and avoided Mom's gaze by plucking miniscule bits of lint off the couch.

"You do realize that's highly unlikely, don't you?" Mom's tone was gentle, but insistent.

"In my saner moments, I do." Picking up a pillow and setting it in her lap, Cass began ridding it of lint. "At night, though, I get a little crazy thinking about them together. Logan pinning on Kira's corsage. The two of them sitting really close and maybe even holding hands in the taxi on the way to the dance. Him kissing her goodnight when he brings her home." She groaned and lifted tormented eyes to Mom. "See what I mean? My imagination tends to spin out of control after a while."

"So don't let it," Mom advised in her no-nonsense way. "It's your imagination. You determine what you think about. If you don't like the direction your thoughts are going in, turn them around."

"It's not that easy," argued Cass.

"I didn't say it was easy." Mom fixed her with a steady stare. "But it is doable. In the proper order of things, you control your thoughts, not the other way around."

Cass' mouth twisted in displeasure. "Why do our conversations usually wind up with you lecturing me?"

Mom laughed. "Because I'm a parent. It's a rotten job, but somebody has to do it."

Tossing aside the pillow, Cass unfolded her legs and stood up. "When I'm a parent, I'm going to have normal discussions with my kids. I won't be harping on them all the time."

"I take it you're not planning on living with your kids then?" Mom's voice held a hint of laughter. "That's the only way you'll be able to avoid lecturing them."

Unable to think of a snappy comeback, Cass turned to head down the hall. "I'm going to my room. You can bring me the dress when you're done."

"Or you can come get it," Mom called after her. "I'm not your slave."

Cass threw her hands up in exasperation, even though she smiled. "More lectures! Honestly, don't you ever get tired of them?"

"Nope," Mom said. "I live to lecture. It's one of my favorite pastimes."

Cass' only response was to growl and slam the door.

CHAPTER 33

The rain arrived shortly after Cass tried on her dress and pronounced it perfect. After reluctantly taking it off and returning it to Mom to be pressed and hung up in anticipation of the dance, she wandered out to the porch to enjoy the storm. Whipped to a frenzy by the wind, the rain pelted the windows with such force that Cass grew uneasy.

"Uh … Dad?" she asked when he joined her after a short while. "Do you get hurricanes around here?"

Dad bit into one of the cookies he'd taken from the jar and offered the other to Cass. "No hurricanes." Just as Cass began to relax, he added, "But we have been known to get hit by an occasional typhoon."

About to take a bite of her cookie, Cass changed her mind and gulped instead. "Are typhoons worse than hurricanes?"

Please say no, she silently implored him.

"Probably not," Dad said and Cass sagged with relief. "The name just sounds scarier. Besides, it's not time for typhoons yet. The season runs from October to April."

Great, Cass grumped. *Just when I was feeling better.*

"There's a typhoon season? Why didn't you mention this before now?"

Dad shrugged. "I guess it slipped my mind. I was too busy bragging about life here."

Crossing her arms, Cass glared suspiciously at him. "Are there any other potential dangers you haven't thought to tell me about?"

"Let's see." Dad slid his hands into his pockets. "You know about the sharks and the beached jellyfish and the possibility of developing coral fever if sand gets into an open wound. Now that you know about typhoons, I think that about covers it. Oops, wait a minute." He looked up, and his grin was wicked. "Have you heard about tsunamis?"

Cass frowned. "What are they?"

"Tidal waves."

Her gaze flew to the window expecting to see one barreling down on them. She licked dry lips. "How … how often do you get them?"

"Never." Dad laughed and reached down to ruffle her hair. "I'm sorry. I couldn't resist teasing you. The last tsunami to come through the Marshall Islands was over thirty years ago, and it didn't even hit anywhere near here. It rolled over a couple of islands farther west."

"Oh, gee, I feel better," Cass drawled. "What that says to me is we're way overdue for another one and it'll probably be our turn next."

"Has anyone ever told you you worry too much?" Dad said, still laughing.

"Somebody in this family has to think ahead," Cass defended herself. "The rest of you are too busy enjoying island life to think about all the possible risks. Boy, what I wouldn't give right now to be back home in Tennessee, where the only sharks and jellyfish are in tanks in the Chattanooga Aquarium, and where they've never even heard of coral fever, typhoons, or tsunamis."

"Sounds pretty boring to me." Dad snapped his fingers. "But that reminds me. Your mom sent me out here to ask you if you'd like to call one of your friends back home. Since there was no mail this week, she thought you might want to call Janette to find out what's going on. She knows you've been waiting for a letter."

Cass was out of her seat before he stopped talking. "I'd love to talk to Janette!" She sprinted past him for the phone. "You've made my day."

Unfortuately, she forgot it was still Friday in Tennessee, eight o'clock in the evening to be exact. Janette's mother answered the phone and informed Cass that Janette was at the high school football game.

"Of course," she added with a laugh, "it's raining and a bit on the chilly side. But I'm sure you remember what football weather's like."

Cass did remember, and she was hit with such a fierce longing to be back in the midst of it that she could hardly bring herself to mumble a garbled goodbye. She hung up and leaned her forehead against the wall while waves of homesickness broke over her.

Tabitha, who'd come into the kitchen in search of lunch, gave her a curious glance. "What's wrong? Did Logan break your date for tonight or something?" she asked.

Glad to have someone to vent her feelings on, Cass whirled around. "Not everything in life revolves around boys. Some people have real problems, you know."

Startled by her wrath, Tabitha backed up a step and raised her hands in surrender. "Whoa—don't jump all over me. All I did was ask a simple question. Who was on the phone, and what did they say that got you so riled up?"

"Dad said I could call Jan." A lump took form in Cass' throat, making it hard for her to talk. "Only I forgot it's yesterday night there, so she's at the football game."

Understanding dawned on Tabitha's face. "And now you're throwing yourself the usual pity party because you're not there and part of what's going on. When are you going to get over being homesick?"

Straightening, Cass glared at her. "Gee, you're so sympathetic," she drawled. "Who are you to talk to me about getting over something when you haven't had to make a single adjustment in your charmed life? When have you ever had anything not go your way?"

"Does having my mother walk out on me count?" Tabitha spoke softly, but her voice shook with fury.

Although Cass was immediately ashamed, she didn't want to show it. "I always forget about that because you never act like it bothers you." She knew it was a lame defense, but it was the best she could do on the spur of the moment.

Tabitha just snorted. "If you'd ever take the time to look closer, you'd see exactly how much it bothers me. I can't help but think of it every day."

Breathing hard with emotion, the girls stared at each other across the kitchen floor. Cass was the first one to break the tense silence.

"Just when I think we're doing better in our relationship, we wind up at each other's throats again." She shook her head, regretting what had been said in the last couple of minutes. "Why do we do that?"

A wry smile curved Tabitha's lips as she shrugged. "Because we're human?"

"I guess." Cass sighed. "It gets so tiring to be always on guard, though. When is this ever going to come naturally?"

"About the time we leave for college?" Tabitha suggested with a laugh. "How should I know? I've never had a stepsister before."

"Yeah." Cass pushed off from the wall to head to the refrigerator. "I keep reminding myself it's not just a relationship. It's an adventure."

Tabitha stepped aside so Cass could open the refrigerator door. "Would you like to talk about how you feel about missing the football game?"

Cass arched an eyebrow at her. "No thanks, Oprah. I appreciate the offer, though."

Tabitha's face fell. "I was just trying to be helpful."

"I know." Cass patted her arm. "And I repaid you by being crabby. Sorry, sometimes I can't help myself." She lowered her voice to confide, "I don't know if you've noticed, but I'm not always a nice person."

Tabitha's yelp of laughter made Cass wince. "Oh, I've noticed all right. It's the worst kept secret on the island."

Cass made a face as she retrieved a package of hot dogs from the meat drawer. "Now who's the sarcastic one?"

"I'll have one," Tabitha said as Cass extracted a hot dog from the package and laid it on a plate. "If you'll cook mine, I'll get the buns ready and pour drinks." When Cass nodded, she returned to the conversation. "Maybe we're twins separated at birth. That would explain how alike we are."

Cass set a small frying pan on the stove and turned on the burner. "I don't think so."

"Why not?" persisted Tabitha. "You look a lot like Dad, and I'm practically Mom's clone."

"Because," Cass stopped and fixed her stepsister with a gaze guaranteed to put an end to the discussion, "if you were really Mom's kid, wild horses couldn't have dragged her away from you. If someone had tried to take you away, she would have fought tooth and nail. It wouldn't have been pretty."

As Cass dropped a pat of butter into the pan to melt,

the utter silence behind her alerted her to the fact that something was wrong. She glanced over her shoulder and saw Tabitha working to choke back tears.

"What?" Cass quickly thought over what she'd said and groaned. "Oh, brother. Someone should string me up for being so stupid. When will I learn to think before I open my big mouth? I didn't mean to imply Mom's better than your mother. I'm sure your mother did what she thought was the right thing at the time."

"It's okay." Tabitha wiped her eyes with a shaky hand. "I know what you meant, and you're right. My Mom did only what was best for her."

Cass hesitated. "Is that why you're crying?"

"I don't know why I'm crying." Tabitha impatiently shook her head. "I've gone for years without giving my mother much thought, and I can't remember the last time I cried about her. Now all of a sudden, it's like I can't think of anything else and I hate it. I don't want her in my head. I want her to go back in the box where I used to keep her, but she won't stay there."

Momentarily distracted by the butter sizzling in the frying pan, Cass turned down the heat and plopped in the two hot dogs. Turning back to Tabitha, she asked, "Have you talked to Dad about what's happening?"

Tabitha looked alarmed. "No, and I don't want you to say anything to him either. He doesn't like talking about my mother. He always gets very uncomfortable whenever I bring her up. I think he wishes I'd just forget about her."

"What about Mom, then?" Cass rolled the hot dogs over so they'd brown evenly. "You said once you've talked to her about the situation, and she obviously didn't mind."

"That's true," Tabitha said, getting out plates, hot dog buns, ketchup, and mustard. "But I feel funny about it. I don't want Mom to think I'm comparing her to my mother or that I wish my mother was in my life. I'm really confused. I can't figure out why she's on my mind so much, and I don't know who to ask to explain it to me."

Cass was stumped too. "Are you close to Kira's mother? Or ... uh ... let's see ... Pastor Thompson?"

Tabitha flatly rejected both suggestions. "Mrs. Alexander's great, but she's not somebody I'd confide in. She's busy with her own family. As for Pastor Thompson, I don't know him that well. I just don't see myself marching into his office and filling him in on all the juicy family secrets."

Frowning, Cass gave the franks a final turn. "Would you be embarrassed talking to him?"

"Sure. Wouldn't you?" Tabitha took two glasses from the cupboard and set them on the counter to fill them with ice.

Cass firmly shook her head. "No way. He's a pastor. You couldn't tell him anything he hasn't heard before."

"I don't care." There was a stubborn set to Tabitha's jaw. "I don't like the thought of him looking at me and knowing all about our private family business."

"He'd never tell anybody," Cass assured Tabitha, in case that was one of her concerns. She turned off the burner and slid the hot dogs onto the plates Tabitha had placed on the counter next to the stove. "Pastors are sworn to secrecy."

"It doesn't matter." Tabitha's tone clearly said the subject was closed.

Cass took the hint. "In other words, it doesn't matter what I say. You're not going to talk to him, right?"

"Finally." Tabitha pretended to mop her brow with relief. "Whew! I practically had to beat you over the head to get it through your thick skull."

"I may be slow, but I do eventually catch on." Cass

traded the ketchup for the mustard when Tabitha was done with it. "You won't talk to our parents or Pastor Thompson about your mother. Who does that leave?"

Tabitha shot her a hopeful look. "You?"

"Me?" Cass raised her eyebrows. "What kind of help would I be? I'm just as clueless as you are."

"You can listen," Tabitha replied quietly. "Just having someone to talk to helps more than you'll ever know."

"Okay." Cass sounded doubtful. "I'm here whenever you need to vent. But," she couldn't resist adding, "I still wish you'd talk to somebody who could actually give you advice."

Grinning, Tabitha flung an arm around her shoulders and gave her a lip-smacking kiss on the cheek. "Hey, you're my sis. I can't think of anyone I'd rather confide in."

"I'm honored," Cass drawled, rolling her eyes and making a show of rubbing her cheek to scrub away Tabitha's kiss.

CHAPTER 34

The two weeks until the formal flew by. Busy with her classes, Cass barely noted the passage of time. Still, there was an ache in her heart and a hollow feeling in the pit of her stomach every time she thought about home and the autumn activities she knew were keeping her friends busy. She and Janette had a brief, unsatisfying conversation that left her more homesick than ever.

She was thinking about it as she lay out at the pool the day before the formal. *Leaves turning. Sweaters. Preparing for homecoming. I'll bet they're all having the time of their lives and I'm here—sweating in the sun.* She frowned, and suddenly heard a laugh beside her.

She opened her eyes to see Rianne bending over her. "Why so sad?"

Cass frowned again. "I'm not sad. I'm tired. It's been a long week. I had three major tests."

"You know what I'm talking about." Rianne sat down on the chair next to hers and Cass groaned. *She wasn't going to let it go this time.* "Half the time you walk around looking like you've lost your best friend. What's going on?"

"I swear I don't know what you mean," Cass insisted. "I'm fine. See?" She produced a brilliant smile to prove her point.

Rianne snorted. “Knock it off. You can’t fool me. I know when something’s bugging you. What is it?” When Cass didn’t respond, she took a deep breath. “Are you upset that you’re going to the dance with Randy?”

Her question was so unexpected that Cass laughed. “You’ve got to be kidding! If I didn’t want to go with Randy, I wouldn’t have told him yes.” Because Rianne didn’t look convinced, Cass decided to tell her the truth. “Honest. It doesn’t have anything to do with Randy. Instead, I’ve developed a raging case of homesickness. I don’t like to talk about it because it makes my mother feel guilty for bringing me here. Plus, you know how Tabitha gets all bent out of shape because she can’t understand how anybody wouldn’t be deliriously happy living on Kwaj, so I’m limited as to who I can talk to.”

“Don’t you know you can talk to me about anything?” Rianne said gently. “Here I’ve been worrying you were trying to think of a way to get out of going to the dance with Randy. But instead, it’s just a simple case of being homesick.”

Cass made a face at her. “It’s not a simple case,” she protested. “Haven’t you been listening? I’m having a major outbreak.”

“I’m sorry.” Rianne reached over to pat her arm. “It’s just that I’m so relieved it has nothing to do with Randy. I didn’t know what I was going to do if you told me you were unhappy about him being your date. Blood is thicker than water, but I didn’t want to risk messing up our friendship.”

For the first time since arriving at the pool, Cass laughed. “Thanks. I needed that. All I’ve been focusing on lately is what I lost when we moved here. I forgot to think about the things I gained, like you as a friend.”

"Stop. You're going to make me cry," Rianne teased. She drew up her legs and clasped her arms around them. "So what do you miss about Tennessee, other than your friends?"

"Actually, I don't miss them all that much. I do, but I don't, if you know what I mean." Cass struggled to find a way to explain it. "They have their own lives to live and so do I. I never thought we'd grow apart, but I guess it was bound to happen. The hardest time I'm having is with the weather. My internal clock says it should be starting to feel like fall. It's still warm back home, but the nights are getting cooler and the leaves are beginning to change. Fall has always been my favorite season, and I miss it so much I feel like crying sometimes."

Rianne's expression turned wistful. "I remember what September and October used to be like. People would start using their fireplaces, and they smelled wonderful, especially at night."

"That's right!" Cass sat up straight, excited to be sharing seasonal memories with somebody. "I love it when there's a nip in the air, and people begin wearing jeans and sweaters, instead of summer clothes."

"Of course," Rianne reminded her, "fall eventually turns into winter. It gets cold and stays cold. There's rain, sleet, ice, and snow. The snow's pretty at first, but then it turns dirty and slushy." She gave a delicate shudder. "No, thank you. I think I'll stick with summer year-round, even if it means missing out on autumn."

Cass wasn't ready to concede defeat. "Nothing's perfect." She was suddenly struck by what she'd said. "You know, that's true," she continued in a reflective tone. "As much as I love Tennessee, it's not paradise. Like you said, I used to get tired of winter, so I shouldn't expect life here to be perfect." She flashed Rianne a crooked smile. "That won't make me stop wishing I were home, going to football games with my friends, and enjoying fall in Tennessee. But maybe it'll keep me from getting too worked up about not being there."

"Wow, you're so wise," teased Rianne. "I'm really glad we're friends. I learn so much from you."

Cass made a face at her. "You're lucky we're not in the pool. You deserve a good dunking for being sarcastic and I'd be happy to give you one."

"Oh, yeah?" challenged Rianne. "You and what army?"

"Don't," Cass wagged a warning finger, "tempt me. I have a sneaking suspicion that the fastest way out of the mood I've been in would be to take it out on someone."

Rianne didn't look the least bit worried. "Nuh-uh. The fastest way out would be to talk about the formal. I don't care how many times we've discussed it, it's still my favorite topic of conversation."

Cass decided she was right, and they launched into a lengthy chat about dresses, flowers, and anything else that might be even remotely connected to the dance the following night.

Saturday morning dawned bright and clear, with not a cloud in the sky. Over breakfast, Cass and Tabitha reviewed the schedule they'd worked out to keep bathroom disputes to a minimum as they prepared for the evening. Cass grinned across the table at her stepsister.

"Two teenage girls getting ready for the dance and one bathroom. This is going to be a real test of how far we've come in our relationship."

"Nah." Tabitha sipped her orange juice. "If worse comes to worst, one of us can always run next door and ask to use the Simpsons' bathroom. I vote it's you since you don't have seniority around here."

Cass' eyebrows drew together in a scowl. "All I can say is it better not come to that. Nothing against the

Simpsons, but I don't want to use their bathroom. If we stick to the schedule, everything should be fine."

As it turned out, it was. While Mom and Dad joined the other parents at the school gym to decorate and set up for the meal that was part of the evening, Tabitha took a leisurely bubble bath. Cass sat on the porch and carefully painted her finger and toe nails the pearly copper Tabitha had assured her would go perfectly with her dress.

Cass had just finished her bubble bath, and the girls were relaxing in the living room when Dad and Mom returned. Spotting the stack of envelopes Dad carried, Cass jumped up from the recliner.

"Ooh, mail! Is there anything for me?"

Dad exchanged an odd look with Mom before sorting through the pile. "You have three letters." He handed the envelopes to Cass, who squealed and carried them back to her chair. After a slight pause, he reluctantly added, "Tabitha, there's a letter here for you."

"Really?" She looked puzzled, but not concerned. "I hardly ever get mail. Who's it from?"

"Your mother," Dad said in a heavy voice.

Cass looked up from her letters. The room had gone very still. She looked her stepsister's stony face. "Are you going to read it?"

Tabitha shrugged nonchalantly, but Cass could see the troubled look in her eyes. "Sure. Why not?" Getting up, she walked to her father. "May I have the letter, please? I'd like to take it to my room and read it alone. Then I'll tell you what it says."

Dad looked unhappy as he handed her the envelope. "I wish you'd stay with us while you read it."

"But Dad," Tabitha protested with a brittle laugh, "this is an event. It's not every day I hear from my mother. It's more like—what?—every five or six years. A letter this special deserves special treatment. I'll be back in a couple of minutes."

With that, she turned on her heel and, holding her back ramrod-straight, marched to her room. The moment she disappeared down the hall, Dad, Mom, and Cass shared uneasy glances.

"I don't like this," Dad muttered. "Why has Beth decided to write to her out of the blue? Something's up."

Mom, who usually tended to put a positive spin on things, didn't have a response. She merely shrugged and looked worried. It fell to Cass to try to come up with a possible explanation. She thought fast.

"Maybe she ... uh ... you know ...had a change of heart," she offered. "That's it," she went on, warming to her theory. "Tabitha told me she had another baby a little while ago. It's probably made her realize how terrible she's been to Tabitha and she wrote to apologize."

Dad snorted. "Nice try, but you don't know Beth. Everything she does has an ulterior motive. Whatever she's cooking up, believe me, she only has her own interests in mind, not Tabitha's." He looked toward the hall and his face tightened.

It was a long five minutes before Tabitha reappeared. With her carefully controlled expression, it was impossible for Cass to guess what she was feeling. She held the letter out to Dad as if it meant nothing to her.

"You can read it for yourself, but I'll sum it up for you." The strain in her voice indicated she wasn't as nonchalant about the situation as she appeared. "She says she's sad circumstances forced her to abandon me and that she regrets all the years we've missed together. She says it's not an excuse, but things between the two of you were more than she could handle, and at the time she thought the best solution was to run away. Now that she has her head on straight—that's a direct quote, by the way—she'd like for us to reestablish a relationship. She wants to know how I'd feel about having her back in my life. She wrote some stuff about the two other children, but that's basically it."

"I see," Dad said quietly.

"You do?" Tabitha's smile was bitter. "Then would you mind explaining it to me? I've gotten along just fine for twelve years without her then—boom!—she wants to be my mother again. What am I supposed to tell her? Never mind, don't answer that," she told Dad when he started to speak. "I don't want to talk about it now. I've been looking forward to tonight for weeks, and I'm not going to let her stupid letter ruin it for me. I'm going to put it—and her—out of my mind and concentrate on getting ready for the dance, just like I planned."

Cass wondered if she was the only one who saw the tears glittering in Tabitha's eyes. Jumping up, she hurried to her stepsister's side and draped her arm around her shoulders.

"Let's go to your room and you can French braid my hair like you promised," she said quickly. "Forget about your mother's letter. It's not worth one more second of your time."

Tabitha flashed her a grateful smile. "My point exactly. Dad, you can do whatever you want with the letter after you finish reading it. If it were up to me, I'd burn it, but it's your call. I don't care."

That settled, Cass and Tabitha left the room to prepare for the evening.

Since the island's taxis couldn't accommodate Randy's wheelchair, he arrived first to escort Cass. He'd offered to meet her at the school while she rode in a taxi, but she'd flatly turned him down. She'd told him in no uncertain terms that he was her date, which meant he'd pick her up and she'd walk the half-mile or so beside him.

When the knock came at the front door shortly before six, Cass' stomach did a triple flip then added one more for good measure. She was waiting in Tabitha's room, and she turned to her stepsister in panic.

"How do I look?" She patted her hair, face, and dress in rapid succession. "Are you sure the dress is okay?" She tugged at the square neckline. "It's not too revealing?"

"You look gorgeous." Laughing, Tabitha turned Cass toward the door and gave her a push. "As far as your dress being revealing, what are the odds Mom would make either of us something that wasn't completely modest? We're lucky our dresses aren't long-sleeved with high collars."

Cass relaxed enough to chuckle. "That's one advantage to living on a tropical island. If the dance were back home, that's exactly what she would've made because she'd have the weather as an excuse."

"Remind me never to live in Tennessee with Mom." Tabitha took her elbow. "Let's go. I want to see the look on Randy's face when he sees you."

Cass let Tabitha guide her out the door. "I won't get to see Micah's expression," she lamented.

"No problem," Tabitha breezily assured her. "Picture what somebody looks like when he sees the Grand Canyon or some other natural wonder for the first time."

Cass laughed. "Wow—you certainly think highly of yourself, don't you?"

"Why not?" Tabitha struck a sultry pose. "I'm a national treasure." Dropping the act, she said, "Come on. Randy's waiting."

Finding she couldn't look at Randy as she entered the living room, Cass' gaze darted from Mom to Dad to the couch. Tabitha gave her a sharp elbow in the side.

"Say hello," she ordered under her breath.

"Hello," Cass obediently echoed.

She finally forced herself to look at Randy and instantly relaxed. When all was said and done, it was Randy. There was no reason to be flustered around him.

Sauntering across the floor, Cass stopped a couple of feet in front of him and grinned. "Well, look at you. That shirt does wonders for your eyes."

Since there wasn't a way to rent tuxedos on the island, the boys had decided to wear either Hawaiian print or white Polynesian shirts. Randy's was a blend of royal blue and purple flowers with an occasional pink parrot thrown in.

Randy glanced down at himself as if he'd forgotten what he had on. "Oh, yeah. Uh ... thanks." He returned his dazzled eyes to Cass. "You look—" he paused, at a temporary loss for words, "incredible."

Cass felt her cheeks burn. "Thank you, kind sir. I'd say we're well-matched then."

Randy fumbled with the box on his lap. "Here's your corsage. I hope you like it. Tabitha said to get you white roses."

Cass' hands trembled as she took the box from Randy. *My first flowers from a boy*, she thought and lifted the lid on the most beautiful corsage she'd ever seen.

"Is it a pin on?" Mom asked. "If it is, I'll do it for you. Men are generally hopeless when it comes to pinning on corsages."

"It's the wrist kind," Cass replied, slipping it on her right arm. She lifted Randy's boutonniere from the box. "But you can pin Randy's rose on for him. My hands are shaking so much, I'd probably wind up sticking him full of holes."

"Yes, please do the honors, Mrs. Spencer," Randy added so fervently that everyone laughed.

Dad had just finished taking pictures when the doorbell rang. Cass glanced at Tabitha, her expression puzzled. "That can't be Micah already, can it?"

Tabitha's eyes danced with mischief. "You never know. Let's see."

She opened the door as a group of grinning teens yelled, "Surprise!"

Randy looked from the group to Tabitha and back again. "What's going on?"

Rianne, trailed by her date, Josh, walked into the house and patted Randy's shoulder. "Come on, Bro. You didn't think we'd let you and Cass go to the dance on your own, did you? We took a vote, and we all decided to walk with you two."

"That's right," Kira piped up.

She preceded Logan through the door. Cass allowed herself one brief, yearning glance at Logan, who winked when he met her gaze. Wincing, she clamped her hands over her ears.

"Ouch," she joked. "That shirt's so loud, I can't hear myself think."

Logan fingered his riotous orange, green, and magenta shirt and pretended to look injured. "Gee, and I thought I looked cute."

Cass patted his cheek. "You do. You look absolutely adorable."

She watched as Micah, resplendent in a gleaming white Polynesian shirt, came up to Tabitha. "I've never seen anyone as beautiful as you are."

Tabitha ducked her head, but not before Cass could see her embarrassed smile. "You don't look so bad yourself."

Holding out a florist's box, Micah removed the lid to reveal an orchid. "Is this okay?"

"It's perfect," Tabitha breathed. Turning, she asked Mom, "Would you pin this on for me?"

Once Tabitha's corsage and Micah's purple carnation were in place, Dad arranged everyone for a group photograph. Cass and Tabitha insisted on standing next to each other with Randy and Micah flanking them.

While Dad adjusted the camera lens, Cass leaned close to Tabitha to whisper, "Going as a group was your idea, wasn't it?"

Tabitha shrugged. "Yes, but don't make a big deal out of it. I wasn't about to let you and Randy get there on your own. It wouldn't have been the same without you two along."

"Are you saying you'd have missed me?" teased Cass.

"Of course," Tabitha said. "Haven't you ever heard the phrase, LYLAS?"

Cass repeated the letters under her breath then shook her head. "Nope, can't say that I have. What does it mean?"

Their hands hidden by their dresses, Tabitha took Cass' and squeezed. "Love you like a sister."

Cass could feel herself close to tears. "We're in this for good, aren't we?"

"Through thick and thin," agreed Tabitha.

"I'll count to three, then take the picture," Dad said the group. "One ..."

"Hey, Tabitha," Cass whispered.

"What?"

"LYLAS."

Their smiles outshone the flash.